# THE PATIENTS

CHARLOTTE STEVENSON

BLOODHOUND
BOOKS

First published in 2026 by Bloodhound Books.



www.bloodhoundbooks.com

Print ISBN: 9781917705417

*For my family. My greatest blessing.*

# 1

# TESS

Tess admires the exterior of the doctor's office and smiles. This place could not be more perfect. As she'd hoped, the building is magnificent and oozes luxury and good taste. Hanging baskets blooming with vibrant flowers flank the beautifully painted blue door. Perfectly on-trend. Tess studies the brass plaque. It bears the doctor's name and title – *Dr Jenna O'Hara, Consultant Psychiatrist* – followed by many impressive-sounding letters and qualifications. Tess flips on her phone's forwards-facing camera and drapes her long black hair across one shoulder. She had it washed and blow-dried yesterday and it looks stunning. She takes a run of selfies with one of the hanging baskets in the background. It's hard to pick the best image. She looks fantastic in all of them.

Her fiancé, Joe, had been reluctant to pay for her to see a private doctor and she couldn't understand why. She spends a fortune on things much less important than her health. Last week, she bought a pair of shoes for over three grand. He didn't bat an eye at that. There is no way Tess is going to slum it when it comes to her mental health. If she needs therapy, she will get the best there is. Granted, *need* is probably a strong word. Tess wants therapy, and what Tess wants, she gets. Joe soon changed his tune. He always does. After a few weeks of ramping up her erratic behaviour to levels even she found unacceptable, he became more agreeable. Tess has learnt which of Joe's buttons to press and how hard to push them and, unfortunately for him, this particular request required a full-throttle approach.

Dr O'Hara's waiting list is long and appointments go like hot cakes. Tess wasn't going to wait around for Joe to change his mind in his own time. But now all is well. She has her hundreds of pounds per hour therapy session, and she even managed to leave him feeling guilty about refusing in the first place. She'll keep those bonus points in her back pocket for a later date. She knows exactly how to play him. It's an art.

Checking her phone, Tess sees she has five minutes to spare until her 9am appointment and decides to wait outside for a few more minutes rather than venturing inside. It's a rare bright and beautiful day in Manchester, and she'd prefer to bask in the sunshine.

Tess stifles a yawn and dabs at her eyes with her fingertips. Her make-up must remain pristine. It's crucial she makes a good first impression. Dr O'Hara is talented, rich, and probably beautiful, too, and Tess hates feeling inferior to anyone in any way. Luckily, this rarely happens. Still, she got up at 7am to perfect her look, which is way earlier than she likes to be out of bed. Even 9am is pushing it. Beauty sleep is a girl's best friend. She even left the house before Joe this morning, which is entirely unheard of.

Joe works as a stockbroker, banker, shares-type person. They've been together for five years and engaged for two. He's quite a bit older than Tess. Twenty years, almost. He's forty... something. Forty-five, maybe? Anyway, he's old and, therefore, she'll always be young and glamorous in his eyes. And by the time she isn't, he'll be demented or dead, and she'll be rich. Tess tries to recall Joe's exact job title. He's told her a million times but it never seems to stick in her brain. Anyway, the most important thing about his occupation is that he makes a ridiculous amount of money, which means she doesn't have to work. Satisfaction blooms in her chest as she replays this thought. *I don't have to work ever again.* It's all she's ever wanted. She breathes in deeply as the morning sunshine warms her face.

When all of Tess's school friends dreamt of becoming lawyers, teachers or nurses, she didn't get it. Of course, she pretended she did. Nobody wants to be the odd one out, so she joined in with the aspirational chatter and invented a pretend vocation of becoming a clinical psychologist. She even went to university to study psychology, for goodness' sake, with little to no idea what being a clinical psychologist entailed. But it seemed to impress people, and her parents were super proud. Now she's older and wiser, she's glad she gave the psychology gig a swerve. As if she wants to spend her time listening to people moan. There wouldn't be enough money in the world to put up with that.

All Tess ever wanted was to meet a rich man and spend her days doing whatever she liked – no stress, no worries, the perfect carefree existence. And that's precisely what she has. She gets up late and goes for lunch or shopping with her friends. It is bliss. And she always makes sure she takes the perfect photos for her Instagram. Currently, she has over one hundred and thirty thousand followers. It's not bad, but she wants more. Lots more. Her followers are primarily women who want to be like her and they fill her feed with praise and well-meaning envy. Honestly, it's pretty much the dream existence.

Tess loves her life, but she's always striving for more. More attention, more adoration. More everything. The devotion and admiration from her online followers is one thing – every time she gets a like or a gushing comment, the little pings of serotonin are lovely. But they're not enough. Not even close. The cyber-love pales in comparison to the satisfaction she gets from one-on-one attention from Joe and, to a lesser extent, her desperate band of hanger-on friends.

Lately, though, Tess has been in a rut. She needs something new and fresh to bring the focus back on her. If she had a choice, she'd probably choose a proper illness of some kind. Not something disgusting or anything that would affect her appearance. Something that would have them fawning, worried, pandering. One of her friends has type 1 diabetes and is constantly banging on about it. She's forever checking her blood levels and piping up in restaurants to ask what's in the food. Everyone falls over themselves asking questions about it and making sure she is okay. She's even got this cute little implant thing on her arm that gets tons of attention. That would be the perfect sort of illness. And oh, how she has tried to find something. But she's disgustingly healthy. Not a thing out of place. Not a blood result even one iota outside of completely normal. So, with options dwindling and armed with a small amount of knowledge from her poorly attended university course, she's giving the psychological trauma thing a whirl.

It's not been a simple task. Tess has had to come up with a whole host of different stories to make it work in a way that meets her needs, and actually, that's been really fun. The people in Tess's life are the chess pieces in her game, nothing more. And she is a skilled player – a grand master.

Tess looks at her ring that twinkles in the morning sunshine. Joe is a keeper. And even if things turn sour, she'll ensure she has a wedding ring alongside the enormous pink diamond engagement ring before she even contemplates leaving him. There is no way she is ever going back to having to fend for herself.

Tess had lots of fun filling out her referral form for her appointment today. There were the usual boring questions: name, age, yada, yada. But she laid it on thick when it came to the 'what can we help you with?' question. Tess painted herself, in a carefully scripted story, as an emotionally depleted and mentally exhausted woman – a saint who has shunned her self-care and given all her energy to others, the years of being a rock to every person in her life finally taking its toll. Tess was so proud of it that she took a photo.

When she told her friends she was going to therapy she got the exact response she wanted. And it felt bloody marvellous. Her cup runneth over with self-satisfaction. There were plenty of hugs and exaltations of what a wonderful, caring human being she is and how she is right to take time to look after herself. Tess couldn't agree more. Looking after herself is priority one. Always.

At twenty-seven years old, Tess has no long-term friends and she doesn't want any. She doesn't see the point in holding on to someone for an extended length of time. She has friends for exactly the duration she needs them, and when she moves on to a different phase of her life, she sheds them and finds new ones. Easy-peasy.

It's 8.59am and Tess decides to go in. She checks for a buzzer or intercom before pushing the door but there isn't one. The rent on this place must be extortionate. A large Victorian red-brick single occupancy business in the heart of Manchester city centre must cost a bomb. Unless Dr O'Hara owns the place. Either way, Tess thinks, the woman must be fucking loaded.

Glancing behind her as she opens the heavy wooden door, Tess sees a short, harried-looking woman shuffling up the steps. Tess squints and then rearranges her face into a welcoming smile, flashing her fabulous white teeth and holding the door open for her. The woman mumbles a thank you, barely making eye contact.

As they walk the short distance to the reception desk, Tess completes a quick appraisal of her new companion. She does this with everyone she meets: a quick top-to-toe assessment. The woman is almost a foot shorter than Tess, who stands at a glorious five foot ten, and over six foot in the heels she wears today, and appears to be in her early forties. Although very practical and even dour in appearance, there are obvious signs of wealth that Tess has taught herself to look out for. The woman wears a well-cut and perfectly fitted charcoal-grey suit. It's just a shame it's on a body the shape of a potato. She's combined this with patent leather flats and a matching tote bag. They are ugly as sin but a high-end designer brand nonetheless, costing well over two thousand pounds combined. Tess shakes her head. What an absolute waste of expensive things on such a plain and unremarkable woman.

# 2

# LEAH

Leah arrives at the doctor's office with barely minutes to spare. A tall, glamorous woman holds the door for her, and an overpowering scent of expensive citrus perfume assaults Leah's nostrils as she dips under her slender arm. Leah doesn't look up. She hates to appear unfriendly, but her face feels hot and damp, and the last thing she wants is for her appearance to be examined directly by a younger, more beautiful, better put-together woman while looking like a clammy toad. She needs to find a bathroom asap; take a few minutes to cool down and do a swift repair job on her make-up, which is currently sliding off her face. It won't do to meet her new psychiatrist looking all red, blotchy, and shiny. She has standards, but perimenopause is making these standards harder and harder to maintain.

Leah's GP has assured her the pills he prescribed for her perimenopause symptoms will start to help soon; she just has to be patient. She's trying to be, but that's easier said than done when you have a full-time job and come face to sweat-laden face with dozens of people every day. It's all so bloody unfair. She's only forty-four, for goodness' sake. Shouldn't she have at least another five years left before her femininity and womanly wiles desert her forever? She's not ready to be a dried-up old husk, even if her child-rearing years are well and truly behind her. Leah's two sons are now hulking young men. Rugby players like their father, and are currently stretching their wings at university. It's not the reproductive aspect of impending menopause that bothers her; it's the fact she finds herself becoming slowly and increasingly less relevant and invisible.

Leah never considered herself a stunner who turned every head in the street, but she was attractive once. She knew it and felt like she owned her space in the world. Despite the disaster that was her high-school years, Leah blossomed in her late teens and early twenties. She became a cute, curvy brunette, full of sass and style. But in the last few years, she's been sinking, losing herself. Fading into the background and disappearing. Old memories have started to resurface and haunt her and to say she has dealt with this poorly is putting it mildly. Leah shakes the thoughts away. There will be plenty of time to revisit those later.

She walks beside the supermodel, taking in her surroundings. The younger woman's heels click and clack irritatingly on the black-and-white Victorian tiles. Leah takes a moment to inspect the flooring. The tiles are the genuine article, not those cheap imitations or, God forbid, linoleum. Leah is beginning to think she will get along well with Dr O'Hara. The woman clearly has taste. The bottom half of the walls are clad with stunning walnut wood panelling, and the remainder is painted with Farrow and Ball Pigeon. She knows the expensive paint colours off by heart. They adorn many of the walls in her own house and are worth every penny. Despite her husband's horror at the cost and insistence that he could buy enough paint to cover the entire street for the price of one pot of 'that poncy stuff', Leah remained insistent that some things are worth paying for.

Leah nods her head in approval. This is almost exactly what she would have chosen for the space. Dr Jenna O'Hara must have the means to afford a very expensive interior designer – a designer like Leah herself.

The glamorous woman hasn't left her side on the short walk to reception, and Leah is beginning to feel a bit put out by having a constant companion. In the absence of anyone manning the desk, she presses the bell before the other woman gets the chance.

Leah researched Dr O'Hara extensively and has waited months for this appointment. She knows Dr O'Hara is the only doctor practising in this building and is, in fact, the sole occupant of this grand space. Her website promised privacy and high-end care, which is precisely what Leah wants. She was assured that appointments are timed to avoid any crossover of patients and that everything would be handled with the utmost discretion. So what is going on here? Leah chose Dr O'Hara specifically to avoid situations like this.

A woman emerges from the door behind the desk and smiles at them, making eye contact with Leah first. Her unwelcome companion speaks.

"Good morning. I have an appointment at 9am. It's Tess Liu."

"Ah, good morning, Ms Liu. I do apologise, but—"

Leah can't help herself and cuts off the receptionist mid-sentence. "No, I have an appointment at 9am. I'm Leah, Leah Jesmond. I've had this appointment booked for months." Her voice sounds a lot more petulant and screechy than she had planned, and both women turn to look at her with something akin to pity. She feels herself shrinking and heat rushes to her already flushed face.

The silence lasts a beat longer than is comfortable before the receptionist speaks again. "Ms Liu, Mrs Jesmond, would you mind taking a seat for a moment while I get this sorted out for you?" She gestures towards two burgundy leather armchairs against the far wall.

Leah looks at the receptionist and then at the woman called Tess, and simply nods, not trusting herself to answer in a calm and collected manner. This is a terrible start and completely unacceptable. Tess shrugs her shoulders, seeming to have not a care in the world, which only angers Leah more. When neither of them take the proffered chairs, the receptionist presses her palms together as though in prayer.

"I am so sorry about this, and I can assure you this is not how I run things here. Nothing like this has happened before and I can only apologise profusely."

Somewhat placated by the woman's professional and sincere apology, Leah is about to take a seat when she speaks again.

"This isn't how I wanted to meet you both, but let me introduce myself. I'm Dr Jenna O'Hara."

# 3

# TESS

Tess walks over to the chairs and sits down. The little woman – Leah, she thinks she's called – is still mumbling away to Dr O'Hara. Tess can't understand why she's making such a big deal over this. The doctor said she'll sort it out, which means she'll sort it out. No point getting all shrill and uppity about it. Tess pulls out her phone and starts scrolling Instagram. Is it too much to post from inside the doctor's office? She doesn't think so, but maybe Dr O'Hara has some weird rules. She'll ask her once she finally gets into her appointment.

Eventually, Leah stops griping, and Tess hears Dr O'Hara's voice. "It's the second door on your right."

Tess watches as Leah shuffles off down the corridor like a grumpy hobbit and opens the door she was directed to. It has the letters WC in brass letters on it. Tess rolls her eyes. That woman definitely seems stressed. Like way too bothered about a little delay to their appointment. But then again, this is a psychiatrist's office. Maybe Tess should try dialling up the anxiety a bit. She doesn't want to come across as too normal right away.

Dr O'Hara walks towards Tess, and she stands up to greet

her. Not out of politeness but because she enjoys towering over people. It puts her exactly where she wants to be in their mind – above them.

"Ms Liu—"

"It's Tess. Tess is fine."

Dr O'Hara smiles graciously, and Tess mirrors her. She hates being called 'Ms'. It screams 'You're not married' – something that will hopefully be rectified soon.

"Of course, Tess. Thank you. It's lovely to meet you, and I do apologise for the unusual circumstances this morning." Tess nods, waiting for the actual explanation of what's going on. "My receptionist hasn't turned up and I can't reach her. She's normally extremely reliable."

Tess notices a flash of concern cross Dr O'Hara's face that piques her interest. It is the exact same 'concerned face' Tess puts on when she is expected to appear worried. It's unlikely anyone else would have picked up on what the doctor just did, but Tess is convinced the doctor is lying. That was definitely a fake face. A good one, but definitely fake. But then the doctor probably *is* lying to her. Most likely, her receptionist went out on a bender last night and has called in sick or something, and Dr O'Hara is using a story that fits with the air of professionalism she wants her office to exude. *Fair enough*, thinks Tess. But something prickles at the nape of her neck as the doctor turns her concerned face back into an amiable smile at the flick of a switch. There's something about Dr O'Hara. Something that makes Tess think there's much more to this woman than meets the eye.

"Not to worry, Dr O'Hara. So, what's happening with the appointments then? Obviously, you can't see both of us at once." Tess keeps her expression neutral. Wary of someone who might be able to read her emotions.

"Well, indeed. I have a proposal for you, Tess, and I

completely understand if this doesn't work, but I spoke with Mrs Jesmond and she can only do the 9am appointment."

Tess puffs out a breath. So that's what the little busybody was doing. Getting in first to snag the appointment.

"As you said, it's simply not possible to see you both at your arranged time so if you could come back, or wait here if you prefer, we could meet at ten fifteen. I've checked my diary and there are no other patients expected. For some reason, Sally, my receptionist, has booked two consultations for nine am and then I have the rest of the morning free. It's clearly just a mistake or a glitch, but I'm so sorry it has impacted you this way."

Tess considers the offer, putting on her best thinking face.

Dr O'Hara must notice as she follows up with, "And, of course, your consultation today would be complimentary. As an apology and a show of gratitude for your flexibility."

Now that gets Tess's attention, but she makes sure not to show her excitement. She wants Dr O'Hara to feel indebted to her; to think this change is terribly inconvenient and that Tess is about to be the better person. That feels like a nice place to start their relationship. It never hurts to have someone feel like they owe you. In actual fact, Tess couldn't care less about having to wait. Her day is hers to do as she pleases. Plus, the money for this consultation will buy her an afternoon at the spa. As soon as Dr O'Hara disappears, she'll make sure to book. She's been dying for one of their hot stone massages.

Tess gives a resigned sigh and a small smile. "It's not ideal, but I can see you're in a very tricky situation. So, yes, I'm happy to have my appointment at quarter past ten."

Dr O'Hara beams and Tess likes the warm feeling it gives her inside. "Thank you so much, Tess. I can assure you this won't happen again."

Tess nods. "That's good to hear."

They both turn at the sound of the bathroom door opening and Leah emerges into the corridor.

Dr O'Hara quickly turns her attention back to Tess. "Will you be leaving and coming back? Or, as I said, you're very welcome to wait."

Tess speaks loud enough for Leah to hear. "I'll wait here. I can get on with some work so I don't end up behind on things today."

The doctor's face returns to an apologetic expression, and Tess drinks it in. She takes a quick glance at Leah, who looks delighted at the fact she will be getting the first appointment. There is not a hint of gratitude, just pure selfish glee.

Dr O'Hara opens the first door to her right and gestures to Tess to enter. "You can wait in here if you like." Dr O'Hara then points to a very impressive coffee machine next to the reception desk. "And please do help yourself to coffee if you wish."

Tess stands at the entrance of the waiting room and looks around. Very nice. An emerald-green velvet Chesterfield sofa and matching chairs surround a chunky antique-looking coffee table. She'll be very happy here for the next hour.

"Now, if you'll excuse us, Tess, I don't want to delay either of you any longer than I absolutely have to, so—"

Tess waves Dr O'Hara away. "Of course. I'll be fine here. Thank you." She smiles likeably and watches as Dr O'Hara and Leah enter the adjacent room. Tess immediately closes the waiting-room door and presses her ear to the wall, excited at the prospect of listening to Leah's consultation. She knows it will be full of 'woe is me' rubbish. Typical dreary middle-aged woman stuff. Tess has no sympathy. Looking after yourself is easy, and she can't understand women who don't make the best of their appearance. There's no excuse for letting yourself get fat and dowdy. Granted, Tess won the genetics lottery. Her mum is French and Tess inherited her height and beauty. She has her dad to thank for her sleek hair and gorgeous skin. But that's not the point. Tess has realised over the years that if you want something, you need to go and get it. You can't act like the world owes you a favour and expect to live a happy and full life. You have to make things happen. And so far, that attitude is serving her pretty well.

Tess eases herself into one of the luxurious chairs and strokes the fabric. On the table is a selection of high-end magazines that look like they've never been opened. The air is filled with the gorgeous scent of Jo Malone Pomegranate Noir, and she spots the diffuser mounted discreetly on the wall.

Tess leans back, crosses her long supple legs and breathes in and out deeply. This is the kind of environment she always wants to be in. Never again will she go back to slumming it with the masses. Opulence and luxury are precisely what she deserves. Tess decides against making herself a coffee. It always makes her bloated and leaves her feeling far too giddy. Instead, she sits back and scrolls through Instagram. She hasn't posted enough today and will need to get on it as soon as she leaves here. Her army of devoted followers want to know every aspect of her life and live vicariously through her fabulous existence. And she is more than happy to share. She adores the little buzz that comes with every like and gushing comment. There is the odd troll or over-obsessive fan, but Tess barely gives them a second thought. Who cares what some sad freak thinks of her. Their jealousy is understandable. Who wouldn't want to be her?

# 4

# LEAH

Leah follows Dr O'Hara into the consultation room. Two cream leather armchairs and a sofa are arranged in a triangle formation, and the doctor gestures towards them.

"Please take a seat, Mrs Jesmond. Wherever you feel most comfortable."

Leah chooses the armchair closest to the door and settles into it, placing her handbag by her feet.

"I'll be with you in one moment. Let me just get a couple of things from my desk."

Dr O'Hara stands and rifles through her drawers. Her back is to Leah, giving her the perfect opportunity to get a proper look at her new psychiatrist. Despite her professional and somewhat strait-laced appearance, Leah loves fashion and can't help checking out people's clothes. She doesn't do it in a mean, judgy way. It's simply something that interests her. Clothing is like your second skin. And the choices you make say a lot about who you are. Leah's expensive perfectly cut suits show her clients she has money and will deliver. Anyone with an eye for tailoring would quickly see that her suit is bespoke. Her look is purposefully classic and non-threatening, allowing her to blend into the background wherever she goes. She's learnt over the years that her clients like this approach. When at work, she is the grey woman.

Dr O'Hara appears very vibrant and youthful. Her skin is glowing and smooth, and Leah strokes her palm along her own sagging jawline, trying in vain to push it back to where it was ten years ago. She was expecting someone a little stuffier and more academic-looking. But that's probably down to her feelings about her own appearance. Leah pushes down the pang of jealousy she feels and takes in the doctor's outfit. She's wearing a cream blouse tucked into navy slim-leg trousers with nude court shoes. Nothing wrong with that in principle, but at first glance everything she is wearing looks relatively cheap. Those shoes are a high-street brand and don't even appear to be leather. Leah chastises herself for being snobby. Not everyone spends silly money on clothes and if Leah looked half as good as Dr O'Hara, she'd probably still shop on the high street too. And the surroundings are very reassuring. In Leah's experience, money equals quality. Dr O'Hara's reputation precedes her, and many glowing testimonies state she is one of the best psychiatrists around. Her choice of clothing is neither here nor there.

With a notebook and pen in hand, Dr O'Hara takes the remaining armchair and crosses her legs. She looks flustered, and although Leah has been irritated by the unwelcome bumps in the road since arriving, she does feel empathy for her. Dr O'Hara has arrived at work to discover her receptionist hasn't turned up and two patients have been booked in at the same time. To be fair, she's done a pretty decent job of finding a solution. Plus, when Leah started protesting that an appointment later than 9am simply wouldn't work for her, the doctor was very apologetic, offered the consultation for free and prioritised her over Tess. All in all, it was a rather good outcome for her.

"Once again, please accept my apologies, Mrs Jesmond."

Leah smiles, she rather likes the doctor apologising to her. "I completely understand. None of this was your fault, and you've done everything possible to be accommodating. So thank you for that."

Noticeable relief spreads across the doctor's face. This woman would be a terrible poker player, Leah surmises. She wears her emotions far too openly.

"How would you like me to address you during our consultation?"

Leah quite likes being referred to as Mrs Jesmond but is worried about what that might say about her. "Oh, do call me Leah."

"Very well. It's lovely to meet you, Leah. Due to this morning's unfortunate events, we're starting our consultation late." Leah looks at her watch and sees it is 9.30am. "My suggestion is this: if you can stay a little later, we can end our consultation at ten fifteen. That will give us fifteen minutes less than usual, but still, I feel, adequate time to have a meaningful session."

Leah nods. She can definitely stay on a little longer. Her earlier insistence that she couldn't return for a later consultation was a complete lie. She has an evening appointment with a client, but otherwise, today is completely free. She only said that because she was irked. She wanted the time she had booked, and it sounded much better if she had a legitimate reason.

"Yes, I can make that work."

"Thank you, Leah. That is much appreciated. Now, what I like to do with any new client is ascertain what you hope to get out of our time together. As you know, my consultations are talking-therapy focused and completely tailored to the individual."

This was another thing that appealed to her. She's had enough of antidepressants and anti-anxiety drugs. She's taken far too many over the years, and they've made her not a lot better and a little bit fatter. It's not ideal for someone who's always struggled to stay slim.

"I've read your patient registration form, but I'd like to hear it from you. So, if you would, tell me why you are here and what you'd like us to work on."

Leah's mouth is suddenly dry, and she looks down at the wooden coffee table with a pile of marble coasters stacked neatly in the middle and a box of tissues next to them. No water. Dr O'Hara must sense what she's looking for and she stands up.

"I'm sorry. Sally would usually set out a water jug and glasses. If you give me two minutes, I'll get you a drink."

Leah clears her throat and swallows. A drink would be nice, but time is ticking on, and she doesn't want to waste more of her already reduced session.

"No. Honestly, it's fine. I'd rather just carry on if that's okay?"

"Yes, of course. I'm sorry this morning is so disorganised." Dr O'Hara sits back down. Again, a pronounced expression of guilt crosses her face. Maybe this is the key to her success. Her genuine and uncensored showing of emotions. "Then tell me. What brought you here today?"

Leah takes a deep breath. It's a huge question with lots of answers, and she doesn't quite know where to start. It's like the 'Why do you want this job?' question during an interview. There is so much to say, but finding an order in which to say it and putting it across well is another matter altogether. So she starts to talk, staring at her knees and hoping it will all come out in some sort of sensical order. "Well, I've felt a bit down for a few years now, and I've no reason to really. I've got a lovely family. My husband loves me, and I've got two wonderful boys. But..."

Dr O'Hara leans forwards and Leah looks up to meet her gaze, her words drifting off.

"Do you mind if I stop you there?"

Leah shakes her head and, embarrassingly, her eyes start to fill up.

"This is your time, Leah. You don't have to apologise for how you feel. You don't have to feel guilty about your thoughts and emotions because you have a lovely family. This is time for you to tell me about you. About how you feel. About your experiences."

Something about the doctor's deep-brown eyes and penetrating stare pulls Leah in. She believes everything Dr O'Hara has just said to her, and suddenly she wants to tell her everything, spill her guts, and divulge her innermost secrets. Leah reaches for the tissue box, takes one, and dabs her eyes.

"Okay. Sorry. I always feel like I should start by saying that. Because it's true. I do have a lovely family. But I hear what you're saying."

Dr O'Hara settles back into her chair and gestures with her hand for Leah to continue. Leah keeps her head up, no longer needing to look down at her knees apologetically. She sees why people are waiting months to speak to Dr O'Hara. She has something that Leah can't quite put her finger on. An indescribable special quality. It's as though she's imploring her to share her deepest secrets.

With Leah's previous doctors, she struggled to open up. But something is different here. She feels the urge to tell her story, all of it. Even... Leah shudders at the thought she almost allowed to the surface and reminds herself that she must hold back on what she reveals to Dr O'Hara.

Of course, Leah needs to talk about her sadness and the things in her past that have made her feel that way. It's why she's here. She has to try to heal.

But some things need to stay hidden. Things she must never say to another person. Otherwise, that beautiful family life she speaks so fondly about will come crashing down around her.

Leah knows she needs to be very careful indeed.

# 5

# TESS

It's been fifteen minutes and Tess is beyond bored. She's taken another selfie, which came out brilliantly even with the complete lack of natural light in here, and posted it on Instagram. She tagged all the brands and named all the skincare products and make-up she's used to create today's effortless no-make-up make-up look. Important to keep those freebies coming. She then added the quote *Self-care means giving the world the best of you instead of what's left of you*. She stole it off someone else's page a few weeks ago and has been waiting for the perfect opportunity to use it.

Her post already has hundreds of likes and many comments.

So powerful. Thank you!

Self-love is the key!

I love this so much!!

And many more similar and equally pointless comments. Yet, for some reason, she's not getting the usual flow of endorphins from the outpouring of love from her followers. After today's session, she'll do an intense and meaningful post about beginning her therapy journey. Maybe she'll make a video. She could cry – her followers would love that. If Dr O'Hara is on board, she could even give her a shout-out. Tag her in the post. Judging by the length of her waiting list, she's not short of clients, but getting more exposure never hurts.

Tess has listened in at the wall a few times but can't hear a single thing – not a peep. She doesn't actually care what boring old Leah has to say, but it's got to be more interesting than sitting here doing nothing. Social media is pretty quiet at this time of day and what else is there to do?

Tess thinks back to her encounter with Dr O'Hara in reception. There was something odd about her. So much so that Tess almost considered scrapping her appointment altogether. When it comes to human emotions and behaviour, Tess is the most astute person she knows. She can't think of anyone who can hold a torch to her understanding of the human mind. It's a gift she has. She knows what everyone is thinking just by reading their faces and body language. Most people will say one thing and be thinking something completely different. Tess knows how to manipulate people. She can move anyone where she needs them to be, sculpt her facial expressions and create the perfect words to get people to think and feel exactly how she wants them to. She's always been able to do it and has spent years testing and perfecting her skills. Honing her craft to perfection. Some people are music prodigies, and others can do complex mathematics without trying. But Tess can read people. It's her thing.

Something about Dr O'Hara's behaviours seemed choreographed, like she'd practised and perfected every word before it left her mouth. But how could that be? They've never met and the only things the doctor knows about Tess are what she wrote on that form.

Even when people are genuine, they still have background

thoughts that muddy the waters. They don't realise it, but it shows all over their face and in the words they speak. When people lie, they are often conflicted or struggling to remember the content of their fabrication and, again, it shows. The truth is hidden deep in their micro-expressions and the unconscious movements of their body, and it takes real skill to control these giveaway signs.

So either Dr O'Hara is the first completely genuine person Tess has ever met, or she is just as skilled at emotional manipulation as Tess. And Tess can't wait to find out which it is. In a perverse way, she hopes she's about to meet her match. A kindred spirit.

But if Dr O'Hara is just like Tess, her career choice feels unusual. What could she possibly be getting out of it? Tess ponders this for a moment, uncrossing and crossing her legs. Money? Maybe. Clearly, this is a very lucrative business. But the doctor will have worked incredibly hard to get where she is, and there's no way Tess would've put in all that effort even if the pay-off was considerable. Imagine having to listen to a bunch of people complaining all day and being unable to talk about yourself. Not a chance in hell! Maybe it's a different type of pay-off. The kind of buzz Tess gets from listening to juicy gossip, spreading rumours, and watching the explosive consequences. She's done that plenty of times and has many friendship break-ups and at least one marriage breakdown on her scorecard. It's so easy. Not to mention fun. People are completely gullible, and her favourite is the 'no smoke without fire' assertion. When something is said enough times, people start to believe it. No evidence is needed. And soon enough, rumours become gospel. People love to be involved with a bit of scandal and will share voraciously if it doesn't affect them negatively. Everyone loves the heat to be on someone else.

Tess hasn't done anything overtly terrible. She's not a

monster. She just likes to have a little fun. The odd white lie here, the occasional anonymous text there. Everyone does it. It's just that nobody does it as well as her. She adores the rush. It makes her feel alive. Everyone around her is an actor in her own personal theatre, where she writes every script. And she is so careful. Nothing she has ever done has been traced back to her. Everyone in her life sees her as kind and caring. She has gotten away scot-free with everything she has ever done.

And she plans to keep it that way.

# 6

## LEAH

Leah gives Dr O'Hara a pleading look. Thankfully, the doctor picks up on it straight away and speaks.

"Okay, I can sense that question was too open for you. I usually start that way to allow my clients to talk about the most important thing to them. To take the lead and avoid me putting my influence into the conversation and steering it in a way that will provide less benefit." Leah nods. That makes sense. "But it's not my intention to overwhelm you. So, let's try something slightly different, shall we?"

"Yes, please." Leah hates how timid her voice sounds, so she clears her throat and reasserts herself. "Yes, I think that would work better for me."

Dr O'Hara beams and Leah feels her heart flutter a little. There is something utterly captivating about this woman. She feels drawn to her but can't quite put her finger on why.

"From your notes, I can see you've experienced anxiety and depression and have taken different medications." Dr O'Hara raises her eyebrows and pauses.

"Yes. Well, that's what they've told me at least. I'm not

taking anything at the moment though. And to be honest, I don't feel worse for it."

Dr O'Hara writes a small note in her book and then meets Leah's eyes again. "And are you interested in trying other medications?"

Leah wrinkles her nose. "No, I don't think so."

"Do you mind telling me why? Depression and anxiety often respond well to medication. It could be that you simply haven't found the right treatment for yourself."

Leah panics a little. Is the doctor trying to palm her off back to her GP, who'll pump her full of drugs just to get rid of her? "But you don't prescribe medication, do you?"

"That's right, I don't. But I do see people who are taking medication prescribed by other doctors. I'm just exploring your reasons and checking you're happy with your decision."

She's been here a while now and hasn't revealed anything of substance. Leah takes a discreet glance at her watch. If she wants to get anything out of today, she really needs to start telling her story. "Yes, I'm happy with that. I'm not averse to taking tablets per se, but..." The events of the past hurtle forwards to the front of her mind and make her stomach churn.

"Go on, Leah. I can sense you're thinking something important. Tell me about it. Tell me your thoughts."

Leah licks her lips and breathes deeply. She's told parts of this story before. But to doctors who haven't shown the slightest bit of interest or care. But this feels different. Dr O'Hara is staring at her intently, ready to drink in Leah's words. "I know I'm not the expert in this and lots of doctors have told me I have depression and anxiety, but I don't think I do."

She examines the doctor's face. She looks immersed in Leah's every word.

"That's very important, Leah. Can you tell me why?"

Leah's face flushes and she wipes her forehead with the back of her hand. Hormones rather than embarrassment this time. But to an observer, they look exactly the same.

"I think so. Yes, I definitely feel sad and worried, but I know exactly why I feel like that. I'm not ill. I don't have a condition. There's just a load of stuff I haven't been able to let go of. I think about it every day. I worry about bumping into people from school even though I've moved away. And the things said and done to me back then still make me feel down. I don't talk to anyone about it because it all sounds so silly. I'm forty-four years old. Nobody wants to listen to me griping about some teenage bullying from school, do they? I should have let it go by now. That's what people will say, won't they?" That all came out very fast, and she's a little out of breath. But she's pretty pleased with what she's said.

Dr O'Hara pushes the box of tissues towards Leah. Her stomach drops in horror – does she really look that sweaty? But then she feels a tear dripping down her cheek and realises she is crying.

"I'm sorry. I hadn't wanted to cry today." It never makes her feel any better, and she always ends up with a blinding headache afterward.

"It's okay. Let your emotions come out in any way they want to. Please don't be concerned about crying. I'd like you to tell me about your experiences during your school days. But first, I want to say a couple of things if you'll allow me?"

Leah dabs her cheeks and manages a small smile. "Yes. Please do." She balls the tissue in her hands and holds it tightly.

"Anything that has happened in your life is relevant to talk about and there is no time limit. If it's affected you negatively, it matters. Your experiences are valid. They are important. Time or perceived severity by others should not be a factor. It's you and your mental health that matters. I can see you want to resolve these things and let them go. And I'm here to help you do that."

Leah absorbs every word. Nobody has ever said anything like this to her before. It feels like a gift. A gift she has been waiting her whole life to receive. The tears come again, and she takes another tissue. But these are not tears of sadness or anger. These are tears of relief. Yet when she looks at Dr O'Hara, there is an unusual smile on her face. It's a peculiar response and reminds her of the expression people make when they've won or achieved something. Leah is taken aback and finds herself staring at the therapist.

Dr O'Hara shifts in her seat and runs her fingers through her long brown hair. The atmosphere has changed, and Leah has no idea what she's done wrong.

"I'm sorry about my reaction there, Leah. Honestly, I just felt a sudden swell of pride for you, and I couldn't keep it in. I'm told I wear my feelings all over my face. Initially, I felt I needed to try to control it, but most clients assured me they appreciated it. It makes them feel like I'm committed to their journey with them. And I am. I loved what you just said and am proud of you for saying it. I valued your reaction to my words, and it made me smile. I hope that's okay?"

Leah thinks about this for a second. It was definitely a weird moment, but the doctor's explanation is actually rather lovely. Is she so used to dour-faced doctors who look down at their knees or desks as she speaks that she is perturbed by a genuine show of emotion from a professional? Most likely.

"Yes, that's okay. I was just thrown off, that's all. I wasn't expecting you to be smiling." Leah gives a little laugh, and Dr O'Hara reciprocates.

"My approach is a little different. I don't stand back. I get involved. It's not for everyone. But if it's for you, I feel privileged to take this journey towards healing with you."

A warm feeling spreads inside Leah's chest. "Yes. I think it's exactly what I need."

"Then let's take the first step. Tell me your story. Tell me what it is that hurts your heart so much."

# 7

# LEAH

Leah wonders where to start. Dr O'Hara talked about reading and reviewing her notes and the bare bones of this story must be in there somewhere. The other doctors must have documented it. They have to, don't they?

"Try not to overthink, Leah. And I hate to bring up the issue of time, but we only have twenty minutes left, and I'd love the chance to discuss what you tell me. Yes, I've read what my colleagues have written in your medical notes, but I'm going to ignore all of that and just listen to you."

Is this woman a mind-reader? Leah rubs her hands down her thighs, straightening out her trousers, and begins her story. "When I was in high school, I was bullied by two girls." Leah pushes down the swell of anger and the bitter taste that appears in her mouth and forces herself to continue. "The worst part is that they started as my friends. We moved from primary to high school together and were so close. 'The Three Musketeers'. We went round to each other's houses at evenings and weekends. Even our mums were friends. We'd get to stay up late while our mums were drinking wine and chatting. It was lovely. Nothing else in the world mattered because we had each other." Leah looks down – remembering those happy days overwhelms her and she allows herself to swim in the sea of wonderful memories for a few seconds.

"Are you okay, Leah?" The doctor's gentle voice jolts Leah out of her reminiscences.

"Yes, sorry. I was just lost in a memory." How Leah wishes she could go back to those wonderful times. She'd find a way to make things different. Keep things as they were somehow and hold on tightly. "Yes. Things changed dramatically. All of a sudden. And I wrack my brain constantly for anything I did wrong. Something I said or did that turned them against me. But I can't. And I think the unfairness of it all haunts me the most. I can honestly say I did nothing wrong. I didn't change."

"But they did?"

Leah sighs and the sadness ebbs away to be replaced by a burning hot resentment. "They did. They changed completely. First, they changed physically. We all used to look the same. We wore the same clothes. Did our hair the same way. It was cool because I was a brunette, Melissa was blonde, and Natalie was a redhead. And did you notice our names?" Dr O'Hara shakes her head but doesn't speak. "L for Leah, M for Melissa, and N for Natalie. We were the LMN crew. We wrote it everywhere and even designed a cool logo with bubble writing. We scratched it into our tin pencil cases with compasses and drew on our hands with biro. We were connected, bonded, best friends."

Leah pauses to collect her thoughts. She needs to stop reverting back to the good parts of their friendship. It's too easy to take solace in the happy memories. She needs to tell Dr O'Hara what happened. "Anyway, enough of that. It was when we came back from the summer holidays in our third year. They both looked so different. They were both a head taller than me. They had boobs, and their skirts were rolled up so high I could see their knickers. And their eyes, something inside of them had changed. There was no fun in there. They laughed at me when I tried to say anything about the LMN crew. Called me a baby. It really hurt." There's a physical pain in Leah's chest. It hurt then and it still hurts now, like a stab to the heart.

"What do you think happened?"

"Well, at first, I thought it was just a development thing. Them going through puberty and leaving me behind."

"But?"

"But it was more than that. I'd barely seen them all summer, and they'd been in each other's pockets. But that had been the way in other school holidays and it hadn't made a difference. Whenever we started back at school, we always picked up like we'd never been apart. And I thought it would be exactly the same this time. I went on a two-week holiday to Spain with my parents every summer. During the rest of the six weeks, I was at my grandma's or auntie's house while my parents were at work. It never bothered me. I liked spending time with my family when I wasn't at school. And we didn't have mobile phones or anything then, so I hardly saw or spoke to Melissa or Natalie the whole time we were off school. It's just the way it was. Maybe I should have made more of an effort."

"Regardless, you did nothing wrong, and as you say, you didn't do anything to make them turn on you."

Leah closes her eyes and nods dejectedly. "I agree. But even after how they treated me, if I could go back and change things, I would."

"So tell me what happened at school that year."

"Melissa and Natalie started getting a lot of attention from boys. And not the ones in our year either. Boys who were fifteen or sixteen. I was worried about them at first because although they thought they were now popular and these older boys liked them, I could see that wasn't really the case."

Leah thinks back to that time. She genuinely felt worried for her friends and wishes she hadn't bothered. If she'd kept her mouth shut maybe things wouldn't have gotten so bad.

"What did you think was happening?"

"Well, I knew the older girls were laughing at them. I heard them being talked about in the toilets. Saying that the boys were using them and trying to get them to do..." Leah feels her cheeks flush again. It's ridiculous to feel embarrassed talking about this now she's a fully grown woman.

"What were the boys trying to get your friends to do?"

"The usual horrible teenage boy stuff. The boys wanted Melissa and Natalie to touch them. And vice versa. You know what I mean." Leah knows she's putting this across very badly. But the thought still disgusts her. They were children. "Sometimes, they even wanted Mel and Nat to touch each other. I mean, that's not right, is it?"

Dr O'Hara nods, a sadness in her eyes.

"I couldn't and wouldn't believe it at first. The Melissa and Natalie I knew would never do things like that." Dr O'Hara raises her eyebrows questioningly. "Don't get me wrong. I'm not naïve. We were thirteen and understood enough about sex and relationships. We'd all had chats about boys and which ones we fancied, but I just couldn't believe they were willing to do things like that with lots of different boys, older boys. I knew that boyfriends were definitely on the cards for us soon. But one, you know. Not loads of horrible older lads with their grubby hands everywhere. It's something I would never have done. And I hated it for them. They were being used and laughed at. It was awful."

Dr O'Hara tilts her head in sympathy. "It must have been hard to watch your friends change like that."

"It was. It was horrible. And I didn't have anyone to tell. If I ever needed to talk to anyone about stuff like that, I would go to Melissa and Natalie."

"What about your parents or a teacher?"

Leah shakes her head vehemently. "No. Definitely not. It was the nineties. Teachers at our school weren't there to confide in like I know they are now. They taught you, and that was it. The school stepped in if there was a big fight or something like... well, like what I'm about to tell you, but otherwise, you were expected to just crack on. It was a different time."

"And your parents?"

Leah smiles, a genuine feeling of love igniting in her at the thought of her parents. Her parents are wonderful. They were then, and they are now. Both her mum and dad are salt-of-the-earth types. They never moved from the village they were raised in and were perfectly happy with their lot.

"I don't mean this in a negative way at all. I had a lovely upbringing. My parents had me late in life, and they were proudly working class. We went to Benidorm once a year. Our food was classic British fayre. Fish and chips, bangers and mash, shepherd's pie." Dr O'Hara smiles warmly, the sides of her eyes crinkling. "I know that might seem off-topic, but I'm just trying to paint a picture. My home life was traditional. And a conversation about my friends – two girls that my parents had known since they were five years old taking part in sexual acts with older boys at school was definitely not on the table. My mum would have probably called the police and my dad would've gone out with a baseball bat. It wouldn't have helped at all."

"Okay, I think I get the picture. So what did you do?"

Leah inhales deeply, her lips fluttering with nervous energy as she breathes out. "I tried to talk to Melissa and Natalie about it. The first week or so had been horrific. They turned off our friendship as easily as flipping a switch. It was like I didn't exist anymore. As though all our years of friendship had meant nothing. I was utterly devastated, and I can honestly say I don't think anything has ever hit me that hard since. And my life has not been short on heartbreak. It was so extreme and sudden, and they had been a huge part of my world until then. They were suddenly hanging out in the popular crowd with the older kids. I could only watch as they started skipping lessons and smoking at the bottom of the school field. I tried to walk over and talk to them a few times. But they literally turned their backs on me." Leah stops and tries to steady her wobbly voice, the sadness she felt as her much-loved friends turned away and treated her like she didn't exist still cutting her deeply. Even though all of this is one hundred per cent true, the humiliation of admitting this still affects her decades later, and is soul-destroying.

"But Melissa and Natalie still walked home the same way as me. After trying unsuccessfully to walk with them the first few days back, I'd started rushing out of class and running home early to avoid them. It was too embarrassing to be knocked back every single time, so I just tried to keep out of their way. But one day, I waited, tucked out of sight on the corner of the street where Melissa lived. I knew it would just be the two of them by then. All their new cronies would have been dropped off along the way. When they turned the corner and saw me, I knew I'd made a huge mistake." Leah's hands are trembling. A new wave of shame washes over her.

"Keep going, Leah. You're doing so well. And please try to banish any thoughts telling you this isn't valid. It is. For you, this was a hugely traumatic event, and it has affected you all these years. Now, tell me. How did you know you'd made a mistake?"

The doctor's words pick Leah up. She is here to fight for her inner happiness. She's tried doing it herself, and it has been a disaster. "It was their faces. They looked at me with the most horrible mixture of pity and disgust. I can still feel it." Leah puts her hand over her heart. "I knew then that our friendship was over. Something had stolen my friends and turned them into these mean girls. Girls I didn't even want to be friends with anymore. At that moment, I realised I didn't want to fight for them. I knew it was over, so I turned and walked away from them."

"And wasn't that a small feeling of power or victory for you?"

"No, not even in the slightest. They shouted at me until I started running. They called me so many horrible, hurtful names. Words I'd never heard them say. I hadn't done anything to them. The next day, I decided I needed to try and make new friends. I knew it wouldn't be easy. Everyone's friend groups were set up and had been for years. But I knew a few girls from when I used to go dancing, and I thought I could get in with them."

"And did that work?"

"Yes, for a few days. Everybody knew what Melissa and Natalie were doing and, like I said, many of the girls were making fun of them behind their backs. People weren't really on their side. So it wasn't as hard as I thought. Until..." Leah puts her head in her hands and lets out a moan. *God, this is awful.* If there was any way she could wipe her mind of that horrible time, she'd do it in a heartbeat. Why does this have to live inside of her like a cancer, eroding her confidence and self-esteem? It's so pitiful she wants to scream.

Leah feels a light touch on her knee and looks up to find Dr O'Hara barely inches from her face. It's way more intimate than she would expect a doctor to be with a patient, but she doesn't mind it. In fact, she rather likes it. Once again, she feels a strange kinship with this woman. Dr O'Hara slowly pulls her hand away.

"You've come this far, Leah. Finish your story. Release it and take away its power. I can see from your notes that nobody has ever heard you. You may have told your story to them, but I know it hasn't truly been heard in the way it needs and deserves to be. But I hear you. And I care."

Leah clenches her fists and digs down deep. Dr O'Hara is right. Nobody has ever made her feel like her story is worth shit, and the only help she has ever received is slightly politer versions of 'get over it' with a side of happy pills.

"When Melissa and Natalie saw me getting on with my life and making new friends, they didn't like it. I didn't see that coming. Yes, they'd changed, but I didn't think they'd become so horrible they'd actively start bullying me. I thought they'd be happy I was leaving them to it with their current circle, but somehow that wasn't enough for them. They called out at me when I passed, and I could see my new friends shrink away from me. Nobody wants attention like that, so I totally understood how they felt. But then the worst part happened."

Leah knows there is much more to this story than she can ever tell. She knows she will never be able to reveal the worst parts to anyone. Ever.

But she needs to at least take a step and disclose what she can.

She's had enough of letting it control her life.

# 8

# LEAH

"We were in art class together. Melissa and Natalie sat away from me and didn't bother me all lesson. I started to feel cautiously optimistic they were getting bored. I wasn't fighting back or responding to anything they did or said. I genuinely thought they were going to leave me alone. They were huddled together on one bench, and I just got on with my painting, occasionally chatting to my friends. It was fine. After art, it was lunch, so everyone made their way towards the hall. Someone grabbed me and suddenly I was being bundled into an empty classroom. There were so many arms on me and bodies pushing me forwards. I didn't know what was happening, and there was nothing I could do. The next thing I found myself on my knees on the floor. Someone had tripped me or pushed me, I wasn't sure. Then I was thrown onto my back, and when I looked up, I saw Melissa's face. She was straddling me. I struggled and tried to push her off, but she was a lot heavier and stronger than me, and then Natalie grabbed my arms and pinned them to my chest."

A sob rises up in Leah's throat and she can't hold it in. Dr O'Hara leans forwards and places her hand on Leah's knee. She has a strange urge to hug the doctor or hold on to her hand. Leah only met this woman an hour ago, yet somehow feels like she knows her. Whilst she has told other doctors about the bullying, she's never gone into this much detail before. Not with anyone. Nobody knows this. Not her parents, not her husband. Only her and those involved.

"Three of the older boys Melissa and Natalie had started hanging out with were blocking the door. They'd closed the blinds, and I could hear the corridors were empty. I knew nobody was coming to help me. The boys started jeering. Telling Melissa and Natalie to take my clothes off. I was terrified and I lost control of my bladder."

Humiliation floods Leah's face. Gritting her teeth, she finishes the story. "Melissa jumped off me after I wet myself. I heard everyone laughing, but I didn't care. My legs weren't pinned down, so I started kicking and bucking. Trying to get free. But then one of the bigger boys held me down by my ankles, and that was it – I was trapped again. Melissa had joined Natalie by my head. I'll never forget the next bit because I'm sure I saw a flash of humanity in Melissa's eyes. A brief moment of regret. I can still see that expression in my mind's eye. And I tried to jump on it. I begged her. I told her I wouldn't tell anyone if she just let me go. I replay that moment in my head every day. And then Melissa actually spoke to me. 'Sorry, Leah,' she said. Her words were so quiet that nobody else but me and Natalie heard them. Then she pulled out a tube of red paint from somewhere and squirted it on my face. I breathed in from shock and some of the paint went up my nose. I did everything I could to get my hands free, but Natalie held them firm, her face turned away from me. Melissa started to rub the paint into my face. It was cold and sticky and had a horrible chemical smell. I could hear the boys screaming with laughter. Then the paint started to trickle into my mouth, and I vomited all over myself."

Leah almost gags at the memory of the horrendous taste of the paint mixed in with her own sick. "At that point, I felt Melissa and Natalie move away, and the room became deathly silent. I rolled onto my side and I was sick again, my vomit spilling all over the floor. I was completely helpless, and I just lay there and watched my friends' feet as they walked away from me and towards the boys. One of the boys kicked me in the back, and I heard Melissa tell him to leave it now. I can remember feeling so pitifully grateful for that tiny show of mercy. Then a voice, a different boy, said, 'You tell anyone and it won't be paint next time, it'll be your blood.' I heard the door of the classroom open and close, and then I was alone. Covered in paint, my own vomit and urine."

Leah sags in her chair, feeling as pathetic now as she did then. The consultation room is silent, and the story and the weight of the emotions Leah has finally set free hang in the air. She grabs a tissue and wipes her face, not caring that she is smearing her make-up everywhere.

"I can see how hard it was for you to tell that terrible story. Thank you for sharing it with me." Leah nods, noticing that the doctor's demeanour seems to have changed again. She's become sort of overly professional all of a sudden. Although time is ticking on, so perhaps she just wants to move things along. "And I don't want to rush you, but when you're ready, can you tell me what you did next?"

Leah blows her nose and crumples the tissue before dropping it into her bag. "Yes. I locked the door to the classroom. Thankfully, it was a science lab, so there were sinks. I cleaned my face and my clothes as best I could. I grabbed a mop and bucket from the cupboard, cleaned the floor, and ran home."

Mindful of the time, Leah keeps it factual. She doesn't mention staring into the mirror above the sink before the clean-up commenced, watching the paint clump and drip down her face, feeling her soul crack and her mind break.

"My parents were at work, but there was always a key under the back doormat. My shirt couldn't be saved, and I didn't want to explain anything to my parents about—"

Dr O'Hara cuts Leah off mid-sentence, her eyes wide. "You didn't tell them?"

"No, I didn't tell a soul. I threw away my shirt, put the rest of my uniform in the washing machine, and went back to school. I was a little late to class after lunch, but I made some excuse, I can't remember what, and I carried on as normal."

"I'm so sorry I butted in there. That was unintentional. I'm sorry. But that must have been so hard for you."

Leah shrugs. "Not really. They said I shouldn't tell anyone or they'd come back for blood. I believed them. I was protecting myself. What else would you have had me do?"

Leah realises her tone is challenging and doesn't mean it to be. But she's always thought she did the right thing, the brave thing, the only thing she could have done to maintain any semblance of a school existence.

Dr O'Hara's face remains unreadable. "And what happened after that?"

"I never once looked Melissa or Natalie in the eye again. Neither they nor the boys wanted me to tell anyone what had happened, and when I didn't, they left me alone. I carried on with my new group of friends. Sure, I was always looking over my shoulder and didn't socialise outside of school. But it wasn't all bad. I got good results in my exams, and I really came into my own at university. Until recently, it hadn't bothered me very much." Leah swallows. Her story has huge glaring omissions and she is convinced they must be written all over her face.

Leah looks up at the wall-mounted clock. If Dr O'Hara is

seeing Tess at 10.15am, they have less than five minutes remaining.

When Dr O'Hara sees her checking the time, she stands up and perches on the coffee table directly before Leah.

"Would you come back at eleven fifteen?" But then the doctor suddenly shakes her head. "Sorry, I forgot, you said you had—"

The words are out of Leah's mouth before she knows it. "No. It's fine. I'll come back. I'll... you know, move things around." Leah smiles meekly, regretting her earlier lie about having a full day.

Dr O'Hara responds warmly. "Thank you. I usually manage the time better in my sessions so we can discuss things more fully. But we had less time than usual, and I didn't want to interrupt your powerful retelling of your past."

*Powerful.* Leah likes that.

"But I don't want to leave things here unless we have to. I feel like you've told me so much, but we haven't had the opportunity to explore any of it together. There's so much more to say. So, if it's okay with you, could we have another hour at eleven fifteen?"

"Yes, another hour sounds good to me." Leah is impressed at how invested Dr O'Hara is. She seems so eager to help and more than willing to go the extra mile.

Dr O'Hara stands, and Leah joins her. "You're welcome to stay in the waiting room if you wish."

Leah picks up her bag. "I think I'll just use the bathroom to freshen up, then head out to grab a coffee. I'll be back just after eleven though." Dr O'Hara doesn't respond, and a weird moment passes between them. The doctor stares at her with such intensity that Leah feels like she is about to hug or grab her. Desperate to break the tension, Leah is about to speak when, thankfully, the doctor's face breaks into a broad smile and she becomes a consummate professional again.

"Perfect. I'll see you then. I look forward to it. And thanks again, Leah." The doctor's words are clipped and spoken through the odd smile she still wears.

Wanting to escape this weird moment, Leah turns and opens the door, holding it for Dr O'Hara and saying her goodbyes on her way to the bathroom without looking back. *What was that?*

When she reaches the toilet, Leah glances over her shoulder and sees Dr O'Hara standing in front of the door to the waiting room. The doctor is clearly lost in her own world, with no idea she is being watched. Leah is surprised at how vulnerable she looks. Like a lost little girl. Dr O'Hara looks up to the ceiling and mutters to herself as though in prayer. Leah knows she should just go into the bathroom and stop being so voyeuristic, but she can't seem to look away. The doctor's behaviour is so at odds with the calm, competent professional she just met. The woman standing outside that waiting room looks tense and anxious. Upset even. Is she okay? Maybe Leah shouldn't come back later. Perhaps this morning has been more stressful for Dr O'Hara than she is letting on.

Eventually, Dr O'Hara smooths down her hair, reaches for the door handle and enters the waiting room. Relieved, Leah escapes to the bathroom to tidy herself up and tries to rid herself of the niggling concerns she feels about what she just saw.

# 9

# TESS

Tess gives an exaggerated sigh of relief and clambers to her feet when she hears the door to the consultation room open and voices in the corridor. Finally, it is her turn. She runs her fingers through her hair and fixes her face into the perfect smile. One that says she's been put out by waiting this long, but because she's such a nice person, she doesn't want to let it show. When Dr O'Hara appears at the door, Tess feels a little disappointed that it doesn't have quite the desired effect.

"Hello, Tess. Thank you so much for waiting. Would you like to come through?"

Tess was expecting something a bit more than that, another apology perhaps. But never mind. She's about to get a whole load of emotional bolstering in the next hour. Add to that the outpouring of support from her online followers and the love and concern she'll receive from Joe when she gets home, and she'll be on top of the world by this evening. Her attention-ometer will be off the scale.

Tess follows Dr O'Hara into the consultation room and sniffs before sitting on one of the chairs. It smells like old lady perfume and sadness in here. Dr O'Hara takes a seat on the chair opposite and crosses her legs. Tess isn't sure what to think of the doctor but reckons she'll have the measure of her by the end of the session. Tess definitely saw something in her earlier. Something that nobody else but she would have noticed. But then, this hasn't been a usual morning for Dr O'Hara, and people deviate from their natural behaviours when things go wrong. If Tess was a famous doctor and her stupid receptionist hadn't bothered to show up, she'd be raging. It could be as simple as that.

Tess smiles and sits back, happy to let the doctor speak first. She thinks that's how these things work. She's never had therapy or counselling – is there a difference? – or seen anyone about her mental health. This is a first for her, and she reckons she's going to love it.

"Thank you for your understanding this morning. As I said, there will be no charge for your consultation today, and I'm happy that we do the full hour if that works for you?"

Tess gives a self-deprecating smile and strokes her arm with her hand. It's supposed to show self-soothing, and she sees the doctor glance at what she's doing. Tess makes a show of pulling her hand away before clasping both in her lap. Perfect. What a great start.

"I can see from your appointment booking that I'm the first doctor you've seen about your mental health and that you self-referred to me. Is that right?"

Tess flits her eyes around the room before looking at the doctor and then down at her hands. "Yes. I've wanted to talk to someone for a while, but I didn't want to be a burden to anyone." Tess bites her lip and crosses her arms, holding her sides. "It's not easy to admit you've got a problem. Well, not for me anyway."

Tess looks up to check how her performance has landed and sees the doctor sitting back casually, watching her curiously. The tip of her pen is in her mouth. It's not the concerned and caring response she was hoping for. Maybe Tess over-egged the nervous body language.

She tries again. "I'm sorry. I'm just new to this and a little nervous."

The doctor nods and gives a pinched smile. She looks almost irritated, and Tess feels her hackles rise.

"Aren't you supposed to be asking me questions or something?" Tess tries to maintain her little-girl-lost veneer, but she can feel it slipping, the doctor's nonchalant reactions getting under her skin.

Dr O'Hara takes the pen out of her mouth and opens her notebook. "Sure. I can ask you questions. Why have you come to see me today? What do you think you need help with?"

The doctor sits poised, ready to take notes. She didn't even look up when she spoke. What is going on here? Tess swallows down her incredulity. Maybe this is some sort of test? Or maybe Dr O'Hara is just a complete bitch.

"Have I done something wrong?"

Dr O'Hara tilts her head and raises her eyebrows comedically. Tess has just about had it with this woman, and they've barely been here two minutes. Who does she think she is, behaving like this? She's out of order, and Tess won't stand for it.

"Why would you say that, Tess? You wanted questions, and I asked you questions. Two, in fact. Was that not sufficient? What were you expecting?"

Tess is rarely lost for words but stares dumbstruck at the doctor. She had imagined many ways this conversation might go and prepared various quotes and stories she could use. But this?

This was not remotely on the cards. And for the first time in a long time, Tess doesn't know what to do or say and, horrifyingly, she wants to cry.

Dr O'Hara points her pen at Tess's face. "There. That's it. That's what I was looking for."

Tess remains flabbergasted. She has lost control of this situation, and it feels horribly uncomfortable. She needs to fight back, or better still, get out of here. This was a big mistake.

"I have no idea what you're talking about, Dr O'Hara, but I'm not here to be spoken to like that. I expect to be treated with respect. This is completely unacceptable, and I'm leaving." Tess begins to push herself up from the sofa. She won't stay with this rude, dismissive woman another minute longer. How she's become the most sought-after therapist in the city Tess will never know.

"That suits me just fine. You know where the door is. And I haven't charged you for this complete waste of my time anyway."

Tess stalls, her hands planted by her sides but still seated. She watches the doctor, who is now examining her nails with absolutely no show of emotion. Tess should storm out, say her piece, and leave. But something is stopping her. She can't leave until she wins back control. The doctor's indifference is killing her, and she needs to regain the upper hand before she goes.

"What are you waiting for, Tess? You've done your announcement, now off you flounce." Dr O'Hara points towards the door, but this time, she meets Tess's eyes and doesn't look away. Tess stares straight back. The doctor's eyes are cold.

Tess leans back and crosses her legs. "No. Actually, I don't think I will."

The doctor mirrors her and they sit across from one another, staring each other down. Minutes pass in silence and apart from the odd blink, nobody moves or makes a sound. Eventually, the doctor speaks, and Tess feels a small pang of victory.

"I know you probably think you've won by me breaking the silence. But you haven't. I could easily sit here saying and doing nothing for the entire hour. You don't bother me one bit." The feeling of triumph dissipates quickly, but Tess maintains her steely and silent demeanour. "I know you think you're special, Tess. But I've seen a hundred of you. I saw it as soon as you walked in the door. You think you can fool me with your acting, but you're actually pretty terrible at it."

Tess swallows as tears threaten again. She'd rather die than cry in here, and she pushes her nails into her palms to distract herself.

"I am not here to be lied to, Tess. There are people out there who genuinely need help. I knew from your referral form what kind of person you would be. And you did not disappoint. You're a narcissist. And if you would like help with that, I'm happy to oblige. But do not come at me with this 'I'm too giving and too caring and it's sapping the life from me' bullshit. It will not wash, and I am not here to be controlled like the poor people who happen to find themselves in your life. So don't even try."

Tess feels as though all the air has been knocked from her lungs. She has not simply met her match, she has been torn to shreds and left for dead. She could try to argue and really turn it on, but she can already see that would be foolish. Or she could get up and walk out quietly. Leave with a shred of dignity and go to the spa like she planned. She never has to see this woman again and can tell Joe and her friends whatever story she pleases. Once she leaves this room, she will be back in control of the narrative. All is not lost.

But these are fleeting thoughts. Tess won't do either of these things. Because not only is she curious, but she is also wholeheartedly impressed. Nobody has ever called her out like this before. In fact, she's pretty sure nobody else has even suspected she is anything other than genuine.

Tess shifts slightly in her seat and takes a deep breath. This is going to be interesting. She's never been totally honest with anyone before.

Let's see what Dr O'Hara can really do.

# 10

## LEAH

After fixing her face and composing herself, Leah does as she planned and walks to the café across the street for a takeaway coffee. She considered hanging around in the waiting room, but there is an energy inside her and she needs to walk it off before returning to speak to Dr O'Hara again. She definitely will go back. She was wrong to spy on the doctor and the woman has had a very stressful morning. She shouldn't be so judgemental. Dr O'Hara can behave however she chooses when she's off the clock. It's nobody else's business.

The day is bright and warm, so she walks, cappuccino in hand, along the street. Most people are at work now, so although there are still a few people around, the streets are not bustling and she can amble easily without getting in anyone's way.

Leah had promised herself she would tell that part of her story in detail today and she managed it. She has spent too many years pushing it away, believing it's stupid and nobody would think it mattered. And it has ruined her. She shouldn't be feeling this way about something that happened thirty years ago and it shouldn't provoke the reactions in her that it does. But she can't seem to fix it by herself. She has tried. And it only seems to get worse.

Until recently, Leah was too busy to ruminate on the past. She was working relentlessly to get her business off the ground while taking care of her boys. From the early years when they needed her direct care and touch to the teenage years when Leah became an unpaid taxi driver and launderer of muddy rugby kits and school uniforms. But she's not needed in that way anymore, in any way, really, and now she has time for herself, her mind is slipping. The raging hormones aren't helping either. She doesn't know whether she's coming or going half the time. Although she still enjoys her work, there isn't the deep-down satisfaction and joy she used to feel after creating beautiful spaces for her clients. It's just a job, simply a way to pay their bills.

Leah takes a sip of her coffee. It is delicious and warms her insides. She spots a bench and takes a seat. She's walked about fifteen minutes from the doctor's office and will need to set off shortly to make it there in time for her second appointment. She reaches inside her handbag and takes out her oversized sunglasses. They are perfect for inconspicuous people-watching.

A delivery van pulls up on the opposite side of the street, and the driver rushes in and out before driving away. A woman walks past pushing a double buggy, one baby in her arm and a toddler holding on to the handle, waddling beside her. Leah smiles. She remembers those days and knows most people will wonder what the woman is doing. Surely she should just put both children in the buggy and push it. But it's not that easy, and young children want their mothers right there with them. Next to their little bodies. Holding and protecting them. A wave of sadness falls over her. Leah and her husband were always planning what to do once the children were grown, looking forward to some time together. And they get to go to dinner regularly now and occasionally the theatre, but Leah hadn't prepared herself for how devastating it would feel not to be needed in that raw way children need their parents. It kept her buoyant and well for many years, but she hadn't realised it until it was gone. Still, Leah is beyond proud of her boys, thrilled that they are self-sufficient and happy, and she hopes grandchildren will be on the horizon in the not-too-distant future.

But one thing Leah doesn't feel any longer is proud of herself. She has allowed herself to spiral into a pit of bitterness and resentment, and she doesn't like herself anymore. Some days, Leah actively hates herself. And she knows why. She also knows she can't tell another soul.

Leah has regrets. Leah has secrets. Things she can't tell Dr O'Hara.

Checking her watch, Leah pushes herself up from the bench and begins the walk back to the doctor's office. She is grateful for the offer of another session today; she wouldn't have liked to leave things as they were. She told her story, but they haven't even scratched the surface about how it made her feel back then or touched upon how it resurfaced only a few years ago. Leah needs to admit out loud she hasn't been coping, that her mind has started to unravel and terrible things have begun to fall out.

But will she ever heal without admitting the whole truth? The answer to that doesn't matter because she knows she can't.

Her life would be over if she did.

# 11

# TESS

"Okay, you got me." Tess smiles and gives Dr O'Hara a slow, sarcastic round of applause. "I'm not sure that gives you the right to be so rude though. Plus, I think you swore at me. That's definitely not allowed. There must be somebody who'd like to hear about that. A professional organisation of some kind I could report that to." Tess raises an eyebrow.

Dr O'Hara barely flinches at her challenge. Instead, she puts her notebook and pen on the chair beside her and exhales an exasperated breath. "You should just leave, Tess. You've jumped from lying to making pathetic threats. Quite frankly, I don't care what you do."

"But I've still got half my session left, so I think I'll stay right here."

Dr O'Hara lets out a shrill laugh, and Tess is annoyed when it makes her flinch. "Oh, you will, will you?"

Tess crosses her arms and nods her head slowly and purposefully. "I will." She's trying her best to look in control, but her insides feel horrible and squirmy. She's nervous, and she's desperate to leave. But she can't go without gaining the upper hand. This bitch won't beat her.

"I promise I can make you leave in the next..." – the doctor checks her watch unnecessarily – "...three minutes."

Tess's heart jolts. Surely, the doctor can't physically remove her. Tess is taller and probably stronger for a start. She's never been in a proper fight but reckons she could handle herself. But the look of confidence and pure certainty in the doctor's eyes is horribly unnerving. *Just leave. This isn't worth it.* Yet still, she doesn't move.

"Very well, but you won't like what I've got to say," Dr O'Hara continues. "Don't say I didn't warn you."

Tess scowls. Dr O'Hara is clearly enjoying this. How can she flip this around? Take back power? There's always a way. She just needs to find it. It's not her fault she's been completely blindsided by the doctor's shitty behaviour. Nobody could have predicted this.

"You've lived in your own little bubble, playing everyone you know and coming out on top. But I promise you, if you continue to sit there in defiance, I will say things, true things, that will cut your soul to shreds." Tess gasps. "You see, Tess. I can see through you as though your skin were transparent. You're a joke. And frankly, I'm astounded you've managed to carry on your charade of a life without anybody noticing. To me, you're as subtle as a pantomime dame." Dr O'Hara laughs again, amused by her own observations, and Tess's whole body breaks out in goosebumps. This isn't worth it. Dented pride or not, she needs to escape before, as the doctor so eloquently put it, her soul is 'cut to shreds'.

"Okay. I'll leave." Tess mutters the words quickly, hating herself for yielding but knowing she needs to protect herself. This woman is off-the-charts crazy, and there's no reasoning with that. She can go to hell. She wonders briefly what kind of experience Leah had. The woman had left before Tess had a chance to see her. Surely not everyone is treated this way here.

She'd have no patients left. And that makes Tess pause for thought. So this must be personal. But why would a doctor give a patient, any patient, no matter what they think of them, such a hard time? It seems completely implausible.

Something isn't right. Tess is missing something and wants to know what it is before she goes. She takes a good look at Dr O'Hara's face. She's definitely younger than Tess was expecting. And she's attractive in that formal businesslike way that some women are. Not feminine or traditionally beautiful like Tess, but alluring, nonetheless.

Tess wracks her brain. Does she know this woman? It's certainly possible. Tess tends to forget a lot of the people she meets unless they're of benefit to her. Most people are just unremarkable and not worth remembering. Has she somehow wronged Dr O'Hara in the past? Could she be a disgruntled follower who has taken umbrage with her? She trawls her memories, but nothing comes. If she has met the doctor before, she has no idea when or where.

"Do I know you? Have we met, or did you know of me before our appointment today?"

The doctor answers coldly. "No. As far as I know, we've never set eyes on each other. Why do you ask?"

"Because this all feels far too much. You're being way too harsh, and I can't wrap my head around it. Yes, I understand you calling me out. But threatening to take me down and destroy me – that seems way overboard for us having just met. Or am I missing something?"

Dr O'Hara nods, looking a little more like the woman she was when they entered the room. Before the vicious tyrant emerged. "I have to agree, Tess. But no, I don't know you. This is indeed the first time we've met, and I know nothing about you other than what I read in your referral form and what I could glean online."

"Online? Why would you look me up online?"

"You put your Instagram handle on your referral form."

Tess flushes. She did do that. And in hindsight, it was probably inappropriate.

"That was a first for me, Tess. I've seen a lot of referral forms in my time, but never one with a social media link. You may as well have written 'I'm a narcissist' in capital letters. But it did get my attention and, actually, made me bump you up the list."

"But why? You said you knew from my form that I would be a waste of time. Did you bring me here just to act like a total bitch? To get your kicks trying to tear me down? What kind of doctor are you?" Tess is fizzing with anger and doesn't care if it shows. Dr O'Hara is abusing her position, and Tess can't think of any good reason for her to do this other than spite.

Dr O'Hara picks up her pen and begins twirling it around and through her fingers. "Okay, let me be frank with you. Yes, I knew you were likely to lie about your life and come begging for attention. But I was intrigued. And actually, I think we can do some good work together if you'll cut the sanctimonious bull—" The doctor puts her hand to her mouth. "Oops, I better stop there. I don't want to offend your sensitive ears with another swear word."

Tess rolls her eyes. She's not being sensitive. Doctors shouldn't be swearing at their patients. That's just a fact. But at least Dr O'Hara has toned down the personal attack, and her last comment actually piqued Tess's interest. "And what work would that be?"

Dr O'Hara leans forwards. "I can help you be the best version of yourself. I can show you how to get all the fuzzy warm feelings you get from being in control and feeling superior without negatively affecting anyone in your life. I can teach you how to feel fulfilled without manipulating your partner, family, or friends. Sometimes we can't change who we are inside, Tess, but you can learn different behaviours."

Tess listens intently. What the doctor is saying sounds pretty good – except for the part about changing behaviours. That sounds like hard work.

"Even though I've known you for a very brief time, I think I can help. You came here under false pretences, but honestly, therapy could actually benefit you. I can guide you towards being a fairer person and stop you from inevitably hurting your loved ones. And more than that, we can make that happen and still have you feeling happier than you do now."

The doctor definitely has Tess's attention now. She feels pretty happy already. But happier – who would turn that down?

"I came at you hard because it was the only way to jolt you out of the prepared narrative you arrived with. You're someone who will lie to the bitter end, even with evidence to the contrary in front of you. I needed you to be shook up. I had to unnerve you so you would listen to me. You rate yourself highly and are rarely usurped, so I needed to do something to place myself higher in your regard, and I think I've succeeded. You do need therapy, Tess. But it won't look like what you were expecting. I know that will make you feel special, and I guess, in this instance, you are."

The doctor is right, this is nothing like what Tess was expecting. But if she can be even more content with life than she is now, what is there to lose? So Tess lays all her cards on the table. In for a penny, in for a pound. It sounds like Dr O'Hara knows exactly who Tess is, so there seems little point in holding back.

"Okay, I'm in. Full disclosure. I'm definitely my number one priority, and I never give anyone more than I need to. I know exactly what I want and usually how to get it. I'm not particularly bothered about how that affects other people. Oh, and I'll do pretty much anything to get what I want as long as it doesn't come back to bite me. That bit's really important." Tess holds out her hands. "There you go. I've never said that to anyone, but it seemed like you knew it already, and I know you can't tell anyone. Confidentiality or something, right?"

Tess knows what she's just said makes her sound inherently unlikeable and selfish. But Dr O'Hara has finally dropped the cold, callous attitude and appears much warmer.

"Indeed. Everything you tell me remains in this room. Can I ask you something though?"

"Of course. I'm an open book, apparently. Who'd have thought it."

Dr O'Hara raises an eyebrow. "You said you'd do almost anything to get what you want. Where do you draw the line?"

Tess tilts her head and thinks for a moment. It's a fascinating question and not one she's ever thought about in depth. Where are her limits? Nothing has ever pushed her to find out.

"That's an excellent question. And do you know, I'm not totally sure. Being the most important person in my life has always felt natural. I don't understand why more people don't feel that way." Tess taps a well-manicured finger against her lip, trying to find a better answer. "I'll think about that for next time. But the best I can do just now is that I've never done anything criminal, like illegal or anything, and I don't think I would, not unless I had to."

Dr O'Hara's eyes gleam with fascination, which gives Tess a thrill. "And why would you have to?"

"No, I mean, if someone threatened me or my..." Tess drifts off before finishing her sentence. She hates any show of vulnerability unless she's faking it.

Dr O'Hara doesn't miss a beat. "Or your...? Come on, Tess.

It's hardly a bad thing to have people in your life you want to protect. Your fiancé, perhaps?"

Tess screws up her face without meaning to, and the doctor smirks.

"So not your fiancé then?"

"No, that wasn't what I was going to say. I mean, I do love him, I think, in my own way. We're happy together, and it's the kind of partnership I want. But no, I think it's his role to protect me if anything. He can look after himself. That's not my job."

Dr O'Hara nods in agreement and makes a quick note on her pad. "I think from your referral form, I can deduce who the one person you would protect is."

Tess furrows her brow, trying to remember what she wrote.

"Your mum. It was obvious to me that you genuinely care about your mum."

She's not sure why, but Tess's cheeks flush. It's hardly unusual to care about your own mother. But she doesn't want to talk about her mum. That's not why she's here. Dr O'Hara promised to make her feel better, not worse.

"It's okay, Tess. I don't plan on discussing your relationship with your mother in any great detail. But it is something that stood out to me. Do you remember the section on the form where I ask prospective patients to write about their circle of support? Everyone in your life, including your fiancé, got barely a sentence whereas your mum had a paragraph all to herself. The tone of your writing changed completely. It was really nice to read."

Tess's eyes fill up but she forces the tears down immediately. Her mum has always supported her no matter what she said or how she behaved. Her dad could be judgemental and pushy, but Tess and her mum have always had an unspoken understanding. She has never felt anything other than unconditional love from her. Love that Tess has not always appreciated or respected, and it is the only thing in her life that makes her feel bad about herself. As such, she keeps her distance from both of her parents.

Tess would like to see her mum more and go for days out together. But she's not a pure, kind person like her mother is and she doesn't want her mum to see her badness, her darkness. So her visits are infrequent, and she tries to see their distant relationship as a sacrifice to get the life she wants.

Tess does her best to summarise her thoughts, leaving out any of the emotional stuff. "Yes, I do love my mum. Don't most people? But I don't see her very often. My dad is always whining at me for not having a career and constantly makes me feel like a disappointment, so I don't go and visit them much."

Dr O'Hara nods. "I understand. And as I said, I don't want to make you talk about your relationship with your mother. I can already see it makes you conflicted. But I will say you should hold on to the feelings you have for her. They are not a weakness, and I think we can use some of how you feel to build on your other relationships and your attitude towards yourself and your place in the world."

Tess folds her arms, the doctor's words hitting a little too close to the bone. She wasn't expecting to feel quite so overwhelmed and doesn't know what to say.

"I know this is all very new to you, Tess. To start with, you've been honest with me. Something very unusual for you. It takes time to get used to the doctor–patient dynamic. It's always unique and forms organically. I can see it isn't comfortable for you to have your true self reflected back at you through my words."

Tess breathes deeply. This realness is giving her a headache, and she wants to escape back to the known and take some time to digest it all.

"What I'd like to focus on in our last ten minutes is your

fiancé and your friends. Can you tell me a bit about those relationships?"

Back on safer ground and with the spirit of honesty she's been asked to adopt, Tess speaks freely. "I don't really have friends. I meet up with a few girls sometimes, but only because we go to places I want. I like going to nice restaurants or the spa and prefer not to always go on my own. But I don't like any of them, and it wouldn't matter to me if they were a different group of people. I think most of them are pathetic, to be honest."

Tess sees the muscles in Dr O'Hara's cheeks twitching. What she is saying is making the doctor uncomfortable. So she ramps it up. It would be nice to get back on an even keel after she was made to feel all emotional about her mum. Tess is not weak, and just because the doctor is able to psychoanalyse her doesn't mean she's going to become all soft and gooey. She has earned her happiness. Will she be willing to make a few tweaks the doctor suggests to make herself even happier? Of course. It would be foolish not to. But Dr O'Hara should not underestimate her.

"And Joe, my fiancé, I've completely landed on my feet with him. He is smitten, and I can wind him around my finger any way I please." Tess watches as Dr O'Hara writes notes, her eyes down and her face taut with tension. Watching the doctor's discomfort is brilliant. This is way better than being the sad, trodden-on doormat she was going to pretend to be. "I don't have to work. He gives me as much money as I want. On the odd occasion he does ask me to cut back or questions me in any way, I turn on the crazy. Just enough to make him feel bad but not enough to ever question wanting to be with me. I've drawn the line beautifully. It's an art." Tess beams and has to hold back a laugh. She can see the doctor simmering. What a sight to behold.

Eventually, Dr O'Hara looks up and smiles but her eyes

are cold. "Thank you for your honesty. It's exactly what I asked you to do, and I can see that now the wall is down, you're an absolute natural. I think there's lots to work with here, and I think you're going to surprise yourself with what you can achieve." Tess soaks in the words as the doctor speaks through clenched teeth. "I can also see you're trying to provoke me. And I must admit, I do find a lot of what you are saying distasteful. But I won't bite or become challenging again because you are being truthful, and I'm here to help you."

That takes the wind out of Tess's sails a little, but not enough for her to stop. "That's good to hear. I hated how you acted before but I see why you did it, and you're right, I do think more of you now." Then Tess remembers how she felt when she first met Dr O'Hara. "You know, I thought I saw something in you when we first met. Your reactions reminded me of mine. Beautifully telegraphed and very convincing but somehow not believable." Tess watches with interest as the doctor mulls this over.

"That's my job. I was stressed this morning but wanted to come across as professional. I was angry and upset at my receptionist. I didn't want my irritation to leach into my interactions with you and Leah. What you saw was simply me doing my job to the best of my ability."

Tess smirks and wags a finger. "Hmm, I'm not so sure. There's definitely something about you."

There's a flicker of fire in the doctor's eyes before she softens her face again and speaks gently. "And what would that 'something' be, Tess?"

Tess leans forwards and stares directly into Dr O'Hara's eyes for several seconds. "You know what, I don't know. Honestly, I don't. You're very tricky to read. I tried to look for it then, seeing if I could find it in your eyes. But I can't work it out.

I know I'm not making much sense, but there is something. Definitely something."

Dr O'Hara gives Tess a thin smile. "As I said, our relationship is developing and it will take a while to settle and find its natural cadence. But do you mind if I ask you one more thing before we close our session today?"

Tess doesn't believe this explanation one bit but decides to leave it alone for now. She'll work out what the doctor's deal is. It'll come to her later. It's this weird environment throwing her off.

"Sure. Fire away."

"How you describe your fiancé and your friends makes them sound disposable. Is that how you see people?"

Tess answers without a second thought. "Yes. Absolutely."

"What if I were to challenge that assertion and say that everyone is equally as important as you. You are just one of over eight billion people in this world, and nothing makes your wants or needs more important than anyone else's."

Tess stifles a laugh. "That's preposterous."

"Really? How so?"

"Because I'm me, and this is my world."

The doctor puffs out a breath and furrows her brow. "Okay, I'd say that's verging on god complex territory."

Tess can't believe she has to spell this out. "No, you misunderstand me completely. I only have this one life. I'm not living anybody else's. So, how can you say I need to treat everyone the same as I treat myself? That's just nonsense. Everyone I meet is a player in my life. That's just how it works. I can't be in their shoes."

"You could try. That's called empathy. It's something lots of people practise on a daily basis. I know I do."

Tess rolls her eyes, frustration rising. "Look, I hear what you're saying. And I don't think I'm actually special, so don't start with the god complex crap. I'm not deluded. But I do live my life for me. Nobody else is going to. And yes, most people are disposable, and I think I'm just as disposable to lots of people too. And rightly so. I'm not going to cry about it. That's just how the world works. I keep people in my life who I want there and only if it serves me to do so. I can't see how that's a bad thing at all." Tess knows this all makes perfect sense, and if Dr O'Hara thinks she's going to get Tess running around after other people's needs all day, she's got another think coming.

"A lot of what you said there is true, Tess. And I actually rather like how you explained it." Tess does a little happy dance inside. Finally, the woman is actually listening to her. "We are all on a spectrum of behaviour, and I'm trying to establish where you fall. I think it's very interesting how you describe yourself and your place in the lives of others, and I'd like to come back to that the next time we speak. But for now, we're out of time."

Tess finds herself feeling a little disappointed. She was just getting into the swing of things. And now their session's over just as she was bringing Dr O'Hara around to her way of thinking.

"Sure. I think I like this. It's nice to say things exactly as they are. Quite refreshing, really. So I'd be happy to come back again. It's definitely been a different experience than I expected, but that's not such a bad thing."

Dr O'Hara smiles and gathers her book and pen before standing and extending her hand. Tess stands up, too, and they shake hands.

"I've got some reading material I'd like to give you before you leave, if that's okay?"

"Like homework?"

Dr O'Hara chuckles. "No, nothing like that. Just some things I think might help you. You can bring them back or throw them away if they aren't for you. No pressure."

"Okay. Fine with me."

Dr O'Hara opens the door. "Would you go back to the waiting room while I dig them out for you? I won't be more than a few minutes."

"That's fine."

Tess watches as the doctor enters the small office behind the reception desk. She feels quite uplifted. She would have tried therapy years ago if she'd known it would have this effect.

When Tess opens the waiting-room door, she is surprised and somewhat disappointed to see Leah plonked in one of the chairs. Why is she still here and why are her eyes so wide? Tess doesn't want to make small talk with this woman. She knows it will only bring down her buoyant mood. So she proffers a polite smile but no other greeting before sitting and turning her head away. Hopefully, this is a clear sign that conversation is not on the table. Tess takes out her phone and starts scrolling.

# 12

# LEAH

When Leah returns to the doctor's office, all is quiet. The door to the consultation room is closed, and she supposes Tess must still be in her session. She feels conspicuous waiting out here and doesn't want to be accused of listening in. Plus, she'd rather not see Tess again. Young beautiful women always have a negative effect on her. She shouldn't be so superficial, but she can't deny the pang of jealousy that hits her every time. She pats her forehead, relieved to find it is relatively dry. Would she be overstepping the mark to go straight to the waiting room? Maybe, but she can blame the absence of a receptionist if Dr O'Hara seems at all put out by her taking the liberty.

She opens the door to the waiting room and peers inside, breathing a sigh of relief when she sees it is empty. She has barely sat down when she hears murmuring and the click-clacking of heels on the tiles outside and she freezes. She has no idea why. She needs to stop being so apologetic for her mere presence. Who cares if they hear her? She's supposed to be here.

Leah finds herself staring wide-eyed as the door opens and Tess walks in, looking about as pleased to see Leah as Leah is to see her. Mercifully, after a perfunctory twitch of her face that

Leah supposes must be an attempt at a smile, Tess pays her no further heed and drops gracefully into the seat beside her before taking out her phone.

Leah wonders if she should go and look for the doctor. She doesn't want to pester her, but she might not know Leah's in here. And why has Tess returned? Perhaps she was offered another consultation too. She risks a glance at her and finds her still absorbed in her phone, a self-satisfied smile on her perfect face. Leah sighs, the noise way louder than she intended and embarrassingly noticeable in the quiet room. Tess visibly stiffens and twists herself farther away from Leah. *Don't worry, I don't want to talk to you either*.

They've barely been alone for a few minutes, but the atmosphere is uncomfortable. Neither of them wants company. Leah waits it out for a few more minutes before deciding to make her way back to reception. There's no point sitting here feeling uncomfortable when she doesn't have to. But before she can move, the door to the waiting room swings open with such force that it clatters off the wall. Even Tess is startled from her phone and cranes her head.

Leah blinks, confusion and terror rising within her. She can't comprehend what she is seeing.

Leah opens her mouth and begins to scream.

# 13

# TESS

Six minutes she's been sitting here with Leah. It feels like a hundred and six. Leah's mere presence seems to suck all the life out of the room, and there's something iffy about her that Tess really doesn't like.

Three minutes ago, she sighed loudly. A hideous gust of air that set Tess's teeth on edge. If that was an attempt at a conversation starter, she can think again. Tess has no desire to give that woman one second of her time and is pissed off she finds herself stuck with her again. Seven minutes now. That's at least six minutes longer than it should take Dr O'Hara to bring her whatever reading stuff she wants her to take home. This is such a waste of her time. If it gets to eight minutes, she's going. Eight minutes is far too long to wait.

What is Leah even doing here? Just hanging around like a bad smell. Her consultation ended ages ago. She'd better not jump in and try to speak to Dr O'Hara first like she did earlier. The spa and an afternoon of relaxation and pampering await.

Finally, Tess hears the door swoosh open, followed by a loud bang. She turns, ready and raring to complain about how long she's had to wait. But then she stops and takes in the sight before her. She can't quite believe what she's looking at.

Tess is not easily frightened. It takes a lot to unnerve her. But what she sees now has her heart hammering in her chest. She hears Leah shriek beside her but doesn't pay her any heed. Tess doesn't take her eyes away from Dr O'Hara.

The doctor is standing in the doorway with a gun in her hand. She moves the weapon from side to side, alternating between pointing it at Leah and then at Tess. It's weirdly hypnotic, and Tess watches, frozen with morbid fascination.

Leah continues to scream in between unintelligible grunts and sobs. Tess wishes she'd cut it out. How can wailing possibly help? And the gun is not the only thing Dr O'Hara has brought with her. There's another even more unsettling addition.

Tess's eyes drift to Dr O'Hara's other hand, which rests on the shoulder of a weeping woman who has a cloth gag wrapped around her mouth. The woman is tied to a desk chair with wheels. Her blotchy, tear-stained face is etched with anguish, and she bucks against her restraints to no great effect. Her eyes are wild and pleading but the gag prevents her from forming intelligible words. She moans pitifully. It is an extraordinarily disturbing sight.

Tess examines the woman in the chair. In her distressed state and with her face partially covered, it is tricky to assess her accurately. She's considerably older than Dr O'Hara. Perhaps pushing fifty. Her mousy brown shoulder-length hair is sticking out at all angles. Black mascara streaks her cheeks. Tess doesn't know this woman, but there must be a reason why the doctor has tied her up and pushed her into the room like some sort of horrific exhibit. Why that might be, Tess has no idea, but she's sure they are about to find out.

Dr O'Hara looks relatively calm and certainly determined. Whatever is going on here is not spur-of-the-moment. Tess has never been one to overreact, and she doesn't now. In fact, by most people's standards, she is seriously underreacting. But neither she nor Leah have any room for manoeuvre here. They have a gun pointed at them. Only a fool would try to leave now. The doctor is an intelligent woman and has obviously planned this, but there is little Tess can do until the reason for this macabre performance is revealed.

Tess turns to Leah, who is now sobbing violently.

"Would you shut up! She has a gun and a woman tied to a chair. What exactly do you think you are going to achieve by crying like a fucking baby? Get a grip."

Tess crosses her arms and looks back to the doctor, who is slowly edging her way into the room, pushing the chair forwards, her eyes never leaving Tess's face. Why is she so focused on her and not Leah? Is this all for Tess's benefit, and is Leah simply an innocent bystander? Tess leans over and shakes Leah's arm, but the doctor shouts before she can speak.

"Don't move, Tess. Can't you see the gun?"

Tess sits back and raises her hands in surrender. "Okay. Calm down. Obviously, I see the gun, but she's shrieking like a banshee. I was only trying to get her to pack it in. Well, that and to ask if she knows her." Tess gestures to Dr O'Hara's captive but doesn't make eye contact. She doesn't want to see her begging eyes again. "Because I don't."

Whoever this woman is, and whatever the reason behind her imprisonment, one thing is certain, Tess won't be playing hero and getting herself shot in the process. If there's a way out of this for her, she'll take it. Every woman for themselves. But the smart move for now is to follow the doctor's instructions and stay exactly where she is. Wait for an opportunity. Wait for Dr O'Hara to slip up.

Leah has at least toned down the dramatics and is now merely snivelling and sniffing unattractively. Although on second thoughts, calming her down might have been an error. It can't hurt Tess's chances to be the most compliant of the two.

The room falls into a weird silence, and Tess turns to find Leah white-faced and still. Is she about to pass out, or has she gone into shock? The last thing this room needs is more drama. The doctor kicks back with her foot, and the door clicks closed, punctuating the stillness. Tess looks up at Dr O'Hara expectantly, knowing this is the moment they will finally discover their fate. Her mouth feels horribly dry, and she has no idea what is about to happen.

Finally, the doctor speaks. "I'm sorry I kept you both waiting so long, but there's someone I would like to introduce you to." The doctor runs a finger down the cheek of the woman strapped to the chair, who flinches and closes her bloodshot eyes tightly. Tess watches the gentle yet sinister gesture, entirely absorbed by the whole twisted act.

"Tess, Leah – may I introduce you to Dr Jenna O'Hara."

# 14

# LEAH

Leah hears the words, but they rattle around her brain, not connecting with anything. She turns as a sharp laugh escapes Tess's mouth and watches as she shakes her head, her glossy black hair swishing. Tess seems almost amused and impressed. It's as though she didn't just hear the same words as Leah.

"Tess, Leah – may I introduce you to Dr Jenna O'Hara."

She must be in some kind of weird dream world. A land of nightmares where nothing makes any sense and unspeakable horrors keep assaulting her. Her brain feels like it's collapsing in on itself.

When the door to the waiting room flew open, Leah found herself screaming. She didn't want to scream but no matter what she tried, she couldn't stop. Her mouth stayed open, and the howls of terror kept pouring out of it. Then the crying began. Again, not of her own volition. The tears simply came, and she sat back, her body refusing to listen to reason.

But now she is numb and lost. She wants to stand up and fight or run away to safety, defend herself somehow. Say something at least. Tess has said lots of things. She has even asked questions, and she's still alive. But Leah finds she can only sit, her head a mess of broken thoughts, her body unable to provide more than the basic functions required to keep her alive.

"Nothing to say, Leah?"

Leah's heart leaps into her mouth, terrified at being addressed directly. She looks up at the woman with the gun. The woman she spent forty-five minutes speaking with this morning. The woman who is not Dr O'Hara. She stares agog at the only person she has ever opened up to about what happened that day at school. She looks both completely different and exactly the same. The shape of her face, her hair, and her clothes are all just as they were an hour ago. But her eyes. Those eyes belong to somebody else. The woman glares, her stare penetrating deep into Leah's very soul. They are hate-filled and Leah knows she is in serious trouble.

"Who... who are you?" Leah is surprised to hear the words come out of her mouth. It's the question that must be asked, but she is terrified of what the answer might be.

The woman's eyes narrow and her mouth breaks into a menacing grin. "Great question, Leah. I thought you'd never ask." The grin becomes a sneer as her eyes continue to bore into her. Leah is transfixed. She hears Tess's voice, but it sounds far away or as though underwater.

"Yes, definitely a good question. Who the hell are you? And what the bloody hell is going on?" Tess sounds annoyed and confident. How can someone act that way when there's a gun pointed at them?

The woman interjects. "Tess, could you stop being such an attention whore for five seconds and let me talk to Leah? If you listen, you'll hear everything you need to. Plus, you'll get your turn."

Leah watches as the woman turns to Tess and winks. Actually winks. What is wrong with these people?

"Anyway, Leah. Apologies for Tess's rude interruption. You'll see during our time here that she is, in fact, a completely selfish and horrible person." Tess gasps at the insult and Leah jumps as the woman raises her voice. "Do you want me to shoot you? Because you're going the right way about it."

Leah is beyond relieved to see that the woman is addressing Tess, not her. Even now, Tess wears an offended and defiant look on her face. She really hopes Tess starts behaving herself. Leah doesn't want to be a witness to her being shot.

With the gun and all of the attention pointed at Tess, Leah wonders briefly if she can make a run for it. The door was only kicked closed, so it shouldn't be locked. Would she be able to get past the prisoner in the chair and out of the door before being shot? She looks at the bound woman in the chair, the woman who she now knows to be the real Dr O'Hara, and sees her shaking her head. A miniscule movement unlikely to be seen by the others in the room. Leah feels her heart sink to her boots but heeds the warning. There is enough space for her to manoeuvre past the chair to the door, but there's no way she would make it. She'd be dead before she even took a step.

Tess and the unknown woman are in a staring match, and Leah wishes she were in this predicament with anyone else. What kind of person tries to win a battle of wills with a woman holding a gun? Tess is going to get them all killed.

"How about this, Tess. I'm going to talk to Leah now. She asked a very good question, and I'm going to be polite and answer it for her. If you make so much as a peep, if you breathe even slightly louder than you need to or move a single muscle while Leah and I are talking, I'm going to shoot you in the ankle. How does that sound? This gun isn't just for killing, you know. I could make your time here very painful. And I don't think those pretty designer heels would look very nice dangling on the end of a mangled stump, do you? So, for once in your life, be a decent human being and shut the hell up!"

Leah winces as the volume of the woman's voice escalates so she's almost shouting.

"Well? A simple yes or no, Tess, please."

"Yes." Tess's voice is croaky and small and Leah sees that for the first time, Tess appears afraid. Leah tries to give her a smile – a small show of solidarity – but Tess only looks down at her lap.

"Good. Finally. Thanks for your patience, Leah. And to answer your question – my name is Sally. I'm Dr O'Hara's receptionist."

Leah looks first at Sally and then at Dr O'Hara, who gives a barely perceptible nod before breaking eye contact and falling still.

Leah doesn't know what to say. Sally may have answered the question, but it doesn't really tell her anything. All Leah has is a name. A name she doesn't recognise. What could Dr O'Hara's receptionist want with Leah and Tess?

Why has she tied the doctor up and imprisoned them all in here together?

And what is she planning to do to them?

# 15

# TESS

Tess is taking things seriously now. She does not want to be shot in the ankle. Or anywhere else, for that matter. It was almost impossible not to react when the gun-wielding woman identified herself as the elusive receptionist. But she did as asked and remained quiet and motionless, regulating her breathing. Tess does not like to be controlled, but let's face it, if there were ever a situation to break from the norm, this is it. Tess wants to walk out of here with her life and all of her limbs intact.

The odds are stacked heavily against her, and she needs to start playing this a bit more shrewdly. To fight against her natural instincts. She has to be obedient. She needs to be quiet and listen. Being passive and compliant doesn't come easily to Tess, but if she wants to remain in one piece, that's what needs to happen.

Tess looks over at Dr O'Hara. It'll take her a while to get used to this new development. So Dr O'Hara has been tied up all this time, and the woman she spoke to this morning, the woman who gave her hell, was actually Sally. Tess can't quite believe it. Sally did a brilliant job. Tess knew there was something off about her, but never in a million years could she have pictured this.

The real Dr O'Hara is no longer struggling or crying. She is slumped in the chair, her eyes downcast. Tess wonders how long the doctor has been strapped to the chair. Did Sally seize her this morning? Probably. Despite her messy hair and make-up-streaked face, Dr O'Hara appears smartly dressed and well-kept. Socks adorn the doctor's feet, making her look somewhat childlike, and her tailored trousers and cashmere jumper are clean. If she'd been held captive for any length of time, she'd look dishevelled and dirty. Plus, she'd likely have needed to use the bathroom, and there's no evidence of urine on her clothes. Tess wrinkles her nose at the thought before forcing her features back into a compliant blank expression.

What did Sally mean by 'you'll get your turn'? Turn to speak? Turn to get a bullet in the head? Whatever it is, she doesn't want her turn. Unless it's her turn to leave. Tess tries to drown out the room and think clearly. Sally obviously wants to speak to Leah first. Does that mean Leah is the main reason behind them being held captive? Leah and Sally must know each other or have a connection. Or is this all about the doctor? Tess checks Dr O'Hara's behaviour once more. She is still sitting quietly and not fighting. The gag covering her mouth looks like a white cloth handkerchief. The kind her dad would use. It seems to be tied pretty tight, but Tess reckons she could speak if she really tried. Although perhaps she's been threatened with the same ankle mutilation as Tess if she does so.

Dr O'Hara's hands are tied behind her back, and her legs are bound separately to the central column of the chair with a thin black-and-white rope. It appears sturdy and the knots look decent enough. Although what Tess knows about knots could be written on the back of a postage stamp. But these are all further signs that this was a planned event. It doesn't look like the kind of rope you'd have lying around a doctor's office. Sally must have brought it with her.

A thought suddenly occurs to Tess. Something that seems obvious, but in amongst all the drama, she hadn't yet had the time to consider. Leah and Tess both having their appointment at 9am was not a mistake. Sally wanted them to arrive together. Tess is relatively sure she doesn't know Leah, and Leah gave no indication they'd ever met. Unless you count her being all weird and sweaty when she arrived.

If Sally wanted them together like this, she could easily have done it first thing this morning. Why did she take the time to put them both through a fake consultation? Why did Sally need to speak to them separately before holding them prisoner? Surely, she was taking a risk by doing so. Either of them could have decided to leave. In fact, Tess was actively told to leave. Oh, how she wishes she could turn back time and just walk out. She'd be lying on a massage bed with hot stones on her back right about now instead of being at the mercy of a psychopath with an unknown agenda. Yet even with all the uncertainty and unanswered questions, Tess is sure nothing this morning has happened by chance.

Sally is pulling the strings and Tess, Leah, and the doctor are all here for a reason. Something must link the three of them.

A shiver runs down Tess's spine as she considers the most important of her unanswered questions. Will any of them get out alive?

## 16

## LEAH

Leah's lack of reaction to Sally revealing her identity seems to irk her. But what is she supposed to do? If Leah speaks, she might end up getting threatened with a bullet in the ankle like Tess. When Sally said that, Leah felt physically sick. Can you imagine how painful that would be? Leah thinks she'd rather be shot in the head and be done with it than bleed out slowly from a mutilated foot.

She breathes out slowly through pursed lips, trying to calm the rising nausea and pushing away the disturbing mental images. No. She mustn't think like that. She needs to get a grip. There must be a way out of here. She just needs to work out what Sally wants. Find a way to get her on side. Make her see she's made a terrible mistake. But how is she supposed to do that when she has no idea why they are here?

"I'm going to sit now." Sally stands in front of the sofa across from Leah and Tess. "Neither of you try anything, okay? You both stay exactly where you are." Sally turns her head and addresses Dr O'Hara. "And you. I know you can't actually move even if you want to, but the same rules apply. You do anything I don't like, and I will hurt you." Sally sits down, crosses her legs and rests the gun on her knee. "This is heavier than it looks, you know." Leah doesn't react and sees in her peripheral vision that Tess's head is still bowed. Sally continues. "Okay. Good. I'm glad you both seem to have settled down a little. I know you're scared, and I'm sure your heads are bursting with questions. But we're going to do this my way. Do you understand?" Leah nods. "Tess? I know I told you to shut up. But you can answer that. My way. Yes?"

Tess lifts her head and gives her one-word answer. "Yes."

"Excellent. I've already told you who I am, but I'm guessing that means nothing to either of you." Leah's heart is racing, and her chest feels tight and constricted. She's not sure she's going to get through this without having a heart attack. "I'm going to tell you both some things you need to know. Answer some of those burning questions I know you must have." Leah swallows. As terrible as this feels right now, she knows it will only get worse. "Neither of you are here by accident. I booked your appointments at the same time this morning. You are both here because I wanted you to be."

An icy chill envelops Leah, yet despite her utter terror, she is still desperate to hear more. Not just about why she is here, but why like this? Why put her through the misery and humiliation of baring her soul. Why not just grab them both when they first arrived? What could Sally possibly have to gain by pretending to be Dr O'Hara?

Leah thinks back to their consultation. Although she doesn't have any significant experience of therapy, Sally certainly came across as believable. She was a little unorthodox in places, but she explained herself really well and seemed caring and concerned. The fact she was able to fake that so convincingly makes this even more frightening.

"In a moment, I'm going to tell you exactly why we are all here and what is going to happen. But first, and in the spirit of the honesty I want to see and hear in this room, I'll allow you each to ask me a question. I don't want this to feel completely one-sided." Tess's head springs up. "Ha. That got your attention, didn't it, Tess? But pop that pretty head of yours back down for just a moment because Leah is going to go first." Sally adjusts her position slightly before tilting her head slowly towards her right shoulder and then her left. Painful clicking and crunching noises emerge as she does so. "Now think carefully, Leah. You only get one question. Use it wisely, and I promise I will answer honestly."

Dozens of questions swim around Leah's head. *Why me? What have I done? Do you know me? Do I know you? Why would you pretend to be Dr O'Hara? Why today? Why here? Why? Why? Why?* Without meaning to, her final thought comes out of her mouth.

"Why?" She knows her voice sounds pathetic, and the pitying look on Sally's face only makes her feel more wretched.

"I'm going to need a little more than that, Leah."

Leah feels as though she might fall apart, her fear, confusion and anger all bubbling and mixing together. Any semblance of self-control is slipping through her fingers. She doesn't want to ask a question. She wants to scream and cry and pull out her hair. To charge at Sally and wrestle the gun off her. This can't be happening. How can any of this possibly be happening? But she can't just sit here like a lump of clay. Dooming herself to whatever Sally has in store for her. So, she does her best to pull herself together and tries to form her thoughts into a question.

"Why? Why have you trapped me in here? Why do you have a gun pointed at me, and why did you pretend to be a doctor and listen to me pour my heart out? Not only that, but then invite me back pretending you want to help me further. Only to do this. And what even is this? Why? That's my question. Why? Fucking why?" Leah feels out of breath and light-headed. That was a lot of questions, and Sally will probably punish her for her disobedience. Leah stiffens, expecting a bullet. For everything to go black or for the explosion of pain in some part of her body. But it doesn't come. There is only silence and the sound of her own breathing. Then she waits for Sally to start shouting, threatening and berating her, but that doesn't come either. When Leah looks up, panting and barely holding it together, she sees an amused smile on Sally's face. She feels a rush of anger, and it takes everything she has not to lunge out of her seat.

"That was quite a performance. You should probably have applied an extra HRT patch this morning, Leah. Wow." Leah grimaces, humiliation burning at her cheeks. "Plus, you've broken the rules and asked more than one question. But I'm feeling generous, so rather than ignore you completely, which I think I'm completely entitled to do, I'll pick something out of that garbled mess of words you just threw at me."

A sense of hopelessness falls over Leah. There is no way to win this game.

"Let's go with 'Why would I pretend to be the doctor?' shall we? I'm sure Tess would like to know that too. Plus, it's one of my favourite parts. So listen up, ladies."

# 17

# TESS

She never thought she'd say this, but Tess is quite impressed with Leah. Granted, she totally lost her shit and looked like a crazy woman doing it, but at least she said something. Sally's comment about HRT was so cutting and absolutely brilliant. It's the kind of thing Tess would have said if she wasn't keeping silent to protect her limbs. Plus, now she's going to get the answer to her question without even having to ask it. She'll pick her follow-up question depending on what Sally says next. This whole situation is weird and unfathomable, but Tess is at a loss as to why Sally would pretend to be Dr O'Hara. Tess and Leah were both here at 9am. She could have just ushered them into this room and immediately cracked on with her madness.

"There are many options for private therapy here in Manchester, and you could have chosen any of them." That's undoubtedly true. "So why did you both pick this one? Why Dr O'Hara?" Sally looks at Tess. "Think back, Tess, and be honest. We've already seen what response you get from me when you try to lie, haven't we?"

Tess crosses her arms. It was fine being honest when she thought she was speaking confidentially to a doctor. But she doesn't want any of the aggro she got from lying earlier, especially not now her interrogator is armed with a deadly weapon. So she decides to tell the truth.

"I don't know. I wanted somewhere that looked nice, you know, luxurious. Top end. I wasn't interested in the actual therapy, so I didn't look very hard. I just picked this one because I saw it on Instagram. It looked plush and the kind of place I could blog about, so I went with it." Leah gives Tess a look of incredulity. "Oh piss off, Leah. Not everyone is a sad old cow like you. Do you want congratulations for needing therapy rather than wanting to try it out? Well done, you."

Leah turns her head quickly away.

"Yeah, keep your opinions to yourself."

Tess worries she has overstepped the mark and is about to be threatened with another maiming, but Sally's eyes are now wholly focused on Leah.

"And you, Leah? Your face suggests you're judging Tess for choosing her therapy from an advert on social media. So why don't you share with the class how you learnt about Dr O'Hara's services?" Sally's eyes glint and a smirk appears on her face. "And don't be lying either, Leah. Tess will tell you I don't take too kindly to that."

Tess watches as Leah clears her throat, her cheeks flushed red.

"Um, Facebook."

Tess can't help herself. She snorts and is about to ridicule Leah when Sally's stern glare stops her in her tracks. Still, Tess basks in her smugness. Facebook is just Instagram for old people. Leah is no better than her. In fact, she's worse. She clearly needs therapy and booked herself in based on a Facebook ad. Hilarious.

"It took a little while to hook you both, but social media

advertising is surprisingly effective at targeting people," Sally says.

Tess is surprised when Leah pipes up to defend herself.

"I did a lot of research, you know. I didn't just see the Facebook advert and immediately book an appointment. I looked Dr O'Hara up and studied her extensively. I did my research. I asked around."

"And that's very admirable, Leah. Yet still, here you are. Exactly where I wanted you. Anyway, I digress, but I wanted you both to understand how relatively simple it was to lure you here. I had backup plans in case the online approach didn't work: leaflets, word of mouth. I'd have knocked on your doors if necessary. But thankfully, it didn't come to that."

As Tess takes in Sally's explanation, she feels increasingly uneasy. Until now, she thought there could be a chance this wasn't personal. But hearing the lengths Sally was prepared to go to, there is simply no way it isn't. Sally has coordinated everything so that Tess, Leah and Dr O'Hara would be here at her mercy this morning, and she is beginning to fear none of them will get out alive.

"To answer your question, I pretended to be Dr O'Hara because I needed to see you both with my own eyes. To hear your stories and see if the things I thought about you were true. And I have to say, neither of you disappointed."

The blood chills in Tess's veins and she sees a similar look of terror on Leah's face. This is not good news. Not good at all. What could she have done to land herself here? She genuinely has no clue. Plus, what did Sally mean by, 'to see if the things I thought about you were true'? Admittedly she pissed off Sally at the start of the consultation by putting on a front. But they got past that. And Tess even showed a brief glimpse of her softer side when Sally brought up her mum. Okay, she then admitted that nobody in her life matters as much as herself. But that doesn't make Tess unique. The world is filled with selfish people. It has to be something more specific than that.

Maybe Sally knows Joe? Tess isn't really interested in his family. She does the perfunctory visits to his parents twice a year and it's been fine. She plays nice and they seem to like her. Joe's only brother died a while ago but he didn't seem too cut up about it, and he doesn't have any mad ex-girlfriends that she knows of. Though she shouldn't dismiss that possibility outright. Sally could be a jilted ex hell-bent on revenge. But then why are Dr O'Hara and Leah here? As far as Tess is aware, there is no connection between the three of them. Nothing that would require this woman to seek out a joint punishment. And that's why Sally holds all the power. She knows everything, and they know nothing. Of course, there must be a connection. And Tess is dying to find out what it is. She could exploit it if she knew. But as things stand, she has no hand to play.

Sally tilts her head and shouts over her shoulder to Dr O'Hara. "Are you listening back there? You're going to want to hear this."

The doctor moans. The drool-soaked rag covering her mouth releasing slimy liquid onto the poor woman's chin. Tess really doesn't want to end up tied and gagged like that. It would put severe constraints on her already limited escape options.

"And, Doc, it was so easy to be you. I can't actually believe you get paid the amount you do for rolling out the same old tired sayings over and over again. Of course, none of your hapless patients know that, do they? And I have to give it to you, you've definitely got a knack for making people feel special."

Tess is intrigued. As soon as she met Sally, she sensed something cunning and she's eager to hear how she pulled pretending to be a psychiatrist off.

"It's unbelievable what you get access to as a receptionist slash personal assistant slash general dogsbody. All those consultation recordings and dictations I listened to and the letters I typed. Every single one had a little nugget or two that I stored away. I practised replicating your voice. Getting the timbre and cadence just right. I memorised phrases. I learnt how to get people to air their dirty laundry. How to behave when someone gets emotional – that would be you, Leah. And how to deal with people you might find unpleasant. The liars. Tess, that's you if you hadn't guessed. I had a plethora of phrases and methods all stored up here." Sally points to her temple with her free hand. "I perfected it all. If I didn't have to do this today, I think I could make a decent career as a therapist." Sally chuckles before the shutter of darkness falls back down on her face.

Sally's self-congratulations are pissing Tess off and she can't help herself. "If you didn't have to do what? What exactly *are* you doing?"

Sally raises an eyebrow and points the gun directly at Tess's face. "Is that your question, Tess? I haven't quite finished with Leah's yet."

"No! No, I have a different question. I want to know if you're going to shoot us, or if this is... something else."

"Well, tough shit. You should have thought of that before you opened your big mouth. Quite frankly, I'm surprised at you. I think it's a rare occurrence for you to say something superfluous and imprudent. But then, we are in unfamiliar waters."

Tess chokes back a biting retort. Sally's flowery language and mocking tone are beyond irritating. Superfluous? Imprudent? Fuck off. But Sally is right. Tess shouldn't have framed that as a question. That was stupid.

"And as I said, I needed to speak with each of you. Alone. I needed to meet with you both to ensure this was the correct course of action. And now I know it is, I can proceed as planned."

Leah sniffs and she has her head in her hands. She's lost it again. Tess wonders what Leah revealed or discussed in her session. Her reaction to what Sally just said could be good news for Tess. Maybe Leah has done something terrible.

To survive this, Tess needs the heat to be on either Leah or Dr O'Hara, and she suspects there is much more to Leah than meets the eye.

# 18

# LEAH

Leah has been clinging on to her sanity by the skin of her teeth, and Sally's assertion that she's going to 'proceed as planned' tips her over the edge. The tears come, and her despair and despondency hit her like a freight train. This is all so indescribably horrific. Far too much for any person to withstand. Sally starts to answer Tess's question and Leah knows she needs to listen. But all she wants to do is curl up and cry.

"So, to your question, Tess. A rubbish question, to be honest, as I've already answered most of it. But what I will say is this. This is going to be a space where we will right some wrongs. This room is going to be a place of honesty. Truths are going to be told and secrets will be revealed." The hairs stand up on the back of Leah's neck. "You see, lies and secrets fester inside you and begin to rot your very being." Leah feels as though her throat is about to close. She can't breathe. Sally won't even need to shoot her; she's going to die right here from terror.

Sally looks at her. "Is that how you feel, Leah? Are your

secrets rotting away inside you? Turning your flesh black. Black like your heart."

Leah can't hold on any longer. She knows there is air in the room, but she can't get it into her lungs. The room starts to close in on her and shadows dance before her eyes. Before she succumbs and passes out into the darkness, she hears Sally one final time.

"You're going to reveal all your secrets, Leah. Just you wait."

---

A slap across Leah's cheek jolts her into consciousness. Tess's out-of-focus face is in front of her and Sally is still sitting exactly where she was before Leah blacked out.

"Sorry I slapped you. She made me."

Leah looks around the room. Her cheek is stinging, but weirdly, she feels somewhat better. As though she's had a reset, although everything is still just as horrific as it was before she passed out. Dr O'Hara remains bound to the chair, and there's still a gun pointed at her, but her most debilitating fears have left her.

Sally looks furious and barks instructions at Leah. "Can you sit back up. I'd have loved to slap you myself, but then that would give Miss World over here a chance to get the gun off me, so I had her do it."

Tess seems pleased with the 'Miss World' remark.

"I couldn't breathe. I didn't mean to—"

Sally cuts Leah off. "You need to breathe. It's easy. You've been doing it since the day you were born. If you pass out like that again, I can't guarantee I'll let you wake up. Do you understand?"

Leah swallows. She does understand and finds she can breathe in and out quite normally now. "I won't pass out again."

"Good. Now, Leah, you came back for a follow-up consultation. And we're going to do it here. Among friends."

Leah's world shatters. She can't. She looks over to Dr O'Hara. Is she going to do the consultation? Is that why she's here?

Sally seems to read her thoughts. "No, not with her. Didn't you hear me? It's money for old rope. Anyone can do it. Plus, Tess and the dear doctor haven't heard your sorry tale yet." Leah's heart sinks at the word 'yet'. "I'll be the one asking the questions. And this time, we'll have a bit of honesty. Okay, Leah? Not the sanitised version where everyone is bad but you."

Leah nods and focuses on keeping a steady stream of air flowing in and out of her body. She may as well accept she has no choice. She is allowed a brief reprieve and time to regroup when Sally turns to Tess.

"It didn't make sense to offer you another consultation, seeing as I needed you to come to the waiting room. But you'll be getting one. Right after Leah's."

Leah waits for Tess's face to fall, for her to look as terrified and filled with dread as she feels. Tess must have dark secrets too. But instead, she just shrugs her shoulders and nods perfunctorily.

"Okay. I've got nothing to hide. Anything I said to you earlier, I'd happily say in front of these two."

"That's very much appreciated, Tess. That attitude will go a long way to making your time here more... comfortable." Dread licks at Leah's insides. That could not be farther from the way she feels. "Did you hear that, Leah? Tess may be a selfish bitch, but at least she's going to be honest. I hate to say it, but you could learn a thing or two from her."

Leah holds back tears. "I'll tell you anything. I won't lie, I promise. If we tell you what you need to hear, will you let us go?"

Sally furrows her brow and puts on an animated thinking face. "That's a tricky one. And before either of you try with the 'we won't tell anyone' nonsense – don't. Because I won't believe it, and I will punish you if you try. You have to appreciate it's a bit hard for me to let you go now I've threatened you with a gun and trapped you in here. It's not really possible, is it? I don't want to end up in jail."

If Sally hadn't warned her not to, Leah would be pleading and begging now. Promising that she wouldn't tell a soul. And genuinely, she thinks she'd keep that promise. She'd do anything to get out of here.

"So here it is. Full disclosure. Not everyone will leave this room alive."

Leah feels all the blood drain from her face, and a low groan escapes from her mouth. Really, she knew this hideous information already but hearing it out loud is beyond terrifying. Tess appears frozen to the spot, her eyes as wide as saucers and she is barely blinking. And the doctor simply sits. Her head bowed, and her shoulders gently bouncing as she sobs.

"But before any of that happens, we will complete your consultations. And I hope I don't have to state the importance of your active participation. This is your chance to put things right. To absolve yourself of your sins. I suggest you both treat this opportunity with the significance it deserves. Bare your soul as though your life depends on it."

The resolute stare on Sally's face chills Leah to the bone.

"Because it does."

# 19

# TESS

Okay, game on. Now Tess knows some of the rules, she can start to play. As she sees it, she is one of three contestants with mad Sally as the game-show host. Yes, it's scary and completely fucked up, but Tess has yet to find a situation where she can't advocate for her own best interests. The prize, if you can call it that, will be walking out of this room alive. The stakes are high and there is no choice but to play. At least one of them is going to end up dead. And she needs to make sure it's not going to be her.

Why she, Leah and Dr O'Hara are here doesn't matter anymore. This is a battle of wills. A fight to the death, and Tess knows she can make it out alive. All she needs to do is be better than her opponents. It's survival of the fittest, a way of life that Tess is familiar with and accomplished at. If she could save everyone in here, she would. Probably. But Sally has made it very clear that's not going to happen.

Tess considers her rivals. One is currently tied up. Tess would put money on the fact Dr O'Hara is leaving with a bullet in her head. How could Sally possibly get away with this otherwise? And the other, Mrs Menopause over there, is about as stable as a one-legged stool. Tess, on the other hand, feels relatively calm. Undoubtedly, she's had moments of genuine fear, shock, and panic. And that's okay. She's probably felt more genuine emotions in the last thirty minutes than she has in the last year, and if she uses them correctly, they could actually help.

A crazy thought jumps into Tess's head. What if all this is a ruse? What if this is some kind of extreme therapy, and they're all going to walk out of here cured and better people? Tess shrugs off the thought. That would be completely mental. It would make a great story though.

She focuses back on the task at hand. If Sally wants honesty, she can have it. If this is some kind of mad confessional where Sally wants to play God and absolve her prisoners of their sins, then so be it.

Tess will lay her entire life out on the table. Tell the room her every poisonous thought and reveal everything she's ever done.

She will survive.

Bring. It. On.

# 20

# LEAH

Succumbing to fear and continually freaking out will not help, but it's almost impossible to do anything else. Leah takes some deep breaths in an attempt to stop her mind from falling apart and her body from sinking into unconsciousness again. She is still hanging on. Barely.

"In our previous consultation, Leah, I took a 'gently does it', tender, coaxing approach. It worked well, if I do say so myself. Although thanking you incessantly and constantly apologising was tiresome, to say the least."

Leah thinks back. Sally did set a lovely atmosphere, and she did feel supported and cared about. If only she'd known.

"But I won't be doing that now. I ask you a question. You answer it. Fully and promptly. Got it?"

Leah nods and clasps her hands together to stop them from shaking. "Yes. I've got it."

"It took me forty-five minutes to drag that story out of you. And I want you to tell it again. Quickly and without all the blubbing."

Leah sees Tess's head turn in her peripheral vision, and she can imagine the smirk on her face. But she can't let shame hold any power here. If Leah wants to live, she needs to follow Sally's instructions to the letter. So she clears her dry throat, stares at her hands and forces herself to speak.

"I had two best friends in high school. Melissa and Natalie. We were close and we did everything together. We used to—"

Sally interrupts. "Get to the point, Leah."

Leah stops picking at her cuticles and forces herself to look Sally in the eye. "Sorry. My friends turned on me, and one day, along with three older boys, they locked me in a classroom." Leah takes a deep breath. She can do this. "Melissa and Natalie held me down and covered my face with red paint. Some went in my mouth and I was sick everywhere. I never told anyone and until recently had forgotten all about it. I booked an appointment with Dr O'Hara because I knew I needed to talk it through with someone. The memories... well, they were making me ill. Changing me."

Leah stops. Realising she can recount the story in a few simple sentences makes it seem so insignificant.

Sally chimes in. "Don't forget that you pissed your pants."

Leah's cheeks flush crimson, and she speaks through gritted teeth. "I did. I was terrified."

"Okay. Can you believe it took her forty-five minutes to tell me that story?" says Sally, addressing no one in particular. Neither Tess nor Dr O'Hara make a sound. "As we all know, I'm not a doctor, but here's my take on it. Teenage girls can be horrible. It's nothing new and pretty much every grown woman in existence has experienced something akin to bullying at some point in their teenage years. What those girls did to you was mean, and I'm shocked you didn't do anything about it. If it was me, I'd probably have gotten them back. Actually, no. I was soft as shit at school, so I'd probably have told the teacher or my mum. I'd have cried about it and thought my life was over for a few days. You know, typical teen girl stuff. But what did you do, Leah?"

"I went home. I cleaned myself up and went back to school. I had never told anyone that story until I told you this morning. I mean, I'd told other people I'd been bullied but never the details."

"Didn't that eat you up inside? Didn't you want... revenge?"

Leah feels the blood drain from her face. "I... I'm not sure. I kind of went on autopilot. I'm not sure why I didn't tell anyone that first day, but then it got harder and harder to say anything. I made some new friends. It was sort of okay. Melissa and Natalie left me alone, and then I just got on with my life and left it behind."

"Until?" Sally's eyes are darker now and filled with danger.

Leah's pulse quickens. "Until it started bothering me again. I... I think I blocked it out for too long, but it affected me more than I realised. I started thinking about it again and it was making me feel weird inside. So... I thought I should probably try talking about it. That's why I came to see you. Well, not you. I mean Dr O'Hara. I..."

Leah's voice drifts off. She's stammering, and her words are garbled. She knows where this conversation is heading but isn't ready to admit it to herself.

Sally leans forwards and moves the gun so she's now holding it in both hands. She points it squarely at Leah's chest. Leah can't risk looking in Tess's direction, but with all of Sally's focus directly on Leah, this could be an opportunity for Tess to attack. She wills Tess to do something, but everyone remains exactly where they are.

"That story is missing a few things, isn't it, Leah?"

Leah squirms in her chair and wipes her sweaty palms on her trousers. Sally can't possibly know, can she? "Um... well, you did say to be brief... I mean prompt. Did you say prompt?" Leah's aware she's rambling, but she can't think straight.

"Shut. Up."

She does as she is told. She knows what's coming. From the moment Leah found herself trapped in this awful room, this is the thing she's been most afraid of. That Sally knows what she did. She can't work out how, but it's becoming increasingly apparent that she does.

Leah has lived in constant fear of being discovered. Yet, nothing has happened. She keeps waking up each morning and living her life. The world keeps turning. She knows she's going to have to admit her sins. They've been warned that lies mean punishment. That her life depends on her being honest. She's going to have to tell her. Which means that even if, by some miracle, she gets to leave this hell alive, her life will never be the same. It won't be worth living anyway.

So Leah sits in silence. As though in front of a firing squad.

After an excruciating wait, Sally finally speaks. "Tell me what's missing from that story, Leah. Tell us all how you got your revenge."

# 21

# TESS

*Oh. My. God. This is getting wild.*

Sally forced Leah to keep her story brief, but Tess would have loved to hear all the details of Leah's bitchy friends' attack on her. It was like something from that film *Carrie* with all the pig's blood. Tess can't wait to hear what happened next. She sits on her hands and presses her lips closed. She needs to keep the attention off herself. Stay still and quiet. Be boring. *Keep playing the game, Tess. You're winning.*

Maybe Leah went all mad psycho bitch when she got back to school, locked all her friends inside and set the place on fire. Though that's probably a bit wild for Leah. She probably just sent a letter. Got them expelled.

Anyway, it's more than obvious that Sally and Leah know each other somehow, and Sally knows Leah's done something terrible. It's just a waiting game now.

Two hours tops and Tess is sure she'll be out of here.

An idea is starting to form at the back of her mind. Little flickers of inspiration. She thinks again to her earlier consultation and what Sally said afterwards: "*...to see if the things I thought about you were true.*"

Tess thinks she gets it now. She reckons she's starting to understand why she's here.

And if she's right, she is more than happy to go along for the ride.

# 22

## LEAH

All of the fight has left Leah's body. It's confession time.

"You know, don't you?"

Sally's face is stone cold. "I do."

A loud sob escapes Leah's mouth.

"Don't start that or I'll do something that will really make you cry."

Leah's hands fly to her mouth. She tries frantically to push back in the sounds of desperation that are trying to escape. "How? How do you know? Who... are you?"

The muscles are twitching in Sally's jaw, and there's a look of pure anger and disgust on her face. "What makes you think you have the right to ask me questions? I will say this once, and if you don't start talking, I will start shooting. Tell me what you did."

This is it.

Leah's life as she knows it is over.

# 23

# LEAH

One year earlier

Leah looks at the pile of antidepressants she has laid out on her bed. All different names she can barely pronounce. Not one of these supposedly happy pills has brought her anything close to happiness. Instead, they've brought her headaches, mood swings and a few extra pounds in weight. All things she's trying to avoid by taking the bloody things. So that's it. She's not taking them anymore and won't be accepting any future prescriptions.

Despite her doctor's protestations that finding the right treatment is trial and error and that they will help not only with her depression and anxiety but with her perimenopausal symptoms, too, Leah is done. She's had it with being a guinea pig. More importantly, she is not depressed and the doctors won't listen. She agrees she's a little anxious, perhaps. But no more than she considers usual. Life is anxiety-provoking. She doesn't need to be dulled. She doesn't want to end up a lump with no emotions at all.

It's getting harder and harder to keep up appearances with Jeff. Since their boys left home, Leah has been sinking and Jeff has noticed. She has become quiet and withdrawn, and last week, he heard her crying in the bathroom. Evidently, the sound of the shower didn't mask her tears as effectively as she thought.

She takes the pile of partially empty blister packs and cardboard boxes and chucks them into a carrier bag before tying the top and taking it outside to the wheelie bin. There. They're gone now. Out of her house. Out of her mind. No more crutches she doesn't need.

Leah has lived a very full and happy life, and as such, the actions of those girls on that horrible day eventually fell away. She didn't think of Melissa or Natalie for years. Decades even. Leah loved her university years. Her parents were sad she moved away from Manchester, but they supported her. Getting away was what she needed. She loved where she grew up and a part of her hoped she could return someday, but she needed to spread her wings. To know that when she walked down the street, there was no chance she would bump into Melissa or Natalie. So Leah headed north of the border to Edinburgh, and that was where she found herself.

At university, she was surrounded by people just like her. People passionate about art and design. She worked hard and partied even harder. Her days were filled with learning and inspiration, and her nights were packed full of laughter and love. Leah blossomed and grew into the person she always knew she could be. No more hiding. No more shame. Her university friends understood her, and she them. She felt loved and accepted, utterly at home. She'd spend hours in her room sketching out beautiful homes and imagining what life would be like once she could do this for a living. She'd glance at the clock and find it was two or three in the morning and that she'd been lost in a world of imagination for hours without even knowing it. And she was brilliant. She knew she was. Her lecturers and friends admired her work with awe. They told her she had a gift, and she felt it too. This was her reward for surviving those horrible years at high school. She was going to be someone. And she was going to be happy.

After university, Leah lived in Edinburgh and cut her teeth working at several established design agencies. She built her portfolio and started to make a name for herself. She was nominated for awards. Never winning but thrilled at the recognition and the networking opportunities. Not to mention the glamorous ceremonies. And then, as her university friends started to settle down and engagements and weddings ensued, she began to feel the pull of home. She'd had a few boyfriends and a lot of fun, but nobody had stolen her heart. Her true love remained with her studies and her work. Leah's mum had always told her that if you do a job you love, you'll never work a day in your life. And Leah was beginning to see this was true. Nothing she did felt like a chore.

But her mum and dad were getting older, and she missed them. And for the first time in years, she thought of Melissa and Natalie. She had heard through her parents that both girls still lived locally. Melissa had married early and had two children in her early twenties. Natalie worked at the local estate agents.

So Leah took a risk. She moved back to the north-west and set up her own design firm. Over two hundred miles away from any of her connections or previous clients in Edinburgh. She couldn't face moving back to her hometown, so she settled in Trafford, less than ten miles away from her parents and with easy access to clients across Greater Manchester. She believed in herself and threw her all into building her business. She quickly built a client list and made enough money to live very comfortably and then some.

Then she met Jeff.

Leah had heard friends talk about love at first sight and how you know somebody is 'the one', but she had never experienced anything like it before. She was beginning to think it would never happen to her. The day she met Jeff was just like any other day. She had a meeting with a repeat client and their architect to discuss a whole home renovation, and as Leah was welcomed into her client's home, there he was.

Jeff. The architect. The man of her dreams. The first man to ever make her heart skip a beat. She knew it in that first second of eye contact and would later learn he felt it too. The meeting passed in a swirl of emotions, and for the first time in her working life, Leah felt unfocused. Half of her mind was proposing ideas and answering questions from her clients, and the other half was running away with dreams about Jeff. She looked at his hands and imagined how they would feel holding her. She was captivated by him: his soft voice, his beautiful dark eyes, the dusting of freckles on his nose. She'd known this man for barely twenty minutes and already he was everything.

And so their love story began. Jeff was not backwards in coming forwards, and within seconds of leaving the meeting, they were in a café gazing into each other's eyes. They were married within two years and parents to their firstborn within three. Leah's parents were ecstatic. They loved Jeff almost as much as she did and were naturals at grandparenting. Life was good. No, life was perfect.

Those years now feel like a dream to Leah. Another life. Another her. She loves Jeff just as much as ever, but the amount of love she has to give has depleted. How is it possible that after decades, her years at high school have come back to haunt her? Why is she having nightmares? Why is she crying alone when her life is still so full of love? She doesn't know. But she does know that Jeff doesn't deserve this version of her. She needs to do something to make herself happy again. And today, she has taken the first step. Job one is done. The mind-dulling antidepressants are gone. And now it's time for job two. She will find Melissa and Natalie, and she will put things right. She needs to remove whatever hold those events have over her. She needs to confront them.

They may ignore or laugh at her and she needs to be prepared for that. But she has to at least try.

# 24

## LEAH

### ONE YEAR EARLIER

It is relatively easy to find Melissa and Natalie on Facebook. She doesn't know if either of them are still married, but they are both using their maiden names.

Natalie's feed is wide open. No security at all, and Leah gets lost for an hour scrolling through pictures of Natalie's friends and family. Middle-aged Natalie looks very different. Her previously red hair is cropped and dyed black, she has arms full of tattoos, and piercings fill her ears and spill out onto her face. She's nothing like Leah would have imagined. There are check-ins at heavy metal concerts and horror movies, but Leah knows it is her. All it takes is a zoom-in on her profile picture. Her eyes are an absolute giveaway. She's seen those eyes laughing with her while they shared stories at sleepovers. She's also seen them staring at her coldly while she pinned Leah to the floor in the science lab.

Suddenly, Leah stops. Her heart begins to hammer in her chest at the picture on the screen before her. A selfie of two smiling women with the caption *Some friendships are like diamonds – timeless and unbreakable*. Leah places the phone down on her lap. Terrified she'll accidentally like the picture and out herself as a stalker.

She stares at the photo of Melissa and Natalie. Natalie may be a cool rock chick, but Melissa has barely changed. Her long blonde hair is exactly the same but with the addition of an elegant side fringe that complements her face. Even if the honey blonde is from a bottle, you can't tell. Her blue eyes sparkle, and her smile is wide and beaming. Her jawline is a little softer, but she looks at least ten years younger than she is. They look so utterly happy together. Friends forever. Just like they always promised they would be. Anger bubbles inside Leah. She should be in that photo. What did she do to make them leave her? Nothing, that's what. Absolutely nothing.

Before she knows what she's doing, Leah is making a fake Facebook profile. She knows this won't be the last time she stalks them, and doing it under a false name is safer. That way, they'll be none the wiser if she accidentally likes a post. It makes good sense. She's not doing anything wrong and doesn't spend long thinking up a name. Jane Brown will suffice. Then she finds a photo of a random sunset online and uploads it as her profile picture. Feeling safer, she quickly scrolls through Natalie's feed and finds the smiling selfie again. Leah takes a screenshot and saves it to her photos. Melissa is tagged in the image, and Leah clicks through to her account only to find her security settings are at the opposite end of the spectrum from Natalie's. Apart from her profile pictures, Leah can't access anything. All her personal information is private, including her friends list. *Bugger!*

She clicks on Melissa's profile pictures. The current one is of her wearing a swimsuit and sarong on a beach, a straw hat dangling elegantly from one of her hands. Her back is to the camera and her long blonde hair cascades down her back. Leah scoffs and sticks two fingers up at her phone screen, which, although childish, makes her feel a little pang of satisfaction. Leah looks at the date and sees the photo was taken this year. *Urgh.* How can Melissa look so thin and young? They're the same age and have both had children, yet Leah puts on three pounds if she even looks at a bowl of pasta. The second and final picture is clearly older and is of Melissa dressed as Daphne from *Scooby-Doo.* The image is grainy and looks like it's been cropped from a bigger group photo. Melissa looks disgustingly adorable and happy.

Leah holds the phone so her nose almost touches the screen and sneers. "Stupid Cow!" Again, childish, but once more, a slight flutter of pleasure stirs inside her. She clicks back over to Natalie's profile. Judging by how much she posts, there will be hours and hours of material to pore over and likely some more 'best friends forever' pics to discover. Uneasy feelings begin to churn inside Leah, and something urges her to stop. What good can possibly come from this?

*You're only torturing yourself. Leave it alone. Move on. Find another way.*

But Leah brushes her internal warnings away without a second thought. She has tried other ways. But they haven't worked. This is the first time she has felt better about this situation since it started climbing back into her thoughts a few years ago. *So fuck off, brain. Let me do my thing.*

Leah starts as Jeff walks in, and she drops the phone onto the bed as though she'd just been caught snorting coke or watching pornography.

Jeff looks at her quizzically and folds his arms. "You okay, love?"

"Um, yeah, fine. Just, you know... work stuff."

Jeff strokes his chin comically and furrows his brow. "You look a bit spooked. I only came in because I heard you shout. You sure you're all right?"

Leah knows she looks guilty but can't tell Jeff what she's been doing. He hates social media. He only uses it for work because he has to, and he wouldn't approve of her stalking her high-school bullies. Leah comes up with a lie on the spot.

"I was looking for some gig tickets for you. A surprise. And you walk in and spoil it." *Gosh, that was convincing*, even if she says so herself.

Jeff's face breaks out into a gorgeous smile, and he rushes over to her and envelops her in a hug. "Aww, Leah. I'm sorry. Thank you. I'd love that. What gig?"

Leah's mind runs a mile a minute, yet she still can't come up with anything plausible. "Er, do you want to completely ruin the surprise or what?"

Jeff laughs and strokes her hair. "Okay. Okay. Well, thank you. I'll leave you to it." He kisses her on top of the head then makes his way towards the door before turning around and giving her a wink. "Comedy or music? You can tell me that much."

Leah gives a pretend huff. "Comedy. Now leave or I'll be going on my own."

Jeff rubs his hands together. "I was hoping you'd say that. No offence, but those warbling singers you like make my ears bleed."

Leah can't help but laugh, and Jeff smiles, blows her a kiss and closes the bedroom door. Shit, she must remember to book comedy tickets once she's done with her investigating. Leah props her pillows against the headboard and sits on her bed, sliding her legs under the covers. May as well get comfy.

Leah dives deep into Natalie's online world. She's a big fan of a motivational quote.

Things like 'the greatest wealth is health' and 'take care of your body, it's the only place you have to live'. That, combined with the various running events she has taken part in for cancer and mental health charities, makes Leah wonder if Natalie has had some sort of illness. Or maybe one of her friends or family. It's not clear, even from the various gushing comments underneath her posts. She looks well enough. A little fatter than she used to be, but who isn't? Melissa, that's who.

Eventually, Leah finds what she's looking for – another BFF selfie. This time it's an arty black-and-white shot. Natalie is in profile kissing a forwards-facing Melissa on the cheek, and they both hold glasses of Prosecco or champagne. Leah checks the date and sees Natalie had posted this on Melissa's birthday. The message accompanying the photo fills Leah with sadness and anger.

> To the best friend anyone could ask for. I love you, Melissa. Here's to many more years of celebrating you!

Leah takes another screenshot. She spends the next ten minutes drawing on their faces – devil horns, moustaches, spots – reverting to the original when she runs out of space and starting again. Then, in a flash of inspiration, she colours both of their faces red.

"How do you like it?" She laughs, but then the brief moment of happiness falls away and she finds herself weeping – pitifully and sadly. What is she even doing? There is nothing therapeutic in this for her, but somehow she can't seem to stop.

Leah jumps as a text buzzes on her phone. It's Jeff. That's weird. She hasn't had a text from inside the house since her boys were teenagers and still living at home.

> I'm treating us to Thai food. Going to pick it up now. Didn't want to make you jump out of your skin again!! Love you xxx

Leah laughs and types a quick reply.

Yum! Thank you. Love you too xxx

She hears the front door and Jeff's car tyres crunching over the gravel on their drive. He knows Thai is her favourite. He's such a good man. Momentarily, her heart feels full. Yes, her life has become smaller since their boys flew the nest. But she has everything she could possibly want in Jeff. And even if her love for her work has dwindled, does that matter? She got so many years of joy out of it. That's more than most people get out of a career. They've made a lot of money and she could probably retire if she wanted to. Maybe they could go travelling? Eat Thai food in actual Thailand or backpack around Australia. Okay, perhaps not backpacking. Hotelling would be more her style. But still, it would be such an adventure for them.

Instead of looking back, shouldn't she be looking forward and planning the rest of their lives together? They're both fit and healthy. They could have thirty or forty years left to enjoy life. Fifty even. But Leah can't make the positive thoughts stick. They trickle away like grains of sand through an egg timer, the emotional hole in her brain allowing them to fall away. So she opens up Facebook again, clicks on Natalie's Facebook Messenger, and, under the guise of Jane Brown with the sunset profile picture, types out one word.

Bitch.

Then she sits and stares at the phone.

# 25

## LEAH

### ONE YEAR EARLIER

Jeff returns with the takeaway, and they sit together in the dining room to eat. Leah knows objectively that the food is delicious – their local Thai restaurant is incredible and Jeff remembered all her favourites – but she can hardly taste anything and every mouthful is a struggle. Her phone is burning a hole in her pocket, and all Leah wants to do is check if Natalie has seen or responded to her message. She shouldn't have sent it. Could she be done for harassment or something? Even though she didn't use her real name, she did use her email address to set up the fake account.

She chokes down the food, smiling at Jeff intermittently. Luckily, their relationship is one of comfortable silence. They're both introverted and she's always valued their ability to simply sit and not feel the need to fill the peace and quiet with inane chatter. After eating barely half of her meal, Leah admits defeat and puts down her spoon and fork.

Jeff looks up, his eyes a mixture of concern and disappointment that makes Leah feel even guiltier.

"You back on one of those diets? I've told you before, you've no need to be. You're as beautiful as ever." He smiles and pops a forkful of noodles in his mouth.

He means well, but Leah can't help feeling irritated. So what if she is on a diet? She doesn't need anyone policing the amount of food she eats or commenting on her body size. It's none of his business. Plus, he's lying. She is fat. The scales don't lie.

"No, nothing like that. I've just got a migraine coming on and I'm feeling a bit woozy. I think I'll keep the rest for later and go lie down if you don't mind? Try and get ahead of it before the headache comes."

Jeff nods enthusiastically. He's familiar with her migraines. Some of them are real. And they hurt like hell. And some, like this one, are just an excuse to go and lie in a dark room and shut out the world.

"Of course, honey. Leave your plate and I'll wrap it and put it in the fridge for you. Go and rest, and I'll check on you in an hour."

Leah smiles as tears prick behind her eyes. "Thanks, Jeff. You're the best."

He grins. "I know."

Leah slopes upstairs to bed and bundles herself under the covers. She needs to listen out for Jeff. Staring at a phone screen in the dark is not something someone with a migraine would do, and she doesn't want to be caught out.

Tentatively, and with her heart racing, she opens Messenger and sees several return messages from Natalie.

What?

Who is this?

Get a life! Don't message me again.

The messages were sent about five minutes apart, and Leah can see she's been blocked. Yet she still finds she can't leave it alone, so she begins investigating. Good old Google. Not only has she learnt that nobody is likely to come looking for her for sending messages like this, but it's also really easy to set up numerous accounts with multiple email addresses and nobody even cares. So now she is armed with three shiny new Facebook profiles. All women's names and all with unremarkable profile pictures of land or seascapes.

Profile one sends Natalie another message:

That wasn't very nice.

While researching whether she would get done for trolling or harassment, Leah learns that the trick is to keep the messages unthreatening.

Within seconds, Natalie replies and blocks her again.

LEAVE ME ALONE.

All capitals this time. Somebody is getting upset. Leah's going to enjoy this. She won't take it too far. Of course she won't. She'll just have some fun for a couple of days. Call it evens and then crack back on with her life. She's only levelling the playing field and she's not actually hurting anybody. Let them have a taste of their own medicine.

Leah quickly deactivates profile one and opens up profile two. She's done enough with Natalie for tonight. It won't do to be freaking her out too much and her getting the police involved. Facebook or otherwise. So she messages Melissa. She only messaged Natalie first because she didn't think she could message someone with a private profile. But guess what? You can message anyone. Unless they block you, of course. She wonders what to write, and then it suddenly comes to her. A flash of inspiration from one of her favourite teen horror movies.

*I know what you did...* Leah cackles to herself. That is brilliant. Inspired. She waits, anticipation and excitement building. She ponders how she'd feel if she got a message like that. Honestly, she'd probably shrug it off. And that's because she's never done anything that could come back to haunt her. Only people who've done bad things would feel worried or scared reading a message like this. And that's on them, not her.

Melissa and Natalie got away scot-free for what they did to her all those years ago, but their past is finally going to catch up with them.

They are about to be haunted by a very determined ghost.

*I know what you did...*

# 26

## LEAH

### ONE YEAR EARLIER

It's 3am and Leah hasn't slept a wink. She feigned sleep when Jeff came in to check on her and again when he came up to bed several hours later. But she hasn't been anywhere near sleep. When Jeff was out like a light after his usual fifteen minutes of tossing and turning, Leah was able to return to her incessant phone checking.

It's been over eight hours since she sent that message to Melissa and it hasn't even been read. The inner fulfilment from riling Natalie has completely worn off and, if anything, she feels worse. She goes to the bathroom for what feels like the gazillionth time, catches sight of herself in the mirror and recoils. She looks like a crazy person. Her eyes are filled with madness. She splashes water on her face and promises herself she'll get some sleep. In the same way as a watched pot never boils, a watched phone never flipping beeps.

She creeps back to bed – Jeff is still snoozing away peacefully – puts her phone on silent and places it in her dressing-table drawer. She won't check it again until morning. Proper morning, not this 3am nonsense. Eventually, exhaustion wins and Leah succumbs to sleep.

---

When Leah wakes, Jeff's side of the bed is empty. He's at work every day this week, finishing a big project. She's between clients at the moment, having just finished a nursery for one of her regulars, and is about to start an orangery for a new client next week. So she has the rest of the week to herself.

She usually loves these periods of free time, but today she could use the distraction. She retrieves her phone from her dressing table and takes it with her when she goes for a wee. It seems she's become one of those people who uses their phone on the toilet. Great.

Her message to Melissa is still unread and a bolt of fury hits her. She types it again.

I know what you did...

Maybe that will make another notification pop up. She waits, but still nothing. *Urgh*, this is beyond infuriating. She returns to the bedroom and checks again. Still nothing. Leah sighs and pulls the covers over her head. What is happening to her? Maybe Melissa doesn't check her Facebook regularly. She might not even use it anymore.

Leah's inner voice of reason tries to pull her away.

*You've got the whole day off. Why not do something nice? Go shopping or get your hair done. Go for a hike, soak up the goodness of nature and get away from all this bitter and twisted nonsense. It's not good for you.*

Instead, she goes downstairs, makes a cappuccino and sits at the kitchen table. While she's waiting for Melissa to get her arse in gear and read her messages, she'll have a bit more fun with Natalie. The reactions she got from her were brilliant. Particularly the *LEAVE ME ALONE* one. *Well, you should have left me alone at school, shouldn't you, Nat? Then neither of us would be in this situation, would we? And it would be the three of us in the best friend birthday snaps and everyone would be happy.*

Leah already knows what she's going to write. If she can't get a bite from Melissa, she'll definitely get one from Natalie.

> I know what you did...

Leah patiently sips her cappuccino.

Barely a minute passes, and the wonderful sight of Natalie typing appears on her phone. Leah's stomach is a bundle of nervous excitement. She can't wait. The typing stops and starts multiple times, but still no message. What is she writing, an essay? Eventually, a message appears and Leah reads it. Her stomach sinks. It's an annoyingly measured, not at all upset response. In fact, it sounds almost pitying.

> Hi, I don't know who you are or why you're messaging me. I think you've probably got the wrong person. But if not, and I've upset you in some way, please just tell me. I'm sure we can work it out. Whoever you are, I hope you're okay.

Leah baulks. This is not what she wanted. Her stomach is churning and she's not sure if she feels guilty or is just plain incensed at getting the wrong type of response. Why does Natalie have to sound so bloody reasonable? She decides to poke the bear one more time.

> I'm going to tell everyone what you're really like.

She presses send. And then, for good measure, adds another message.

Watch your back.

She presses send again then immediately rethinks it. That's a proper threat, isn't it? And she's supposed to be avoiding doing that. But the message has already been seen and Natalie is typing again. A frisson of anticipation builds inside Leah. *Fuck it.* She hopes Natalie does feel threatened. She deserves it. Why should she feel all safe and happy after what she did?

A message pops up.

I tried being nice, but clearly you're just a sick troll. Go away. I won't be reading or responding to any of your messages again.

And with that, she is blocked again. Leah grins. Natalie will be bothered. Even if she never responds in the future, Leah knows she has gotten under her skin. And the feeling is rather delightful.

---

Six hours later, Leah is back in bed. She's eaten three rounds of cheese on toast and feels fat and burpy. She's also drunk almost half a bottle of red wine. A cheese and wine afternoon. La-di-da.

Along the way, she's made five new Facebook profiles and sent the same message to Natalie from each.

I know what you did...

True to her word, Natalie hasn't responded to any of the messages and has blocked each account immediately. She's definitely got good self-control. Leah thought she might kick off again by at least profile three. But alas, nothing.

Melissa is still annoyingly absent and Leah knows she can't continue doing this. She now has so many email addresses that she can't keep up with what she's doing. Instead, she's booked a manicure and pedicure for the next day and arranged to meet a friend for a late lunch. This will be a today-only activity. Normal service will resume tomorrow.

She'll play ill again tonight with Jeff, get it all out of her system, and wake up a new woman. Perhaps she'll try yoga or therapy.

Leave the past behind.

One naughty day can't hurt.

# 27

# LEAH

One year earlier

Jeff was full of tea and sympathy when he got home and found Leah still laid up in bed. She told him the migraine had passed but had left her feeling exhausted. He agreed she should just stay in bed.

She'd hid the now-empty bottle of wine under the bed and sprayed her deodorant liberally around the room to hide any wine or cheesy aromas. He's currently in the kitchen making macaroni cheese for her, which she loves but is worried it will put her in a cheese coma.

She's been pretty good the last few hours. She hasn't sent a single message or checked Facebook once. The madness appears to be leaving her. There's a light tap on the door and Jeff peeps his head around.

"Want your tea up here, love?"

Leah's heart swells and she smiles at her loving husband. "Oh yes, please."

"No worries. I'll do a tray and bring it up. Glass of vino?"

He winks and Leah smiles. "Or is that not a good thing with migraines?"

"No, it's fine. It's never food or wine that triggers it. My headache is gone and I think it will help me nod off. I'm shattered, but hopefully I'll feel completely better after a good night's sleep."

"I'll make it a large one then." Jeff returns ten minutes later with the promised tray, an empty wine glass resting atop it with a steaming bowl of macaroni cheese. An unopened bottle of red wine nestles under his arm. "I didn't trust myself to bring up a full glass, not with those slippery floors and fancy rugs of yours."

"Thank you. Are you eating too?" The thought of them eating bowls of pasta and drinking wine together in bed is quite lovely, and Leah hopes he says yes.

"Nah, I'm going to leave you to it. I've said I'll meet Fred at the pub for a quick pint, and then I've got a drawing to finish for work tomorrow. So I'll say goodnight now and let you rest." He leans over and places a soft kiss on her forehead. "And I'll sleep in the spare bedroom tonight so I don't wake you when I come to bed. I'll check on you before I get off to work tomorrow."

"Sounds like a plan. Have fun and say hi to Fred for me."

"Will do. Feel better, love."

Leah wolfs down the delicious pasta. Her stomach feels and looks like she's six months pregnant, but she couldn't care less. She pours a large glass of red and sips as she hears Jeff head out to the pub.

Tomorrow will be a new day. Leah grabs her book from her nightstand. It's the fourth in a cracking thriller series she's been blasting through, and she knows it will keep her mind off Melissa and Natalie. With no TV in their bedroom, her only options for entertainment are reading, her phone, or her mind. And reading is definitely the safest option of the three.

The wine is delicious, much better than the bottle she

picked out earlier. One glass becomes two, but she's not feeling sleepy yet. Jeff came back about an hour ago and headed straight into his office. It's weird him being in another room. She briefly considers going to invite him back to bed with her. But she's sweaty, bloated and a little bit pissed. Not the most attractive combination. She'll make it up to him tomorrow night. Cook something special for him for a change. He'll like that.

Eventually, Leah's eyelids start to droop. It's almost 11pm and she hears Jeff go into the spare room.

Putting down her paperback and switching off her bedside light, she reaches for her phone to set the alarm. She wants to see Jeff before he heads out to work tomorrow. Curiosity tugs at her as she moves to place her phone on her bedside table. One last time. One last check. Then she'll leave it alone. She won't be able to sleep unless she knows. She clicks on the Messenger app and sees that her message to Melissa is still unread. She knew it would be. She desperately wants to let it go, but the uncertainty of this message hanging over her is too much. So, she quickly deletes the profile. Good. Now she'll never know and will just have to move past it. Be the bigger person. In the interest of putting everything to bed properly, she looks up Natalie on Facebook one final time. But Natalie's profile has disappeared. Leah feels a surge of panic before it shifts to a swell of satisfaction and achievement. She did this. She made Natalie paranoid enough to delete it.

Leah is sure that whatever Natalie feels tonight will soon ebb away and she'll return to her life. She bets Natalie hasn't thought of her in years and probably never will again. There is nothing to worry about and she should just focus on the small act of revenge she has managed to inflict. It's been a bizarre day. Leah has done things she never thought she would. Things that are entirely out of character. A good night's sleep will sort her out. Reset everything.

Leah starts to drift off, finding herself in that weird not-asleep-not-awake middle world that her mind often inhabits after too much wine. She tries to focus on the good: Jeff and the boys, her successful business, a pampering session and a lovely lunch tomorrow. But instead, her head is filled with haunting images of the past. Her friend's faces. Their mocking laughs and cruel words. And then she's being pushed to the floor. She can almost feel the arms grabbing her, forcing her down, violating her. The pressure on her chest is too much and she's struggling to breathe. Overwhelming nausea rises in her throat and she chokes back a disgusting mouthful of vomit. Next, she sees the paint and Natalie and Melissa's faces bearing down on her. Their stupid, betraying, evil faces. Then the paint is in her mouth and hair, sticky and disgusting against her skin. She cries out, but nobody hears her. And then she wakes suddenly, sitting up stiff as a board. Her face and hair are gummy with sweat, and the faint glow from the streetlight through the curtains creates shadows in her room.

Leah reaches for Jeff. Desperate for him to hold her and chase the nightmares away. She shivers uncontrollably and tears of despair tumble from her eyes. This will never be over. Why won't this leave her? What does she have to do to make these nightmares go away? Leah runs out of the bedroom and down the stairs. In search of what, she has no clue. She's not concerned about waking Jeff. He sleeps like the dead. She's seen him sleep through fireworks, thunderstorms and even that time when their drunken teenage neighbour kicked a football through their living-room window at two in the morning. It would take a sledgehammer to wake him.

Sitting at the kitchen table, her head in her hands, Leah feels about as helpless as she can ever remember feeling. All she wants is to be happy. Melissa is happy. Natalie is happy. Why not her? It's Melissa she's the angriest with. At least she's managed to get back at Natalie, even if only in a very small and petty way. But Melissa, Melissa is seemingly untouchable. And she's the one who is the most to blame. She smeared the paint all over Leah's face and what has she done to make up for it? Nothing. Has she had to suffer because of her disgusting actions? No. Not one iota. She needs Melissa to hear what she has to say. To feel the fear and helplessness she inflicted upon her. Why must Leah continue to suffer? It's not fair.

Leah can feel herself slowly falling apart. She pushes her hands hard against her temples. Is this what it feels like to have a breakdown? Grabbing roughly at her hair, Leah opens her mouth as wide as she can and screams silently at the world.

# 28

# LEAH

One year earlier

It's 2am and Leah is sitting in her car. She has achieved quite a lot in the last hour. First, she found out where Melissa lives. It really wasn't that hard. A quick Google search and she discovered that Melissa runs a yoga business. That explains her fabulous body.

A click on the website later and voilà, Melissa's home address. She really should be more careful. It's three doors down from the house she grew up in. Leah can't decide if that's rather lovely or completely sad.

Armed with the address, Leah got herself dressed and drove here. It's the middle of the night and she should definitely be at home in bed rather than staking out Melissa's house. Common sense occasionally creeps through and tries to make her return home, but it's been wholly unsuccessful so far. Not to mention that she's had far too much wine to be driving. But coming here feels urgent. Necessary. She doesn't think she can sleep until she's given Melissa her message.

It was pretty pleasant driving around the empty M60.

Much less stressful than the rush hour traffic she's used to. She knows she looks like a complete sight, but then, if all goes to plan, nobody is going to see her. She's still wearing her pyjama top with accompanying cheese sauce stains and no bra. She swapped her pyjama bottoms for black jogging bottoms and pulled on her oldest trainers. Completing the ensemble is an old black fleece of Jeff's she found in the coat closet and one of his beanie hats, with all her hair tucked inside. She looks like a teenage boy. Just as she intended.

Many times on the drive over, she almost pulled off the motorway. Her inner conscience becoming more and more vocal as she neared her destination. *Go home, you mad bitch. What do you think you're doing?*

Yet, here she sits. And now she is here, she may as well go through with it. All she wants is for Melissa to hear her and it's not Leah's fault she won't answer her messages. What else was she supposed to do? Leah realises things have gone a bit wonky inside her head. She knows coming here is wrong, but she can't make herself stop. Normal rules don't seem to apply. She will get her message to Melissa, and what better way to do it than in big fuck-off letters painted on the wall of her house. That way, everyone will see it. Questions will be asked. People will talk and, hopefully, they'll all understand she's not the sweet-as-pie person she fooled them into thinking she was.

Melissa's street is empty. The houses are sleeping and all is still. Hardly surprising for 2am on a Wednesday in a quiet Manchester suburb. Leah's heart is thumping against her chest but she has to do this to try to save her sanity. She's tried so many normal ways to calm her thoughts and feel better inside and if they'd worked, she wouldn't be here. But somehow this feels right, so she has to go with it. So she waits around the corner from Melissa's home, ready to send her message.

Leah exits the car and quietly opens the boot. Scanning the

street, she's relieved there isn't a soul to be seen and no lights have turned on in the surrounding houses. There is only her. Her and her vengeance. Scrabbling around inside the boot, she quickly finds what she needs. She takes out a 3M respirator face mask and pulls it over her face before searching through the box of leftover paints from the nursery she just finished decorating. They wanted a circus theme so Leah used stencils and spray paint to create a feature wall. She thought it looked far too garish for a newborn, but clients want what they want. The fact she has all this ready in her car somehow justifies her actions. This was supposed to happen. The universe was clearly pointing her in this direction. Never in her working life has she used red spray paint and she hardly ever does any of the painting herself. It's definitely a sign.

Clicking the boot closed as quietly as she can, Leah takes a deep breath. She has to go for it. The longer she hangs around, the higher her chances of being seen. She walks with purpose, her trainers hardly making any sound on the pavement.

Melissa's house is a typical seventies semi-detached in a street full of similar properties. When she arrives outside, the address is clearly visible in large silver numbers on the gate, and Leah's relieved to see there is no doorbell camera. Although she looks nothing like herself, she still doesn't want any evidence of what she is about to do. The black paint on the gate is peeling in places and looks a little rusty. Will it squeak and alert them to her presence? Until now, Leah hadn't considered who might be in the house. Melissa's children are grown, but they could still live at home. And what about her husband? She has no idea if they are still together. Damn Melissa's overly private Facebook settings.

Leah risks the gate and it opens silently. Sneaking through like a middle-aged ninja, she makes sure it doesn't bang behind her. There's a large area of wall right by the front door that looks perfect, and she gives the spray can a shake. She winces as a terrible clanking noise pierces the soundless night and looks around frantically. She needs to shake it again and probably several more times to write what she needs to. It simply won't work otherwise. Leah's skin crawls and all the moisture disappears from her mouth. She's losing her nerve. It's so exposed here and just because this house doesn't have security cameras, the neighbours might.

Desperate for cover, she sneaks down the side of the house and into the back garden, squeezing past the overgrown hedge. She catches sight of herself as she passes the large kitchen window. She looks like a criminal. A dangerous individual to be avoided and feared. She doesn't recognise the person staring back at her but rather than feeling ashamed, she smiles at the empowerment this gives her. She shakes the can again, ignoring the noise, and walks towards the pale pebbledashed wall to the side of the back door.

An uneven but perfectly acceptable canvas.

It's time.

# 29

# LEAH

One year earlier

As the paint flows from the can, Leah feels spikes of fear and exhilaration but remains largely calm. She is doing something for her. She is fixing things. Making everything right and just. But Leah barely finishes the first letter when she's sure she hears a noise from inside the house. She freezes. Eyes wide and listening intently. But all is still and the house remains in darkness. Maybe she imagined it. She wants to rip the mask from her face and gulp in some air, but forces herself to stay entirely still and waits for her breathing to normalise. She can't leave now when she has come so far.

The back door swings open without warning and a figure emerges. Leah stares, adrenaline crashing around her body as she comes face to face with her old friend. Melissa is wrapped in a dressing gown and there is a surprisingly genial look on her face, as though she was expecting to greet someone familiar. But within seconds, her face morphs into one of horror, her lips pulled taut and the whites of her eyes showing, gleaming in the moonlight.

Leah can't breathe or move. What is she supposed to do? She should run. Of course she should run. *For goodness' sake, Leah, run!* Instead, she stands there, transfixed by the woman she once knew, drinking in the look of pure terror on her face. Relishing in the soothing feeling it gives her. It is the most incredible sense of justice. Leah has the upper hand now. This is way better than any online message.

She waits for Melissa to run back inside and slam the door. That's undoubtedly what Leah would do. Call the police and report an intruder. But Melissa remains frozen, a stricken look on her face. As though she is in some kind of fear-induced trance. Time seems to slow down and Leah simply watches, fascinated. It's clear Melissa doesn't recognise her and the sense of power that envelops her is like a drug. She luxuriates in the wonderful sensation, watching the woman who wronged her so terribly all those years ago, looking helpless and afraid. Just as Leah was.

Until Melissa screams.

The blood-curdling cry is so loud that Leah stumbles backwards. But Melissa doesn't move. She stands as still as a statue, her hands balled in fists by her side, screaming at the top of her lungs.

*Please stop. Stop screaming.*

Leah wants to run but her feet won't move. No sound comes from inside the house, and the neighbouring houses show no sign of life.

*Stop screaming. Please.*

Leah often replays what happened next, and even to this day, she can't remember making the decision to do it. It was as though something else took over – a completely unconscious act.

Leah holds up the can of paint and sprays Melissa full in the face, covering every inch of skin. Melissa's screaming instantly ceases, and the world seems to stop turning briefly. Leah watches aghast as her old friend's trembling hands fly up to her face and begin frantically wiping at her eyes. Moans and guttural gurgling noises now falling from her mouth. Leah looks down at the can of paint in her hand. Did she really just do that? She can't have. She would never... She has to do something but her body won't let her run away.

Thoughts are coming thick and fast, and time has begun to speed up. Should she go inside with Melissa and come clean about the whole thing? Perhaps Melissa will understand. She's not hurt, just scared. Maybe they'll even laugh about it once all the paint is cleaned up. Become friends again. But she is lying to herself. Melissa's moans are escalating now and she will begin shrieking again at any moment. Leah needs to get away from here, right now, and so without thinking, she pushes Melissa hard in the centre of her chest. Leah watches as she falls backwards through her doorway into the inky blackness before slamming the door and running as fast as she can to her car. Not once does she look back.

Within seconds, Leah is driving. Her heart is pulsing painfully and she can't seem to find any air. She yanks off the mask and throws it into the footwell to join the can of red spray paint, gulping in oxygen and trying to steady her nerves. She has never felt more terrified. With her head swimming and her vision unfocused, she knows driving isn't safe, but she needs to get away. Far, far away. She has crossed over into a different version of reality. None of this can possibly be happening. What is she going to do now?

Leah lets out a strangled cry. She's just committed a crime. A very serious crime. She has assaulted someone. Trespassed on their property and attacked them on their own doorstep. That's got to mean prison, surely? Nobody will believe she didn't mean to do it, and even if they do, it won't matter. Leah's family will be heartbroken. Jeff will leave her and her boys will disown her.

How could she have been so careless with all of their lives? Black spots surface in her peripheral vision. She needs to keep breathing or she's going to lose consciousness. All that matters now is putting as much distance between her and Melissa's house as humanly possible. She can work everything else out once she's home.

Everything will be okay as long as she can get back unseen. She was never here. She was at home in bed all night, sleeping off the after-effects of a migraine. Jeff will vouch for her. Nobody will ever know. And why would anyone even suspect her? Leah darts her eyes around furiously, constantly checking the road and her mirrors for flashing blue lights. She's sure she'll hear the wail of police sirens any minute. But she continues to drive on through the empty streets, and the farther she gets, the calmer she feels. She doesn't meet another vehicle until she hits the motorway. She keeps an eye on her speed. Maintaining a steady seventy miles per hour gives her something to concentrate on. She banishes all thoughts of Melissa. Melissa will be shaken up, but ultimately, everything will be fine, and regardless, Leah can't think about that now. Before she knows it, and not entirely sure how, Leah is home.

Parking her car quietly, she returns the mask and paint to the boot before sneaking into the house. She does everything in reverse. She places Jeff's coat and hat back in the cloakroom before creeping up the stairs and putting her pyjama bottoms back on. The house is reassuringly still. She tiptoes across the hall and opens the door to the spare bedroom. Jeff is still asleep. Leah returns to her room and gets into bed. She has never felt more relieved to climb under the covers in her whole life.

Nothing about the last couple of hours feels real. If someone told her it was all a fever dream, she'd probably believe them, and this sense of unreality is most welcome. She knows the truth of her actions will eventually hit her. But what happened was an accident. Nothing more. And is what she did to Melissa any worse than what Melissa did to her? Not really. Plus, Leah's actions were unplanned. She was only going to write on the wall. If Melissa hadn't come out of the house and started screaming incessantly, none of this would have happened. With all that in mind, the critical question is whether Leah can live with what she's done. Will she be able to keep her reckless and malicious actions a secret? Yes, she thinks. Yes. She will never breathe a word and, if anything, she may now be able to move on. And although Leah should be horribly ashamed, calling the emergency services and handing herself in, that's not at all how she feels.

Now she is home and safe, she feels alive and vindicated and within minutes, Leah is deep in a nightmare-free sleep.

Because revenge has been served. And now, life can go on.

# 30

# TESS

*Holy. Shit.*

Tess can barely pull her jaw off the floor. That was some story and she was utterly mesmerised throughout the whole thing. Who would have thought that mousy old lady had it in her? Tess is all for revenge but in, like, a normal way. What Leah did was something else. Who would even do that? A psycho, that's who. Just goes to show you can never judge a book by its plain, drab cover.

Tess leans back in her chair. After hearing Leah's confession, she feels like she's sitting pretty in this weird room of judgement. She has never done anything like that in her entire life. Whatever Sally is going to pull out of her hat about her, it will pale in comparison to the red-paint-in-the-face story. Tess is definitely winning.

Leah told the whole story staring at the wall like a weird robot. And now she's just stopped. She looks like an empty shell. Tess sort of feels sorry for her. Gun-toting Sally is sure to have something to say or do. Tess surreptitiously flicks her eyes to Sally. She looks mad. And not angry mad. Crazy mad.

Tess has always known she's not exactly normal herself.

Sally probably thinks she's dropped a bombshell on Tess with her verdicts about her. But Tess isn't stupid. She knows her feelings are different to most people's. It's pretty difficult to look on the bright side in this room, but Tess has to say she's starting to feel like a pretty good person. She is at least the second-sanest person in this room. Who would have thought it?

Tess holds her breath as Sally starts to speak.

Take your seats, everyone. The next act is beginning.

31

# LEAH

Leah is completely drained. A husk of a human being. She didn't look at Sally the entire time she recounted her story. She couldn't risk being derailed. The words came out surprisingly easily once she knew the game was up. She left nothing out. Probably gave them too much detail, even recounting how she met Jeff and what a wonderful life they've had. She should probably have left that out. Hearing how happy she's been isn't going to ingratiate her. But what's the point in holding back now? Leah has no idea what happened to Melissa after that day, but she fears the worst now and knows she's about to find out.

After that first night, when she'd felt a peculiar sense of detached satisfaction, the crippling anxiety and dread set in. Every phone call or knock at the door filled her with sheer terror. She cancelled her next job, citing a family emergency. The clients were understandably annoyed, but she didn't care. She didn't care about anything other than her family never finding out what she'd done. Gradually, as days and weeks passed uneventfully, and when nobody came looking for her, she started to believe that everything would be okay. On the surface, at least.

Thankfully Jeff was still in a busy patch at work. He kept apologising about leaving early and coming back late. Leah couldn't let on how relieved she was, so she behaved as she would under normal circumstances. She never did buy those bloody comedy show tickets.

Unable to handle the guillotine hanging over her head any longer, Leah looks up at Sally. They stare at each other in silence. Sally's deranged expression should frighten her, but Leah feels nothing but defeat. Sally's hands are no longer steady. The gun is trembling in her grasp. Is this the effect of hearing Leah's story, or is it because she is about to use it? Leah can't bring herself to care.

"How do you feel about what you did?" Leah wasn't expecting that question. "Answer honestly." There is a crack in Sally's voice and Leah wonders again who she is and why she is doing this.

Leah stares at the wall again before giving a genuine answer. "I was scared. I hadn't planned to spray her in the face. But I did. I knew what I'd done was terrible but when I got home, it almost felt like it hadn't happened. I only wanted to protect my husband and children from what I'd done."

"Did you ever think about Melissa?"

"I did. But honestly, I did everything I could not to. I tried to carry on with my life as normal, but it didn't work. I started getting horrible flashbacks of that night. Melissa's... Melissa's face. I see it everywhere. I have horrific nightmares and I know it's because I've lied." Leah looks down at her hands. Her hands that committed that terrible deed. She'd do anything to reverse time and take it all back. It was a moment of madness, that's all. She never meant to do it.

"Well, boo fucking hoo."

Leah jolts her head up and meets Sally's thunderous gaze.

"I'm not trying to get sympathy. I'm just being honest, and you asked me—"

Sally suddenly stands up and pushes the gun hard against Leah's forehead. Leah closes her eyes and braces herself. She says her goodbyes to her family and prays they will be okay.

"No, Leah, I didn't ask for any of that. I asked if you thought about Melissa and you went off on a self-involved rant about yourself." Sally pushes Leah's head back with the gun's muzzle and takes her seat again, the weapon once again pointed at Leah's chest.

Leah's mind is going a thousand miles a minute. She can't believe she's still alive and is sure she's going to throw up. She alternates swallowing and sucking in air, trying desperately to dampen the roiling nausea.

"Working as a doctor's receptionist, you see people from all walks of life. People who've suffered indescribable trauma and tragedy. It's impossible not to feel for them, to want to help them. The doc back there does what she can."

Leah looks at Dr O'Hara. The woman has barely moved or made a single sound throughout all of this. Apart from Sally referring to her once or twice, she has been a purely silent observer and Leah shudders as she considers what fate awaits her.

"But sometimes just talking isn't enough. Sometimes, you need to take action. And you know all about that, don't you, Leah?"

Leah nods. She wants to say that she feels nothing but regret after taking action and that seeking revenge is never the way, but she knows that will only enrage the already furious Sally further.

"Dr O'Hara spoke with Melissa lots of times. And no offence, Doc, but it did sweet fuck all." Leah gulps. Melissa was a patient here! "Melissa has been suffering and you've been merrily burying your head in the sand for the last year. Living your charmed life with no consequences for what you did. Now, that doesn't sit well with me. That doesn't sit well with me at all." Sally's eyes burn into Leah. "So I'm going to tell you what happened to Melissa after that night and I want you to hear it. To really feel it and understand what you did. Okay?" Leah nods again, holding back tears. She knows this can't be good. If Melissa was well, this wouldn't be happening. "I said, okay?"

"Okay... yes, okay." Leah can barely get the words out.

"When you callously pushed Melissa in the doorway that night and ran away like a coward, she hit her head and it knocked her out."

Leah feels all the air leave her lungs. She had no idea. Is Melissa dead?

"She was out cold and that paint you sprayed stayed in her eyes the whole time. Can you imagine that? Just burning away while she was unconscious. Go ahead, Leah, take a minute and imagine what that would actually feel like."

Leah shouldn't cry as any show of emotion will only be misconstrued as self-pity, but try as she might, the tears still come. She sobs silently. Even in her worst nightmares, she couldn't have imagined her stupid childish actions having consequences as grave as this.

"Melissa was alone in the house that night. When she heard the noises, she thought it might have been her son trying to get in. He was out clubbing and she said she never slept well until he was home safe."

Leah shivers, remembering the door springing open and how Melissa initially greeted her with warmth before the fear set in. As a parent, Leah knows that feeling well. She could never relax until her boys were safely tucked up in bed after a night out.

"But it wasn't her son. It was you. You coming to seek revenge for something that happened thirty years ago! I've tried to wrap my head around that but I still can't. Even if the consequences weren't what they are, that's still completely unhinged."

Leah should wait to be asked a question before speaking but she's desperate to explain. Sally needs to hear how filled with self-hatred and remorse she is. "I know. I had... I don't know, a breakdown or something. I don't know what came over me. I wasn't myself. You have to believe me."

Leah immediately regrets her words, wishing she hadn't led with something quite so selfish. Even to her own ears, it sounded pathetic and whiny.

"I don't have to do anything. That poor woman is blind because of you. You completely ruined her life!"

Leah can't hold it in now. Big, fat sobs erupt from her and her whole body convulses with the weight of what she has just heard. "I... I had no—"

"I don't care. You did that. You! And do you know the worst part? Melissa barely engaged with the police. Her family tried, but she was adamant. Can you believe that? And do you know what I think? I think she knew it was you, and I reckon she thought she deserved it. Can you imagine? No, I bet you can't. There isn't a part of you that could understand being such a kind and caring person that you thought you deserved going blind because of a stupid prank you played as a teenager."

Sally is out of breath and Leah can see the rage and hatred flowing from her every pore. Not for the first time, Leah thinks Sally can't just be Dr O'Hara's receptionist. Leah must know her. Melissa must know her. Otherwise, why would she be this angry and go to such extreme lengths to punish her?

"I'm a truth-seeker, Leah. Some things in this world are just plain wrong. Terrible things happen to people and they don't get the justice they deserve. I can't sit back and let that happen anymore. Sometimes, someone has to step up and put things right. And that is why we are all here."

Leah takes in Sally's words but knows there's more to this than meets the eye.

This is personal.

# 32

## TESS

Tess is beginning to think she could just slip out and nobody would notice. The atmosphere is beyond intense. So Sally is some kind of modern-day vigilante dishing out justice like Robin Hood. No, that's not right. That was giving money to the poor, wasn't it?

Anyway, clearly she has lost the plot and is going on some mad eye-for-an-eye crusade with Dr O'Hara's patients. Maybe there's a whole slew of them in other rooms waiting to have their fate dished out by Sally and her sword of Damocles. Who knows?

This has been a very weird watch, but Tess has been able to glean a few things.

One – Sally is not going to kill anyone. At first, Tess thought she might. But she just can't see it. The ankle-shooting thing, maybe, but even then, Tess isn't totally convinced.

Two – Sally is no longer the same calculating woman Tess spoke with earlier. She may have been able to keep it together when everything was ordered and planned out, but now that things have ramped up, she has lost it. The Sally they're dealing with now is a slave to her emotions and Tess will be able to use that.

While Leah was telling her story, Tess was able to come up with a couple of things that Sally may be about to spring on her. The online trolling thing. Yes, she's done a bit of that. If one of those people – Tess can't come up with any names – has ended up as a patient here, it could be that.

The only other thing that could be worthy of Sally's wrath was when she left her last job. She had been working part-time at a make-up counter. It lasted all of three months and she was only there for the perks and freebies. When Tess left, she set it up so it looked like her supervisor had been stealing and made an anonymous report that she'd been bullying her staff. But she was genuinely a horrible cow and totally deserved it.

Although judging how Leah spiralled after a bit of meanness from a couple of her friends, it could be just about anything. It's like that film, *The Butterfly Effect*. Tess has never really considered the knock-on effects of anything she does. Maybe there's someone somewhere baying for her blood because she once said she didn't like their shoes.

But the most important thing is that Tess is now sure she's a secondary character in all of this. She just needs to work out why.

# 33

## LEAH

Everything is out in the open now. What will be will be. Leah is utterly devastated at what happened to Melissa, and even though none of it was intentional, it is undoubtedly her doing and she must face the consequences.

Her chest feels hollow, like there is a big hole where her heart used to be. What a horrific and unimaginably cruel way to learn a lesson. Leah can't think what there is left to say. Is this the point at which Sally dispatches with her?

Leah thinks back to some of the things Sally said.

*This is going to be a space where we will right some wrongs.*

*Sometimes, someone has to step up and put things right.*

And when she was talking about Dr O'Hara and the work she does: *No offence, Doc, but it did sweet fuck all.*

Will Sally punish the doctor for not helping Melissa, or is Dr O'Hara's role here to 'put things right'?

Leah's chest constricts, and her mind starts to run wild. Revenge. Justice. Is Sally going to make the doctor blind Leah? Is she about to have paint forced into her eyes again? The thought is sick and terrifying. Yet, from what Sally has said and how she is acting, it feels horrifyingly plausible.

"I've got some good news and some bad news for you, Leah. Which one would you like first?"

Leah's flabbergasted that there is any good news to hear. "Er, good, please."

"I thought you might say that. The good news is that I'm done with you now." Leah's heart rate skyrockets and she clutches her chest. "No, I don't mean that. I mean, I'm going to talk to Tess now."

Sally looks over to Tess. "You ready for this?" Tess doesn't answer but weirdly doesn't look afraid, just curious. "You're going to get some thinking time, Leah. Some time to reflect and repent. Use that time wisely. And the bad news – I think you know this already, but I want to reiterate my intentions. You won't be getting away with what you've done. Before you leave this room, you will pay for your sins. It's the only way."

With the as yet unnamed threat hanging in the air and Leah barely holding her body upright, Sally shifts slightly in her seat and turns to Tess.

# 34

## TESS

*Oh goodie. It's my turn. Which of the nine circles of hell is Sally about to unleash?*

It doesn't matter what Sally says, Tess is pretty sure she's worked out what's going on. Sally will start with a story that paints Tess as a bad person – something terrible she did once upon a time that had dire consequences, yada yada. She is confident she knows how this whole thing will play out.

"Leah and Dr O'Hara haven't had the pleasure of your company yet, Tess, so I'm going to give them a little flavour of who you are."

Tess's eyebrows raise. Did Sally just slip up?

"Don't get excited. Anything I say will be because I mean to. They don't know you. I hadn't met you until today. Stop thinking you're going to get one up on me. You're really not as smart as you think you are."

Tess ignores the insult and takes in the information. It sounds positive. She was worried there was some actual connection between her and Sally, and she was about to drop a bombshell, like Sally being her long-lost sister or something.

"Tess is a narcissist and a psychopath."

"Hey!" Tess had planned to listen, observe and let any slights on her character wash over her, but she's not having that. She is not a psycho, and she's certainly not about to be called one by someone who's holding people hostage with a gun. That's slanderous.

"Urgh. Fine. Let's get technical for a moment. Are you listening, Tess? You might even learn something. I'll start with narcissism. Narcissists are entitled and self-important people. They love being admired and think they're better than everyone. They'll happily exploit others for their own gains and they lack any real empathy. Ringing any bells?"

Tess gives Sally a pinched smile. The narcissist bit wasn't really what she had a problem with, and yes, it rings all the bells. Ding-a-ling-ling.

"Psychopaths aren't all that different. They manipulate and they are dishonest. They often do rather well for themselves in life and can have what look like successful relationships. But they're not real connections. Everything is superficial. Psychopaths fake their emotions and they don't feel guilt or remorse for any of it."

Tess furrows her brow. That's not what a psychopath is. Psychopaths boil bunnies and have heads in their freezers. She is nothing like that and she feels a spark of irritation when Sally smirks at her.

"No need for you to wear a mood ring with that face of yours!"

Tess breathes deeply and centres herself. She needs to keep cool and control her reactions. No more knee-jerk responses to Sally's jibes.

"Okay, fine. That sounds like me. But I'm not a psychopath. I'm just looking out for myself in a world where nobody else will. It makes good sense. Look at Leah over there. Does she look like an armed attacker ready to break into your house and blind you? No, exactly. There are scary people everywhere. You have to keep your guard up. Look out for number one. That way, you don't get hurt."

Tess doesn't look at Leah. She doesn't care if that upset her. She shouldn't go around blinding people.

"I get that, Tess. I really do. But everything you just said fits completely. You don't have to be Jeffrey Dahmer to be a psychopath."

Tess is confused but she keeps her face neutral. There's clearly no reasoning with this woman. She thinks she knows everything, and as soon as Tess gets out of here, she's googling what a psychopath is. Sally is definitely wrong.

"You probably think I'm about to make you confess to some terrible deed and tell you that you're about to atone for your sins."

Tess can't hold back. Sally thinks she's so superior and that she can read Tess like a book. But she couldn't be more wrong. "No, actually. That's not what I think at all. I know exactly why I'm here."

Sally sits back and raises her eyebrows. "Wow. I can't wait to hear this. Do share with the class."

Tess crosses her legs slowly and runs her fingers through her hair, dragging out the moment. "I think you're mad at her." Tess points a finger at Leah. "And I think you're pissed off with Dr O'Hara because all she did was talk to this woman, Melissa. I think you got to know Melissa. Maybe you're best friends now, lovers even. I don't care. And you've decided to dish out some good old-fashioned eye-for-an-eye justice. I haven't quite worked that bit out yet. You're going to do something like poke her eyes out. Maybe you'll make Dr O'Hara do it, or even better, Melissa is about to join us as a surprise special guest armed with a bottle of acid. Anyway, this whole charade isn't about me. I think you'll tell a story about something awful I did. I can't wait for that bit, by the way. But you're not going to punish me for it. You're going to use it as leverage. As blackmail. Because you need me here."

Tess gives Sally a big smile before delivering the big finish.

"I'm. Your. Alibi." If Tess had a mic, she would drop it.

"That is quite the story you've come up with." Sally attempts to keep up the mocking tone, but Tess can see she's impressed.

"But I'm right, aren't I? You wanted to check that I was the perfect person to go along with your plan. You need someone who you have no connection to but will corroborate your story without feeling guilty about it. Someone without a conscience."

Tess should feel upset or outraged by Sally's assumptions about her, but she doesn't really care. She wants out of here. If she has to lie to the police and parrot back whatever story Sally gives her, then she'll do it. She just wants to go home. Plus, what Leah did was gross. Sally's methods of evening things up and serving justice may be completely warped, but she seems pretty committed to the cause. And Tess isn't about to stick her neck out for some woman she barely knows and who attacked and maimed her own friend.

"That's not bad, Tess. Not bad at all. But unfortunately, it's almost completely incorrect."

Tess is stunned. She was so confident. Is Sally testing her? "Almost? So I'm right about something."

"Yes, you are." Sally stares at her, and Tess stares straight back. If Sally wants something from her, she will have to say it. "I brought you here because of the type of person you are. That much is true. But I'm not about to tell any kind of story about you. There isn't one specific event I'm going to ask you to recount. And do you know why that is?"

Tess looks down at her nails, feigning disinterest. "Nope. But I guess you're about to tell me."

"It's because you're not a decent person who did a bad thing. Prisons are full of people who committed heinous crimes. But often, if you hear their friends and family speak about them, they'll say 'I couldn't believe they could do something like that' or 'he was such a lovely, normal guy'. But not you. You are one huge bundle of unpleasantness. Your entire existence and every small action you take is filled with poison. You're a bad person deep down in your soul."

Tess shrugs. There are a lot of insults in there and under normal circumstances, she'd be going crazy and tearing Sally down. But why should she care what Sally thinks of her? The woman is a lunatic. "This verbal abuse is getting a little tiresome. If you're trying to provoke or get me to defend myself, you're barking up the wrong tree. You think I'm an awful person. So what? Tell me something I don't know."

Sally smiles. "Oh, I'm about to."

Apprehension sparks inside Tess. Sally looks far too confident and pleased with herself. What has she missed?

"You will get to leave this room alive and unharmed." Although already relatively confident of this fact, it is still a massive relief to Tess to hear it said explicitly. "No, actually, let me rephrase that. You'll leave this room alive and unharmed if you do exactly as I say. I am being one hundred per cent serious when I say I will hurt you, kill you if needed, should this not go precisely as I planned."

Tess nods. She's genuinely nervous now. It's not a feeling she's used to and she hates it. Will Sally just hurry up already?

"I'm not like you, Tess. In fact, I think we might be exact opposites. I care about people fiercely. And not just those close to me. I hate to see wrong in the world. If there's a way I can help someone in need, then I will do it."

Tess doesn't respond. *Get to the point, Mother Teresa.*

"I'm not going to hurt anyone in this room unless I have to."

Tess feels her blood run cold. She sees it now and knows the horrendous words Sally is going to say before she even opens her mouth.

"But *you* are. You will leave this room alive and unharmed. But you will also leave here as a murderer."

# 35

## TESS

All the moisture has left Tess's mouth and her body begins to tremble. She detests showing fear but after hearing those words, she no longer has the ability to appear strong and brave. Sally's words have shaken her to her core.

No. Absolutely not.

The things Sally said about her may be true. But this? Sally has got this very wrong. Tess may be many things, but she is not a murderer.

She glances at Leah, who appears to have turned to stone. She stares back at Tess, unblinking and statue-like. Tess then looks to Dr O'Hara. The bound woman's eyes are wet with tears and her face is filled with hopelessness. Had she already been made aware of Sally's plans?

This is utter madness. Tess is not going to murder a complete stranger for no reason. Sally has the wrong person. And doesn't this prove Tess's point from earlier? She's not the psychopath here.

Sally continues to stare at her. Waiting, watching. And Tess needs to say something. Make it very clear from the get-go that Sally has made an enormous mistake.

Tess stumbles through her words but eventually gets them out. "No. I'm not... going to murder... anyone."

"Oh, but you are. Trust me, soon you'll feel very differently."

"I doubt that very much. If you want—" Tess can't finish the sentence, realising she doesn't know who Sally expects her to kill. Leah presumably. But what about Dr O'Hara? Tess takes a deep breath and digs deep. "Actually, what is it that you do want? I've said it already, but I'll say it again because I don't think it's something I can say too many times – I am not going to murder anyone. But is it Leah or Dr O'Hara or both? And again, just in case you didn't hear me – I'm not going to murder anyone."

Sally keeps her body still but turns her head to look first at Dr O'Hara and then at Leah.

"It's Leah. She needs to pay for what she's done."

Tess knew the cacophony of screeching was coming before it started, yet it still alarms her. Leah begins screaming relentlessly. Tess watches the display with dismay. This woman has no self-control. Leah's eyes are wide and saucer-like as she writhes and cries in her chair as though being attacked by an imaginary wild animal. What the actual fuck is she doing? Sally is watching Leah with a similar look of distaste.

If Sally isn't going to stop this, she will. "Leah, will you shut the fuck up!"

Leah instantly stops screaming, but the relief is short-lived. Next comes the babbling and mewling. Leah's shaking hands come to her lips and she stuffs her fingers into her mouth. She looks possessed or like she's high on drugs.

"Well, that's a bit better than the screaming, I suppose. Could you get a grip of yourself? Didn't you hear me? I'm not going to do anything to you. It doesn't matter what she says. But, if you don't shut up, I reckon you're in danger of getting us all killed." Tess turns to Sally for agreement. "Right?"

Sally nods and points the gun at Leah. "Tess is right. If you don't stop moaning or you start that god-awful screaming again, I will shoot you. I reckon I'll aim for your knee." Sally twists the gun from side to side in her hands. "But from this angle and with you squirming around like a toddler, there's no guarantee I won't hit something more serious. Even shooting your knee might kill you. It'd be sore, too. Don't you reckon? Ouch. Really sore."

Leah is clearly trying to calm down and be quiet, but she's hyperventilating and sounds like an injured seal. It's really hard on the ears.

Tess tries once again to reach her. "Leah, listen to me. Please. I'm not going to hurt you. She can't make me. But she can and will kill you herself if you don't be quiet. You need to calm down. You need to breathe. Go to your happy place or something."

Leah nods and, slowly, she begins to calm down.

Now that's dealt with, Tess can begin to negotiate with Sally. And there is room for negotiation. The most important thing is that she gets out of here alive. The second most important thing is that she gets out of here without having to kill anyone. Tess won't do it. Why would she? This isn't a 'her vs me' situation. If it was, Tess would throw Leah under the bus in a second. But Sally isn't threatening Tess's life. In fact, she's actively said she will leave this room alive. So, if Sally wants Leah dead, she will have to do the deed herself. And if she does, that's none of Tess's business. That's between Leah and Sally. And if, as she initially thought, she can be Sally's alibi, she'll do it. Of course, it's still a bad thing to do. But nothing like actually killing someone, and it's definitely a lie worth telling to remain alive. She reckons most people would go for that deal under these circumstances.

Now all she needs to do is appeal to Sally. Get her on board with this improved plan. "Good. Now, can we please—" Tess stops barely halfway through her plea when she notices Sally is holding out a sealed white envelope. Where did that come from?

"Take it. Open it." Sally's tone is brusque and she waggles the envelope in irritation when Tess doesn't immediately take it.

"What's this?" Tess is reluctant to take it, but she guesses she won't have a choice.

"You'll see when you open it. Take it. Now."

Tess reaches out and turns the envelope over in her hands. There's a handwritten note on the front.

*Follow the instructions in here. Do NOT deviate.*

Fear crawls up Tess's spine. This note was clearly pre-prepared. She can't imagine what could be in it. There is nothing that would make her carry out Sally's instructions and murder Leah. It doesn't matter what Sally threatens her with. There is nothing Sally could reveal that would warrant Tess resorting to murder. If Sally is about to ruin her life, she can go ahead. If she's going to destroy her relationship with Joe, then Tess will start again. If she needs to leave the country, she will.

Then why is she so hesitant to open the envelope? Tess takes a deep breath and tears it open. As she reads, her whole world comes crashing down. She was convinced she had thought of everything. But this? This never even crossed her mind. Her eyes fill with tears. This can't be true. Sally is lying. Tess looks up at Sally and sees there is actually a hint of regret on her face. Even Sally must know this is wrong. How could anyone be so cruel?

"No. Please, no."

The remorse in Sally's eyes falls away and is replaced by a determined stare. "You do as I ask and everything will be fine."

Tess's stomach churns and her heart aches. Sally is a monster.

"Read it again and make sure you understand every word."

Tess wipes her eyes and does as she is told. She must have misread it the first time. This can't be happening.

*Tess,*

*Do not read this aloud.*

*At this moment, a friend of mine is at your parents' house.*

*They are posing as a friend of yours. Her name is Claire and she has told your parents you used to work together.*

*Your mother will remain unharmed if you do exactly what I tell you to do.*

*I am about to call Claire. You will take the phone and she will allow you to speak to your mother. When you speak to your mother, be natural. Tell her you've received a text message informing you that Claire is at their house and you will drive over to visit with her.*

*Do NOT raise the alarm. Do NOT tell them what is happening here.*

*Your parents will remain safe unless I give the word.*

*Once you have killed Leah, Claire will leave, and I will prove to you that your parents are okay.*

*Do this for your mum.*

Tess can't believe what she has just read. The note itself is annoyingly wordy, but the message is as clear as day. She can't even summon up any anger. Only devastation. This is the worst possible thing that could have happened and she feels completely broken.

*Maman.* Her mum. Her wonderful, caring mum. Sally thinks she is in pursuit of justice, but how can that possibly be true? Tess's parents are innocent. How can she be willing to harm them and still think she is a good person? She is deranged.

Tess looks up and nods solemnly at Sally. Her parents' lives are on the line and she can't take any chances. She has to at least take the phone call. There will be a way out of this where she doesn't have to kill Leah, but the call needs to be made first. She needs to know her mum is safe. Needs to hear her voice.

Tess doesn't know how she'll get through this without crying and screaming down the phone, but she must.

She has to put on a brave face. Her mother's life depends on it.

# 36

## TESS

Tess closes her eyes and gathers all of her strength and self-discipline. Taking a deep calming breath, she opens her eyes. Everything she is feeling has to be put to one side for now. She is in fight mode.

"Have you read and understood everything?"

"Yes. I understand completely."

"Good." Sally takes out a phone. It's small and black and looks like it's from the nineties. A burner phone? Tess has only seen phones like that in movies with FBI agents and serial killers.

Sally types in the number and hands the phone to Tess. She takes it without hesitation and puts it to her ear. Each time her nerves or anger try to resurface, she pushes them way down into the pit of her stomach. When tears threaten, she forces them back. She can do this. She has no other choice.

The phone seems to ring forever, and horrendous images of her mother being tied up and threatened or beaten run through her mind. Eventually, the ringing stops and a woman answers. Tess doesn't recognise the voice and her breezy tone throws her off guard.

"Hi, Tess. How are you?"

*How am I? I'm terrified and furious. Get away from my parents, you evil bitch.*

Tess attempts to match the woman's cheery demeanour. "Hi... Claire. I'm fine. How are you?"

"I'm good. I'm so sorry to drop in like this, but I was passing and popped in on the off-chance you might be here. I'm just having a cup of tea with your mum and dad. They've been so lovely."

Tess can hear her own breathing. She wants to climb down the phone and rip this woman's throat out with her bare hands. Forget all that 'I'm not a murderer' bullshit, she deserves to die. And this story is so ridiculous. Who pops into someone's parents' house they've never met?

Keeping calm and speaking politely may be one of the hardest things Tess has ever done in her whole life. But somehow, she does it. "Can I speak to my mum, please?" Tess's voice almost cracks but she makes it through the sentence.

"Of course. I'll just get her for you." The woman's next words are muffled and Tess feels her blood boil as she hears her call her mum's name. "Margot, Tess is on the phone. She wants to speak to you."

*How dare you speak her name, you disgusting creature from hell.*

When this is over, Tess will find this 'Claire' and she will make her pay. Tess had never thought of herself as someone who could physically torture another person, but that was before this horror of a human being lied their way into her parents' home and threatened their safety. Now, she'd quite happily pull every one of this woman's teeth out with a smile on her face.

Tess knows her mum is holding the phone before she

speaks. Her soft, sweet breathing hits Tess's ears, and she almost faints with relief.

"Hello. Is that you, Thérèse?"

Tess drinks in her mum's voice. She would give anything to be there to protect her. She doesn't even care that her mum uses her full name. Tess doesn't know how to answer without breaking down, but a click of Sally's fingers and a waggle of the gun pulls her back to reality.

"Hi, yes, Mum, it's me. How are you? Is Dad there?"

"Yes, dear. Jun, Thérèse wants—"

"No!" Tess winces at the volume of her own voice and her outburst earns her a serious look from Sally.

*Keep it together, Tess. Keep it together for Maman.*

"Sorry, Mum. I just meant no, I don't want to speak to Dad. I was just checking that you weren't alone."

Tess isn't sure whether that was stepping over the line, but Sally doesn't seem angrier.

"No, dear. He's speaking with that lovely friend of yours, Claire. What a nice surprise. I don't think we've met her before, but having some company is nice. I was saying to your dad..." Her mum's words begin to blend and merge inside Tess's ears. She can't cope with this anymore. She needs to get that woman out of their house. She can't have anyone hurting her mum. It would be... she can't even finish the sentence. It's unthinkable.

When the line finally goes quiet, and hoping that her mum hasn't asked her a direct question, Tess follows the instructions in Sally's note. She will play this game and get her parents to safety, and then she will unleash holy hell on Sally and her accomplice. Maybe not today, but she will get her revenge, and it will be sweet.

"I'm not far away. I'll come over and visit with you all. Are you and Dad okay to wait there with Claire until I make it? I won't be long." Tess hears a little squeak of excitement from her mum and her heart breaks a little.

"Of course. I'll make sandwiches. How lovely."

Tess hears a scratching noise through the earpiece and she can see her mum in her mind's eye, pressing the phone against her chest as she relays the news.

"Jun, Thérèse is going to come over." A tear escapes and rolls down Tess's cheek. Hearing how happy her mum is that she's going to visit is devastating. When this is over, she will do better. She will be a better daughter. The daughter her mum deserves. "Shall I put your friend back on the phone?"

"No. I'll see you soon. And... I love you, Maman." Tess hears her mum's intake of breath. She is surprised at hearing those three simple words and her preferred name, which Tess has always shunned. Words that she should say to her mum all the time yet never does.

"I love you too, Thérèse. Est-ce que tout va bien?"

Tess feels Sally's heated stare before she even meets her eye. Tess hadn't thought of this. Could she get a message to her mum in French? Perhaps. But she can't take the risk. She knows she's already behaved unusually by telling her mum she loves her, but she couldn't miss the opportunity. What if it's the last chance she gets? Tess grits her teeth. No, it will not be the last time. She will make sure of it. Tess answers perfunctorily and in English.

"Everything's fine. I won't be long, okay?"

"Okay. Bye."

"Bye." Tess ends the call and hangs her head.

"Well done, Tess."

Tess doesn't look up. That was awful and she is barely holding herself together. She is not surprised that her mum let a complete stranger into her house. She has such a gentle and trusting nature, and Tess hates Sally with every fibre of her being for abusing that trust.

"How could you?" Tess raises her head and glares at Sally with pure hatred. "Seriously, how could you? My parents have done nothing to you. They are completely innocent." Sally squirms in her seat. "See? You don't have anything to say. And do you know why that is? Because what you are doing is horrible. All this talk about righting wrongs, getting justice. How can this be justice?" Tess shakes the phone at Sally.

"I can see you're upset. But—"

"Of course I'm upset. Who wouldn't be upset? You've kidnapped my mum and you're using her as ransom. Can't you see how appalling that is?" Tess feels a glimmer of hope as, once again, Sally shows a flicker of remorse.

"Yes, but I didn't have a choice."

"What!" Tess doesn't even try to control the volume of her voice and Sally flinches. "You didn't have a choice? I've never heard anything so utterly absurd in my entire life. You did this. All of this. Us in here. My parents. You made all of this happen. Is anyone holding you at gunpoint? Is anyone threatening your life or your safety? Is anyone threatening your mum's life?"

Tess stops. She had more to say but the change in Sally's face stopped her in her tracks. She hit a nerve when she mentioned someone threatening her mum's life and maybe, if she stays silent, Sally will elaborate.

Their consultation feels like a million years ago, but Tess remembers Sally taking a lot of interest in how she felt about her mum. It was the thing that made Sally soften and stopped her giving her a hard time. She may be on the warpath, but Tess senses she's not entirely happy with this part of the plan. She's already seen a couple of glimmers of guilt in her eyes. Tess must try to use this to her advantage. If Sally loves her mum or is a mum herself, she could appeal to her better nature. Obviously she's crazy, but there must still be some good in there.

Maybe Tess can change her mind. She's already planted the

idea of her being the alibi. That's what she'll do. She'll beg for her mum's safety and promise Sally she'll tell whatever story she needs her to. "Look, Sally. I can see why you're doing all of this. I understand. But what I can't understand is why you would be prepared to hurt my innocent parents. That's just cruel, and you don't strike me as cruel." Tess nearly chokes on that lie. Sally is cruelty personified. But she'll say anything to get her on side. "You've already told me you care about people fiercely and your actions are only to protect those who need it. Well, my parents need it right now. They're good people, I promise you. Me? We already know I'm selfish and awful. But they're nothing like me. They're kind and caring. I think you'd like them."

Tess is pleased with that speech. Considering it was off the cuff, it came out brilliantly. Tess tries desperately to make eye contact with Sally, but she remains staring at the wall.

"Sally, please look at me. I'm begging you. Please don't hurt my parents. I can see you don't want to."

Sally's eyes flick to Tess. They are swimming with sadness. Yet when she speaks, her voice is robotic and monotone and Tess's heart sinks. She's not going to be able to reason with her. Something fundamental inside her has broken. Logic won't work. She's unreachable.

"It's out of my hands now. The ball is in your court, Tess. But for what it's worth, you're right. I don't want to hurt your mum and dad. But in any war, there are innocent lives lost." Sally resumes her emotionless wall-staring.

Panic starts to rise. What does she mean by 'war'? This is not a war. Tess had thought she was dealing with someone with twisted intentions but who still had some sort of grip on reality. But now she's not so sure. Tess looks to Leah. She hasn't heard a peep out of her in a while, and she finds her curled in a foetal ball in the chair, her lips twitching as though she is talking to herself or perhaps praying. Could Tess actually kill this woman if she was left with no other choice?

Sally reaches down the side of the sofa, pulls out a kitchen knife and places it across her knee. Tess's mouth falls open. Has that been there the whole time?

"Two chairs and a sofa. Nobody ever chooses the sofa." Sally's voice is calmer and quieter than it's been so far and it's horribly unnerving. "Leah, would you sit up, please. I have some things I want to say to you."

Leah does as she is asked. Her movements are slow and she continues to mutter faintly to herself. Tess scans the room. Dr O'Hara remains motionless and defeated. Tess hasn't heard her struggle or try to speak in ages. Leah is in some weird child-like state and Sally's behaviour is getting more and more deranged. Tess is the only person in this room with a shred of normalcy left, and if it weren't for the threat against her parents, she would risk an attack. Tess reckons she could get that gun or the knife and storm her way out of here. Leave Sally to whatever she wishes to do with her two remaining prisoners. But she can't risk it. She has to wait it out a little longer.

Tess fears the knife is for her and after whatever Sally is planning to say to Leah, she's going to make her kill Leah with it. That's even worse than the gun. Where would she even stab her? In the chest? In the neck? But Tess can't. Her overriding thoughts remain with her mum and not just her being in danger. If her mum found out she'd killed someone, even if the very act was to save their lives, it would break her. Her mum already feels like a failure because of how Tess has turned out. Of course, she would never say that to her, she's too kind. But her dad has alluded to it on many occasions.

*"Look at what you're doing to your mother."*

*"Think of your mother."*

Her mum loves her, but deep down Tess also knows she is ashamed of her.

Tess can't kill Leah. Knowing she murdered someone would be a fate worse than death for her mum. So she's going to have to call Sally's bluff. Try and find a way out. Pray that the woman calling herself Claire won't go through with it.

A lot of ifs that ultimately might result in her sentencing her parents to death.

# 37

## LEAH

Leah has resigned herself to her fate. When she woke up this morning, she thought she was taking the first step on the road to getting better. Doing something to make herself well again. But that can't happen now. She won't be able to live with what she did to Melissa. She still can't believe her flippant moment of madness caused such irreversible damage and a lifetime of pain. Even if she got out of here, she'd go to jail. And she can't have that.

She's drifted in and out of listening to the conversation between Sally and Tess. Sally has undoubtedly gone to extreme lengths to plan all of this. And Leah gets it. Look at what she herself did under the veil of retribution, from trolling Natalie to driving to Melissa's house in the middle of the night. Both things she could never have imagined herself doing, and it all snowballed so quickly. Leah knows from experience how easily and rapidly madness can take hold. She's sure Sally never imagined herself here, doing this, but revenge is an evil beast. It takes over and makes you do horrific things. Sally isn't doing this because she wants to, she's doing it because vengeance has her in its claws. And there are no rules when you are under its spell.

It's a sickness and Leah can no more easily reason with Sally than anyone could have reasoned with her that fateful night. Retribution is the only thing that matters.

Weirdly, Leah feels calm. She's screamed and shouted but she's done with that now. And so she sits, putting the world to rights inside her head. She speaks to Melissa, telling her she's sorry and asking for forgiveness, which she knows she doesn't deserve. She tells her everything. How she loved her so dearly when they were young. How losing that friendship broke her heart and how the incident with the paint in the classroom wounded her so deeply. She tells her all the things she would if she were able to see her one last time. And it's soothing. Leah has no control over what is about to happen and succumbing to the helplessness brings with it a serenity. A peacefulness she hasn't felt for years.

Then she talks to her boys and her dear Jeff. They will be fine without her, and she only hopes they don't find out what she's done. She doesn't know if Sally is going to let them find her body. Will they think she's missing? She wouldn't want that either. Years of anguish without any understanding or answers. But Leah lets these concerns float away. These things aren't her choice. This is her Judgement Day and she doesn't get to decide her fate.

Sally's voice jolts her out of her dreamland. "Leah, would you sit up, please. I have some things I want to say to you."

Leah slopes up and tries to focus, hoping she'll get more time to say her goodbyes to her family. Sally has a knife now, yet she doesn't even feel her heart quicken or the desire to shout out and beg for her life. A knife is no worse than a gun.

"Leah, are you listening?"

"Yes."

"You look completely out of it."

Leah nods, her head swaying as she does so. She does feel

very woozy. Maybe this is her body's way of protecting herself. She won't fight it. She quite likes this odd feeling of serenity.

"Sorry. I'm feeling a little off. I think it was all the screaming. And I'm sorry about that, too, by the way. I'll listen and I won't do anything."

Sally seems put off by her agreeable nature, annoyed even. But Leah can't summon up the energy to do anything else.

*You beat me, Sally. Do your worst.*

"I've spent the last year thinking I played a cruel prank on Melissa. That I scared her. I knew it was a nasty thing to do, but I had no idea what damage I'd caused. I guess I feel differently about this whole kidnapping thing now."

Sally looks shocked. "If you think you're going to get out of this by behaving like... like whatever this is, you're wrong. You can't fool me, Leah."

Leah smiles. "No, that's not it. Honestly." Sally continues to glare at her with contempt. "What did you want to say to me?"

Sally's face turns scarlet and she looks like she is about to explode. "What are you doing? You're supposed to be scared. You're supposed to be begging for your life. Why are you doing this? You're ruining everything!"

Leah is lost for words. Upsetting Sally was not her intention but even in her weird resigned-to-death state, she can see the ludicrousness of Sally being irritated that she's not frightened enough. A tiny spark begins to flicker inside her. If she remains calm, is there a chance she could talk Sally down? Will her repentance remove the need for violent revenge? And outside of here, if Leah were honest and explained to her family that she had some kind of mental breakdown and did something dreadful, is there a chance they would forgive her? She'll hold her hands up to her horrific mistake that had consequences she couldn't have imagined in her worst nightmares. If she handed herself into the police and took the punishments handed out to her by a real court, could she still have a life? She doesn't know. But it's worth a try. She owes it to Jeff and the boys to at least try.

"Believe me, I am scared. But I don't think I deserve to die for what I did. I should have to face the consequences though. And I haven't, which is wrong. I'd like the opportunity to put that right. But I don't think you're going to give me that chance. So I'm just waiting. That's all. I was scared before knowing about Melissa, but now I only feel sad. I feel guilty and horrible. That's what you're seeing. And I'm sorry it's making you feel like this."

Leah's words have the opposite effect than intended. Sally is downright furious.

"No!" She is screaming now. "No. You don't get to do that. You don't get to make me feel bad."

"I'm not trying—"

"Shut up! Just shut up. Do you have any idea what you have done? Do you know what it has done to our family?"

The room falls silent. *Our family*. Leah had suspected some connection between Sally and Melissa, so she studies Sally's face, looking for, but not finding, any noticeable resemblance to Melissa.

"Melissa is my mum. You blinded my mum. You ruined her life and you ruined mine. I hate you and wanting you dead has taken over my entire life. Well, no more. I'm taking our lives back. I will get justice for Mum."

Leah looks down at her hands. She didn't think it was possible to feel any more ashamed. But seeing how traumatised Melissa's daughter is is simply soul-destroying.

"You know Mum told me once that she thought it might be you. She wasn't sure and wouldn't tell anyone else or let me tell anyone. I can't live like that anymore. Do you know what she said? Look at me, Leah." Leah obliges and meets Sally's distraught gaze. "She said she thought if it was you, she deserved it. Can you imagine?" Sally's voice is barely a whisper, and another piece of Leah's heart shatters. "She may have been a shitty teenager, but she was a wonderful woman. A wonderful mum. But you took that away. You broke her. She's a recluse now. She just sits in a chair. She doesn't eat. She barely sleeps. Do you know what it's like to watch someone so full of life fade before your very eyes?" Leah shakes her head. She doesn't know and she can't even imagine. "So you may think I've lost my mind, that what I'm doing is way over the top. But I assure you it's not. You took my mum's life. The woman I loved is dead."

The only sound in the room is Sally's ragged breathing.

"I'm sorry." Leah's words feel pointless and don't even come close to expressing her regret, but she says them anyway.

And then she retreats back inside herself.

Shutting out the world and waiting once again for her sentence to be carried out.

# 38

## SALLY

### ONE YEAR EARLIER

Sally bursts through the hospital ward door and almost screams at the poor nurse manning the reception desk.

"My mum. Melissa Johnson."

Sally's brother, Grant, runs up and puts his arm around her. "Don't run off, Sal. We need to stay together."

Sally wants to push him away, to scream at him that none of this would have happened if he wasn't out getting pissed with his mates as usual. But she falls into his arms and lets him hold her. It's not his fault; she wasn't there either. They hug and Sally cries into his chest. Deep wracking sobs. How could this have happened to their wonderful mum? Cancer stole Dad five years ago and Sally doesn't know what she'd do without Mum. She's the backbone of their little family. Her rock, her everything.

When Sally and Grant are ushered to their mum's room, Sally prepares herself for the worst. On the way to the hospital, her mind was filled with visions of her mum's burnt, misshapen face, her eyes black and unseeing. Yet when they enter the room, Mum looks relatively normal. There's a bandage over one eye but her skin looks okay, and although red and a little swollen, her visible eye looks fine. She even smiles.

Sally rushes over and kneels by the side of the bed, grasping her hands, squeezing and shaking them with relief. Her mind had gone to a very dark place when she got the call from Grant, but he must've been given the wrong information or misunderstood what they had told him. None of that matters now. Mum is okay.

Tears of relief wash away tears of anguish, and Sally looks up at her mum's face and smiles. Grant perches on the other side of the bed and rests his hand on Mum's shoulder.

Sally's voice judders as she speaks. "How are you, Mum?" Even though she looks fine, Sally knows she's been through a terrifying ordeal. Also, didn't Grant say she banged her head and was knocked unconscious? There could still be things wrong. Things they can't see.

Sally is desperate to hear her mum's voice and fresh tears come when she finally speaks.

"Don't cry, love. I'm fine. Well, not fine, but you know."

"What happened? Are you okay? Is... everything going to be okay?"

"I think so. They've washed my eyes out about a million times. I don't think anyone has cleaner eyes than me right now. One is a bit more damaged than the other." Mum points to the bandage. "This one has a bigger burn on the front. But they told me both would be fine eventually. And I can sort of see out of this other one. It's a bit hazy and I can't see all of the bits of your face, but I've gotten up and been to the loo no problem."

Sally gasps with relief. She has a sudden urge to pray or cross herself even though she's not the slightest bit religious.

"That's amazing, Mum. And what about your head? Grant said you were knocked out."

Mum purses her lips. "That bloody hooligan pushed me

back into the house. I slipped and cracked my head on one of those bar stools. Knocked me clean out. I don't remember a thing until your brother came in, and even that's a bit of a blur. But I've had a scan and I'm fine. My head is as good as it's ever been."

Sally bites down hard on her bottom lip as she thinks of the person who did this. Was it just random, or was their house targeted? She looks across at Grant. Was it someone looking for him? Sally takes a deep breath. She needs to stop feeling resentment towards Grant. It won't help anyone and it would definitely upset Mum.

"Did you see them? Do you know who it was?" Mum's lips start to tremble and Sally feels her blood boil. If she ever finds out who did this, she'll beat the shit out of them. Her brother rubs the back of his neck before wringing his hands together. Clearly he's thinking the same thing.

"No. He was quite short. It was the first thing I noticed when I realised it wasn't you, Grant. So I reckon a teenager rather than a man. He had a big coat and one of those beanie hats pulled down. He even had a COVID mask on. I couldn't make out any of him really, and I was proper terrified when I saw him." Sally has so many other questions about her mum's attacker, but she doesn't want to upset her any further. "But one thing that was weird..."

Sally's heart rate picks up. "Go on."

"He seemed surprised to see me."

"What do you mean?"

"Well, I went downstairs because I could hear footsteps and weird noises. I figured Grant had forgotten his keys, and when I opened the door, the boy in the mask looked terrified. I think if I'd closed the door then and there, he'd have just run away. But I don't know what came over me. I just screamed and then, before I knew it, he'd sprayed the paint on me. I think he panicked or something. I'm not sure what he was doing, but I don't think he was there to break into the house or attack me."

Grant pipes up, trying to control his fury through gritted teeth. "There was some paint on the back wall. I wonder if it was just some scumbag vandal and you disturbed them. You need to talk to the police properly, Mum. Get them checking other houses and speaking to the neighbours. Looking at those doorbell cameras."

Grant looks down. Sally understands his guilt. Mum only opened the door because she thought it was him. If she'd stayed inside, she'd be fine, and they'd all be moaning about having to clean graffiti off the wall rather than sitting around a hospital bed. But it's not his fault, and when Sally calms down and gets her head back on straight, she'll make sure he knows that.

Sally's prevailing emotion is anger. Anger at her mum for opening the door in the first place. Why couldn't she just stay inside? Anger at herself and Grant for not being there. All of this anger is misplaced and unhealthy, and she knows that. It will pass but until then, she needs to watch what she lets out of her mouth.

"Well, all that matters is that you're going to be okay. When can you come home?"

Mum puffs out a breath. "What I wouldn't give to come home with you both now. But because I banged my head, I've got to stay in for a bit. They keep asking me the same questions and checking me over every five minutes. It's just routine, they say, but it's bloody annoying."

Sally nods. She'd give anything to take Mum home now, too, but only once they know she's okay.

"I've got lots of eye drops, I'll need some help with those by the way, and I've got to come back in for check-ups, but they won't keep me in longer than they need to. My head's a bit sore, but they've given me painkillers and I can take those home too."

Sally feels completely choked up by her mum's bravery. What a terrible thing to have happened to someone so kind and giving. Mum wouldn't hurt a fly.

"I'll come and stay with you for a bit. No arguments. It'll be nice. We can—" Sally almost says *watch movies together* but catches herself just in time. "We can catch up."

Mum smirks. "You were going to say watch TV, weren't you? You silly bugger." And then Mum laughs and Grant grins.

"Yeah, I reckon she was, Mum."

Sally finds herself laughing too. A knock at the door brings them out of the moment, and a nurse peers in.

"Melissa needs some rest now and the doctor will be in soon."

She doesn't actively tell them to leave, but Sally knows what she's hinting at. "Can we have two more minutes and then we'll go?"

"Of course. Do you need anything, Melissa? More water?"

"Yes, please, water would be good."

"I'll be back in a tick." The nurse closes the door gently.

Sally grips her mum's hand tightly. "I'll find out when we can come back, okay? One of us will be here whenever we're allowed to be."

Mum nods and smiles wistfully. "I can't wait to go home."

"You'll be home before you know it. Just rest and listen to the doctors. We need you." Sally's voice cracks on the last sentence. She hopes Mum realises just how much she is loved and needed. Sally stands and leans over to kiss her mum on the forehead. Grant does the same and they say their goodbyes.

As soon as they get out of the room, Sally breaks down. Relief, sadness and anger boil over and hit her like a tidal wave. Grant places a protective arm around her shoulder and they walk out of the hospital together.

"Honestly, Grant, I was so scared. You won't believe what I

was imagining when you told me. But she's going to be all right, isn't she?"

"Yeah. She is. I was expecting something a lot worse too. Not to say this isn't bad, but I wasn't expecting her to look so, you know, normal. I had to swallow down some choice words in there though. I'd love to get my hands on whoever did this. I'd wring their scrawny neck."

"Same. And I don't care what Mum says. It doesn't matter if they only meant to spray-paint the house. They didn't. And even though Mum is going to be all right, she might not have been. They could have done some serious damage. Never mind that they could have killed her."

Grant squeezes her tighter and they silently walk back to the car.

# 39

## SALLY

### SIX MONTHS EARLIER

These last few months have been the worst of Sally's life.

Mum did not leave the hospital after a day or two armed with painkillers and lots of drops. Not even close. They were told by the doctors there could be rare complications with such an injury. Sally only half-listened at the time. She knew they had to warn you about these things but she didn't really think it would happen.

But those complications started to occur. Every single one. And no matter what the doctors did, the outcome was always the worst-case scenario. Mum has been through the mill and then some. There have been infections, raised pressure inside her eye, tortuous pain, lasers and surgery.

It has been a living hell.

So here Sally stands, waiting for the kettle to boil in her mum's kitchen. Mum is in her usual seat on the sofa. Nowadays, she is either on that sofa or in bed. She just sits or sleeps. There is no music, no conversation, no movement or noise of any kind. All signs of life have left the house. A house that used to be brimming with love and laughter.

Sally knows it is fruitless to suggest going out or even doing something together in the house. Mum always refuses and even the suggestions themselves make her angry or upset. Visitors have dried up, and Mum doesn't want them anyway. Her best friend, Natalie, whom she's known since they were children, refuses to give up. She is the only person other than Sally or Grant that her mum will engage with, and despite Natalie's insistence that she'll never stop trying, Sally is scared it won't last much longer.

Mum lost almost all of the vision in one eye. In fact, she nearly lost her actual eye. And she needs an operation for a cataract and some laser treatment in her other eye. But she's refusing and so, as things stand, she can see virtually nothing. They've had lots of arguments about it. The doctors have said she'll get a good level of vision back if she has the procedures. Enough to make her independent again. But Mum won't listen. She's scared and doesn't believe them, and although Sally disagrees with her mum's decision, she can at least understand. She has been through so much in the pursuit of making her vision better. Yet nothing has worked and invariably, things have got worse.

Mum has lost all faith and she's terrified of losing the tiny bit of sight she has left. How has everything gone so horribly wrong? On that first day, the day of the attack, they told her everything would be fine. She was supposed to be fine.

Sally takes two cups of tea to the living room and sits on the sofa beside Mum. She knows she won't drink it, but Sally feels she needs to keep some normality. Otherwise, they'd just sit here all day doing absolutely nothing.

"Natalie messaged. She's going to pop in and see you at about eleven o'clock. That okay?"

Mum's face barely moves as she speaks. "No, it's not okay. But that won't stop her."

Sally thinks she sees her Mum give a slight smile, but it is fleeting and disappears quickly. Her face has changed so much. She looks sunken and so very tired. She no longer has her hair coloured or wears any make-up. Sally has offered to take her to the hairdressers and help her do her make-up, but she always refuses.

*There's no point, Sally.*

At times, Sally wants to shake her and remind her that she has so much to live for. If she would agree to the cataract operation and the laser treatment, then they could try to get back to normal. But she won't have any of it. At first, Sally hoped her refusal would be temporary, and as the trauma of what she'd been through began to wear off, Mum would start to feel differently. But every day is the same. And she refuses to engage with her GP about her plummeting mood. They've offered therapy and medication but she won't even entertain the idea.

Hopefully, Natalie's visit will lift her spirits. Sally likes Natalie. They've been in each other's lives for years and she's like a member of the family.

"Maybe when Natalie comes, we could all go out for coffee or something?"

Mum closes her eyes and takes a deep breath as though trying to keep her patience. Sally knows she wants her to stop pushing, to stop suggesting she do anything other than sit here all day, but she won't. That would be admitting defeat and Sally will never give up on her. If the roles were reversed, Mum would do everything in her power to help. Sally holds on to the hope that one day her persistence might work.

"If Natalie insists on coming, she can sit here. I don't want to go out. And I wish you would stop asking. You know it irritates me, right?"

"Yes, but—"

Mum interrupts before she can finish telling her that she

will always keep asking, that she loves her, and will never stop trying. "Do you believe in karma?"

Sally's heart sinks. Not this again. When they were going through the worst of it, and Mum was on lots of pain medications that sent her doolally, she would often babble nonsensically about karma. Saying this was her payback or something. She never explained herself or told Sally what she thought she was being punished for. Sally just assumed it was a mixture of the drugs and her trying to make sense of all the horrible things that were happening to her. She simply did her best to be reassuring. She's barely gone more than a few days without seeing her mum her whole life, and she knows her mum has nothing to feel guilty about. She is a good person. But this is the first time Mum has mentioned karma while lucid and a creeping unease comes over Sally. Is her mum about to reveal some deep, dark secret?

"Er, no. No, I don't think so. Do you?"

Mum ignores her question. "When Natalie and I were young, we did something terrible." Sally reckons she must be exaggerating. She'd always imagined her mum as studious and well-behaved when she was younger. A teacher's pet. "We had a friend. Her name was Leah." Sally has never heard that name before. She doesn't interrupt, sensing Mum has something she needs to get off her chest. With all these hours sitting in silence and only her own thoughts to keep her busy, she must have had time to think through every event in her life. It's probably nothing serious. "Leah, Natalie and I were the best of friends for years. But when we got older, she started becoming annoying. Clingy. We tried to pull away, but it didn't work." Sally nods. People fall in and out of friendships all the time at that age. It's nothing to feel guilty about. "Then Natalie and I got in with a group of older boys. We were so excited at the time, and thought we were so grown up. Looking back, I don't even recognise myself in those few years. I wasn't a nice person."

Sally leans over, puts her hand on her mum's shoulder and rubs it gently. "That's hardly unusual. Do you remember me as a teen? All slamming doors and thinking I knew it all. I'm sure I was an absolute nightmare. It's just a phase though. All girls go through it."

Mum takes Sally's hand off her shoulder and holds it. Her hands are cold and dry. "I know that. But we did something awful to Leah."

Sally listens attentively as her mum recounts how they, alongside this crew of older boys, pushed Leah into a classroom at school and covered her face in red paint. Sally grimaces as her mum describes how Leah wet herself and vomited everywhere.

"And then we just left her. And do you know what? At the time, I actually thought it was funny. It was years before I realised how disgusting it was. How it must have made her feel. Leah had been a good friend. Okay, we didn't want to hang around with her anymore, but by doing that, we were monsters."

The look of deep sadness and regret on her mum's face is heartbreaking, and Sally envelops her in a hug.

"Leah never told anyone, you know. Well, at least nobody came asking us about it. She just carried on and made new friends. That's the kind of person she was. I've never paid for what I did to her. Until now."

And then Mum breaks down. She weeps openly and Sally holds her in her arms. It's the most emotion she's seen from her in weeks.

"Don't you dare think that. Playing a dumb prank as a child has nothing to do with this. You do not deserve what has happened to you. This is not karma. Do you understand?"

Sally is being blunter and more forceful than she would like, but her mum needs to hear this. This is not how the world works. Mum has been through indescribable torture and suffering. Not to mention already having to deal with the death of her husband at such a young age.

Mum sniffs and raises her head. "I think you're wrong."

"I'm not wrong. Speak to Natalie, she'll tell you. She was there, too, and nothing happened to her. What you've been through is dreadful and completely unfair, and I won't have you blaming yourself."

Mum shrugs and pulls away, sniffing and wringing her hands. Closing down and disappearing deep inside herself again. Shutting her out. Sally wants to scream. Mum is going through enough without adding self-flagellation to the already unmanageable pain.

Natalie will be here shortly and she can set things straight. Mum even said herself that her friend Leah carried on with her life as usual. It can't have been that traumatic for her. Teenagers do shitty things every day. Leah probably doesn't even remember it.

# 40

## SALLY

### SIX MONTHS EARLIER

Sally is waiting by the front door and before Natalie can knock, she goes outside and joins her on the doorstep, pressing a finger to her lips. Mum can't see them from here.

"Is she asleep?"

"No, I just wanted to talk to you before you go in. She told me something and I wanted to ask you about it."

Natalie looks puzzled and a little worried. "Sure. Go ahead."

"She told me about something that happened when you guys were at school, and she's trying to say that her being attacked is some sort of karma." Sally stops when she sees Natalie's eyes fall.

"She told you about Leah?"

"Yes. Is it true?"

Natalie swallows and nods her head. "Yeah, sadly, it is. We were such little bitches. And you know, I've been thinking about the karma thing too."

Sally can't hold back. "What! Do you think someone did this to Mum on purpose?"

"No, nothing like that. Just, it's weird, and I haven't told Melissa this by the way, so please don't."

Sally agrees, desperate to hear what Natalie has to say. "I won't tell her anything. What is it?"

"Something weird happened to me just before your mum was attacked. I started getting all these horrible messages from unknown profiles on Facebook. Saying stuff like 'I know what you did' and threatening me, telling me they were coming after me. I was going to tell Melissa about it, but then all this happened and I couldn't. Then the messages just stopped and I kind of forgot about it."

"Who was it? Did you report them?"

"I was planning to, but then with your mum being in hospital and just life, I guess, I didn't. All the profiles have been deleted, too, so I'm not sure there is anything I can do."

"Why didn't you tell me?"

"Honestly, with everything you were all going through, I couldn't add to it. Your mum seemed sure it was a teenage boy and that it was just a random attack. And she's right, Sally. This isn't anything. It's just a set of weird coincidences. We haven't seen Leah in years. What we did back then has nothing to do with your mum being attacked."

"How do you know? Maybe she has a teenage son. We need to tell the police."

Natalie looks sheepish. "I've done a bit of digging on Leah. She does have a son. Two, in fact. But they're adults."

"So you do think there could be something in this."

"No, I don't. Leah would never do anything like that. Melissa's just upset because what's happened makes her think about how we treated Leah back then. It was a horrible thing to do and we got away with it. But..."

"But what?"

"I do still think it could have been Leah messaging me. I've thought a few times about tracking her down and confronting her. I've even asked around, and I know her married name, but I've no idea where she lives or anything."

"Then let's do that. Let's find her and ask her."

Natalie shakes her head. "No. Can you imagine what that would do to your mum? Trust me, Sal, it wasn't her. Melissa's in a bad place and she's just grasping at straws. What good would it do to drag up painful memories? All we can do is be here and try to support her."

Sally's voice cracks in frustration and a torrent of pent-up emotions flow out of her. "But she won't let me support her. I've tried. She's completely broken. It's like she's died. Can't you see? If there's even the slightest chance that this Leah was involved, we need to find out."

Natalie reaches out and places her hands on Sally's forearms. "I know this is hard."

"Hard? That's the fucking understatement of the century."

"I know. But don't let it take you off on some mad witch hunt. You need to stay focused on what matters. You and your mum. I know you're saying she's not looking after herself, but neither are you."

Sally's shoulders sag. Natalie is right. Almost everything Sally has said about her mum, she's doing too. She's not eating properly and hasn't been out or seen any of her friends since it happened. But none of that matters.

"Well, I'm going back to work on Monday. Just mornings. I thought about getting another sick note but Mum was insistent I go back. Plus, I thought if she saw me getting on with things, it might encourage her to do the same." Sally looks up at Natalie expectantly. Desperate to hear something positive.

"Good. And I think you're right. And this stuff about karma and Leah will pass. It's okay for Melissa to feel low right now. But I've known her almost my whole life. She will pick herself up eventually. The fight will come back, I know it. We just have to weather the storm." Natalie pulls Sally into a tight embrace and she yields. Falling into her and letting the tension in her body drop.

"You're right. Thank you." Sally wipes her eyes and they walk back into the house together.

"You take some time while I visit with your mum. I've got loads to tell her, and I reckon I can get at least one smile out of her today."

Sally makes her way to the kitchen.

"Hi, Melissa, I'm here to piss you off again. Cuppa?"

"Not you again. Don't you ever listen?"

"Nope. You know me. Listening is not one of my strong points. Talking, on the other hand, is my speciality, so buckle up, buttercup, I've got plenty of gossip."

Sally's heart brightens as she sees her mum give a small silent chuckle, the colour returning to her cheeks. Sally heads upstairs and gets comfy on the bed in her room. She may have told Natalie she was right. But deep down, Sally knows Leah is somehow involved. Coincidences don't exist and it would be stupid to ignore the obvious connection. She will track her down and find out if she is responsible for her mum's pain and misery.

And woe betide her if she is.

If Leah has destroyed her mum, Sally will not wait for karma.

She will become karma.

# 41

## LEAH

This just gets worse and worse. Poor Melissa. Leah continues to be astonished at the knock-on effect of what she's done. She tries to tell herself she can't be held responsible for every consequence and complication. But she is lying to herself. She started a chain reaction of events. She lit the fuse. Every single thing that happened after is of her making.

"I... I don't know what to say."

"No, I should think you don't. And I'm not finished yet. Mum got even worse after that. She's pretty much mute now and barely makes eye contact. Natalie remains a faithful friend. Something you couldn't possibly comprehend."

Leah wants to object. Sally is making it sound like she was the one who broke their friendship, and that's at least one thing she's not guilty of – maybe the only one. But that would make her sound bitter and sulky.

Sally continues. "She never spoke to me about you again after that day, but I knew you were to blame. Something inside me, something bigger than all of us, told me it was you. And I was right. I've let it take over my life, and I know I've neglected Mum. But after today, I'll be able to focus on her one hundred per cent. We can start the healing journey once your dark presence is extinguished."

Leah knows her curiosity will likely only get her killed sooner, but there is still so much she can't figure out. "I understand why you'd want to get back at me. But why all of this? Why not just come to my house or something? You've already said you know where I live." Leah is surprised by her own bravery. Since being in this room, she's acted in ways she can't comprehend. She's screamed bloody murder, she's cried like a baby, she's fallen into semi-conscious despair, and now she's somehow emerged calmer, braver and accepting. All in such a short space of time.

"Good question, Leah. When I decided to seek revenge for you killing my mother." Sally looks up and catches Leah's gaping mouth. "Don't argue with that statement. You don't know. You killed her. She died." Leah closes her mouth and folds her arms, knowing there is no point in arguing. "I found you pretty quickly. Natalie told me your surname and, as I've said before, you weren't hard to find and coax here."

Leah thinks. She remembers Sally saying she targeted her through Facebook, but how on earth could she know Leah was looking for therapy? She doesn't dare ask, and what does it matter anyway?

"I spent weeks following you. I have to say, you lead a pretty nice life. Expensive clothes, beautiful home. I noticed you often went to the doctor, which got me wondering. I remember standing behind you in the queue at the pharmacy to collect your antidepressants. It took everything I had not to bash your skull in. But, you see, Mum needs me and I know she can come back to life once you're gone. As soon as everything has been put right, we will heal."

Leah listens intently. Okay, that answers the bit about knowing she was suffering with her mental health. But why bring two other innocent people in on this crusade of vengeance?

"But why here? And why are you punishing them too?" Leah doesn't look at either Tess or Dr O'Hara. How they must hate her. They're entirely innocent.

"I can't take the chance I might get caught. Even though what I am doing is justified and should, in my opinion, be legal, sadly it's not. Mum can't lose me. So that's why Tess is going to do the honours."

Sally turns the gun on Tess briefly, who doesn't move a muscle until Sally's eyes are firmly focused on Leah again. Then Tess shakes her head and Leah sees her silently mouth "No". Even though Tess's life isn't being threatened Leah feels horribly guilty that she's become tangled up in this.

"But why Dr O'Hara?" Leah hadn't meant to say this out loud. But thankfully, Sally doesn't seem to mind.

"Ah, the doctor." Sally turns her head. "Are you okay back there?"

The doctor's head is raised now and she is staring at Leah with pure hatred. Who can blame her? She's yet another victim of Leah's actions, and from what she read about Dr O'Hara before coming here, she's nothing but a kind and caring professional who's helped many people. Of the three of them, she must be the most confused and angry at her current predicament. Dr O'Hara doesn't answer Sally's question.

"Ah, I forgot, you can't speak properly with that gag in your mouth. Let's fix that, shall we?" Sally jumps up, the knife in one hand, the gun in the other. Leah's heart jumps into her throat as she watches Sally take up position behind the doctor. The knife pressed to her throat.

Leah begs, "No, please." She can't watch this poor woman get her throat cut. She has to do something. "Please. Don't hurt her." The knife glints as Sally slices through the gag and throws it, the wet material hitting the tiled floor with a thud. Leah can't bear to watch, yet she seems unable to turn away.

"Dr O'Hara is a good woman, you know. She's dedicated her life to helping people. And in the time I've worked for her, I've seen it first-hand. She helps people heal purely through listening and talking to them. It's quite special."

Leah's nerves are on edge. The knife is still uncomfortably close to the doctor's neck, and although the gag has been removed, she is still tied to the chair and unable to move or defend herself. Sally praising the doctor is confusing and there must be a 'but' coming. Dr O'Hara doesn't speak and remains facing forwards, staring at Leah. Her stoicism is impressive.

"I haven't done very well for myself workwise. I've always been a bit of a flake with jobs and I've never known what I want to do with my life. But Dr O'Hara gave me a chance and I will always be grateful. It's led me here. To the most meaningful and important thing I'll ever do."

Sally's grandiose attitude is back, and Leah imagines how much Dr O'Hara regrets her decision to hire Sally. Leah truly hopes the doctor makes it out alive. She deserves to live more than any of them.

"And now I think it's time."

Panic rises inside Leah's chest. Time for what? She leans forwards, her arms outstretched, pleading with Sally. But then a thought occurs to her. Sally has already stated she won't kill Leah herself. That she can't run the risk of being caught. Then surely Dr O'Hara is safe? Not to mention, the doctor is someone Sally clearly admires and is thankful for. She won't hurt her. She would go to prison. She would still be unable to support her mum. But Leah's trying to apply rationality to an illogical situation. Sally's mind isn't working. Things don't have to make sense.

"Sit. Back." Leah does as she is told. Sally slowly moves the knife away from Dr O'Hara's neck and points it at her back. Relief floods through Leah. If she has to watch the doctor be stabbed, in the back would be a less unpleasant sight. What an utterly horrific and selfish thing to think.

Sally slices upwards with the knife and Leah clamps her eyes closed, waiting for the tortuous screams to follow. But all is quiet. Leah opens one eye, her heart racing, and sees Dr O'Hara move for the first time. Her arms are in front of her, rubbing at her wrists. Then Sally bends down quickly and dispatches the ties around Dr O'Hara's ankles with another quick flick of the blade. Leah watches, relieved and bewildered in equal measure.

The doctor stands and stretches out her neck and back, rolling her head from side to side. Leah is frozen to the spot. Is Sally going to let her go? Even with the gun and the knife in her possession, Sally's taking a huge risk by setting Dr O'Hara free. Sally drops the knife onto the chair recently vacated by the doctor, the gun still trained on Leah. Leah flicks her eyes to Tess, who looks equally gobsmacked by what has just occurred. Sally holds her free hand up as though about to swear an oath and Dr O'Hara turns and high-fives her. They smile at each other warmly, tears pricking at their eyes. Leah's head is spinning.

"Come on, Jenna, join me on the sofa. You must have been so uncomfortable in that chair all this time."

Dr O'Hara nods before focusing her eyes on Leah and then Tess, flashing them a wicked smile.

Leah feels like she is going to pass out.

# 42

# TESS

*What. The. Actual. Fuck.*

Nothing, absolutely nothing, would surprise Tess now. These women are evil geniuses. Tess looks at Sally and Dr O'Hara as they sit next to each other on the sofa. They are holding hands and sitting in the exact same position. They remind her of the little girls from *The Shining*.

Tess almost pissed her pants when they high-fived. They actually high-fived! It was a very cool move. Not to mention creepy. It gave her goosebumps.

The last ten minutes were fascinating to watch, and Tess has to give it to Sally and Dr O'Hara. They had her. She still can't quite believe what she is looking at. Why the hell would they do that? For theatrics? If so, it definitely worked. It was like watching Keyser Söze stop limping. And being immersed in their performance was a bit of welcome relief from the horrible fear she feels for her mum.

Since they've been in this room, it's been a peculiar turn-taking approach between her and Leah, and Tess is trying to use the time when the heat is off her to regroup and come up with options. She doesn't have much. Pretty much nothing, to be honest. And the revelation that Dr O'Hara is on Sally's side does not work in Tess's favour. Sally has an accomplice. She already has an alibi, which means Tess needs to rethink what she can offer outside of being the one who carries out Leah's murder.

With some time to reflect, Tess feels relatively sure her parents are not at risk. Okay, so these two women are batshit crazy, but there is at least a reason, no matter how warped. Sally is avenging her mum. Surely that means Sally wouldn't hurt Tess's mum for no reason. It's a bluff. It has to be. Tess can't ruin her whole life and end Leah's on what is almost certainly just an empty threat. Tess waits with bated breath for what Sally and Dr O'Hara are about to do and say next. It could literally be anything.

"Tying Jenna up in the chair was her idea. I didn't want to. But she insisted, and who am I to argue. She's the expert." Sally's enamoured smile and deference to Dr O'Hara is unnerving, and her tone is light and airy. Unhinged does not even come close.

Dr O'Hara gives Sally a businesslike nod before pulling her hand away from Sally's and crossing her legs. She straightens her hair with long elegant fingers, tucking the strands that were stuck to her face behind her ears.

"It was simply the best strategy." It's the first time they have heard the doctor's voice. It is deeper than Tess was expecting and has a sultry tone. Perfect for a therapist. "When we decided to do this, I researched the theory of hostage-taking quite extensively." Is this woman for real? Tess can't believe they are about to be subjected to a lecture. "In the initial hostage-taking stage, emotions are running wild. This was the greatest risk to our plan. Both of you would have reduced decision-making capacity. In layman's terms, you'd likely do something stupid and ruin everything. My feeling was if it was a very obvious two against two situation, you might try to overpower us. And as Sally has stated, we don't want to have to hurt either of you ourselves. But be assured, we have discussed this at length and will dispatch with either or both of you if needed. I have worked through every eventuality so that Sally and I can return to normal life after this."

Tess gawps at the doctor in amazement. It's as though another person has entered the room. The woman speaking to them now and the one tied up mere moments ago are two completely different animals. Dr O'Hara is one hell of an actress. The fear and emotion Tess witnessed earlier were so believable. Yet there is not a hint of feeling when she speaks to them. It's as though she's reading a bus timetable. All facts and technical information. And the worst thing about it all is Tess believes her. She has no doubt that Dr O'Hara has everything mapped out with pinpoint accuracy.

Sally holds all the emotion and Dr O'Hara is cool and calculating. They are a perfect team. Tess and Leah are well and truly fucked.

"We needed Sally to establish control. As well as being a distraction and diluting your own felt sense of threat, my presence added weight to Sally's dominance. She had overpowered me. I was silent and subservient. I behaved as though I was afraid and showed no fight to escape. Seeing this will have subconsciously encouraged you to do the same. With my professional standing, you would have seen me as a person who makes good, measured decisions. If I wasn't fighting, you wouldn't either."

Tess can't help but be fascinated. Could this be any more messed up? Everything Dr O'Hara says makes perfect sense. They must have been planning this for months.

Dr O'Hara reaches out and places her hand on Sally's forearm. "As the situation developed, I knew Sally would get emotional and make threats." Sally turns to look at her accomplice. Her face filled with apologies. "No, please don't feel bad. It's the natural progression of the situation. I needed to be in a position where I could monitor you all, establish trends in your behaviour and watch your relationships develop. Look for weak points and assess your motivations. Plus, I could have intervened at any point. Those ties had a mechanism I could use to get myself free if needed. Like I said, every eventuality."

Tess looks across at Leah, who has returned to her weird state of nothingness.

The doctor continues. "And now we are in the most effective and productive phase of proceedings. You may not feel it, but you have all made considerable progress. We still have some way to go to reach the acceptance stage. You in particular, Tess, are very challenging to assess. Under different circumstances, I'd have enjoyed the opportunity to work with you."

Dr O'Hara gives Tess a small smile. It looks weird on her face. *Not a chance in hell*, thinks Tess. She wouldn't let this woman anywhere near her brain.

"What I'm about to say next falls outside the normal order of things." Tess scoffs internally. Normal? Normal went out of the window a very long time ago. "But I feel it's important to lay my cards on the table."

Tess has given up trying to predict what will happen next. She wouldn't be surprised if Sally and Dr O'Hara suddenly peeled off rubber masks and revealed they were actually Ant and Dec.

So she waits, thinking about her mum and praying that what the doctor is about to reveal somehow means her mum is actually safe.

# 43

# LEAH

Leah's mind has hit its limit. Nothing else is going in. She caught some of what Dr O'Hara said but can't seem to process it. It's as though her body has turned off all but the most essential of functions. She's still breathing and blinking but not much else. Sally had been the overriding presence and the dynamic shift is odd. Not in a bad way. Leah prefers the doctor's stiff tone and factual words to Sally's emotional outbursts and threats. The doctor continues, and Sally remains quiet and submissive.

"For privacy, I practise under my mother's maiden name – O'Hara – but my given name is Jenna McGill."

That gets Leah's attention. McGill, as in Natalie McGill. Dr O'Hara nods as she sees the realisation dawn on Leah's face.

Sally is Melissa's daughter and Dr O'Hara is Natalie's sister.

Sally chimes in. "Jenna gave me this job just over a year ago as a favour to my mum."

Dr O'Hara reaches out for Sally's hand and retakes charge of the conversation. "My sister, Natalie, and Melissa have remained best friends. We see each other as family. We support and care for each other, and we'd do anything to keep each other safe. As you can well see. I love Sally as though she were my own daughter." The tips of Sally's cheeks redden and her eyes become glassy. "I knew Sally was struggling to find work, so I reached out. None of what has happened today was on the cards at that point. In fact, it was just before that terrible night."

"Three weeks before. I completely left you in the lurch. Yet you still kept the job open when I was ready to return."

They smile lovingly at each other.

"Well of course, you needed my support more than ever."

Leah scrutinises their exchange, baffled by the shift in the conversation.

Then Dr O'Hara addresses her directly and Leah's skin prickles. "I look at you sitting there, Leah, and I wonder if you will ever truly comprehend what you have done." Leah swallows. She knows what she has done. It's been explained to her in painstaking detail, and she's having her life threatened because of it. "And I don't mean knowing the specifics. I mean, feeling it. Like we do." Leah remains mute. It's clear what happened to Melissa has crushed them and she supposes she'll never be able to feel that pain. But terrible things happen to families every day and they don't go around on murderous plots of revenge. Of course, Leah is sorry but she can't comprehend how they both think their actions are right.

Dr O'Hara continues. "Natalie is the exact opposite of me. I'm quiet and reserved. Academic and introverted. She is gregarious and fierce. Creative and extroverted. Yet we've always gotten along wonderfully together. I wonder if you remember me from when you were a child?"

Leah tries to think, but her brain is mush. She takes herself back to those wonderful nights when she, Melissa and Natalie would hang out at each other's houses. She has a vague recollection of an older sister but can't ever remember meeting her properly. "No. I'm sorry. I don't."

"I'm four years older than Natalie. By the time your friendship had ended, I had moved on to college. I remember you being at my house a few times. Not many, but I spent most of my time in my room. I was always that way. Only liked the company of a few people, namely my family, at that age, and routinely retreated to my bedroom whenever we had visitors."

Leah can't comprehend why they are having this mundane conversation, and she doesn't have the brain space or inclination to engage.

"You should know your brief flirtation with trolling devastated my sister." Leah's heart jolts. She wasn't expecting that. "I feel like I should also say that I abhor what they did to you at school." Leah nods. It's the first piece of validation she's had. "But you were children. And now you are women. I won't bore you with the development of emotions and behaviour from adolescence to adulthood, but suffice to say, what you did to Melissa and what they did to you as children do not compare. What they did was unkind. They bullied you and that is unacceptable. They should have been punished in an appropriate manner for their age and the severity of their actions. But what you did was a crime. And I will echo Sally's sentiments. The Melissa we all know and love died that day, and the consequences gravely wounded so many of us. Sally in particular."

Leah doesn't want to hear all this again. How many times do they need to twist the knife?

"And I've had to support my sister through the consequences of your trolling. You dulled her light. You made her afraid. And whilst that pales in comparison to what you did to Melissa, I must tell you I hate you for it."

Leah has never heard anyone say the words 'I hate you' in such a perfunctory and factual manner before. But she gets it. She'd feel the same if the shoe was on the other foot.

"So when I discovered Sally was planning to seek retribution, I stepped in to help. She shouldn't have to suffer for what you've done and after much deliberation, I agreed with her assessment. To all intents and purposes, you have taken a life. And I think it would be better for all concerned if you paid with yours."

She says it just like that, like a statement of fact. And somehow, that makes it hit harder. Dr O'Hara isn't crazed and fuelled by misguided love and devotion. Are they right? Does Leah deserve to have her life taken away? Or is Jenna O'Hara just as unhinged as Sally, but in a completely different way?

Dr O'Hara turns to Sally. "I'd like a little more time to talk with Leah, but I'm concerned this is taking longer than anticipated. I think it would be wise for you to check in with Claire at Tess's parents' house. We don't want her worrying and jumping the gun, so to speak."

Sally nods. "Tess, wake up. We need to call your folks again." Sally moves herself and the gun closer to Tess and takes out her phone.

Leah focuses on Dr O'Hara, dreading what their private chat might involve.

"I did manage a brief conversation with Sally after she met with you this morning, but I have some questions I'd like to ask if you'll oblige?"

Leah can't think of any reason not to. They know everything already, and she'd rather answer questions than hear further details about Melissa's condition or have insults thrown at her. "Sure. Ask whatever you want."

Dr O'Hara looks around the room. "Sorry, this just feels rather odd without my notebook, but then I guess this is odd." She makes a little snorting sound that Leah assumes is supposed to be a laugh. There's nothing remotely funny here, and Leah screws up her face. "I apologise. I'm a little socially awkward. I like order and follow the same process whenever I speak with patients."

Leah is pissed off now. "But I'm not your patient, am I? I'm your prisoner. So if I have to talk against my will whilst being threatened with a gun, I'm sure you can ask questions without your notebook."

Dr O'Hara's cheeks redden and Leah feels a small flush of satisfaction.

"Well, indeed." Dr O'Hara recovers quickly and clasps her hands together. "What I'd like to know, Leah, is why. Why then? So many years have passed and you have a successful life. Why would you do something completely out of character, so ill thought out, and risk everything?" The doctor's eyes are boring into Leah. "And I won't judge. We've already done that part based on your actions. Your words won't change that. I'd just like to understand."

The tiniest flicker of hope ignites inside Leah. Even though Dr O'Hara's words suggest her fate has already been decided, what if she could make the doctor understand? If she can show her that none of this was intentional, could she make them reconsider?

"You're right. I look back on that day and honestly can't believe it was me. And hearing everything that happened afterwards has made it a hundred times worse. I'm not a monster. But I've done something monstrous and I know that." Leah looks into Dr O'Hara's eyes, but there is no indication of how this is landing. "I don't know how or why it happened, but the events of that day at school started popping up in my mind. First, they were just fleeting thoughts. Then they came daily, then hourly, until they consumed my every waking thought and kept me awake at night."

Dr O'Hara's eyebrows flicker with interest. Everything Leah has just said is the truth. This woman is a mental health professional. Surely if Leah can prove she was unwell when she hurt Melissa, she will have to rethink. Temporary insanity is a thing, isn't it? Even for murder. Could they really execute – because that's what this is, an execution – a woman who was mentally ill at the time of her crime?

"I started having nightmares, I began having hallucinations, and I still do to this day."

Okay, so that is a bit of a white lie. Leah regularly has bad dreams and she does get flashbacks, but hallucinations might be stretching the truth.

"The trolling of Natalie came first. I sent those messages and something started happening to me. I just lost control, couldn't hold back even if I tried." Leah knows the next part is risky, but she has to go for it. "Melissa was ignoring my messages and I couldn't take it. I needed her to hear me. I was obsessed. Things snowballed and I was in the car driving to her house before I knew what I was doing." She takes a deep breath. "All I was going to do was spray-paint her house. That's it, I promise you. Write my message so she could see it. I know you've already heard the story, and it doesn't excuse what happened, but I need you to know that. I don't know why I did it. It was a moment of temporary insanity. I had no intention of hurting her and if I could take it back, I would. I swear on my children's lives." That's it. That's all Leah can say or do. Dr O'Hara doesn't react. Leah adds, "I'm so very sorry. Truly sorry."

Dr O'Hara clears her throat. An irritated look on her face. "That was a lot of words to essentially say you don't know."

Leah tries to find something else to say. Something to add weight to her plea. "I'd lost my mind. I was out of control—"

Dr O'Hara holds up a hand. "That's enough. Genuinely, I've heard more than enough."

Leah's blood runs cold. She's made it worse. How, she's not

sure, but the doctor is definitely angrier with her than she was before she asked her question.

"I was going to ask another question but I'm not keen to hear more excuses, so I think I'll leave it." The doctor turns as though she's about to summon Sally over.

"No, please. Let me answer. Let me try."

Dr O'Hara sighs, her face a blend of boredom and exasperation. "I was going to ask why you didn't come forward and admit to what you'd done. If your assertion that you felt remorse and guilt is true, wouldn't that be the natural course of action? But as I've said, I really don't care to hear the answer." Dr O'Hara cranes her neck and calls to Sally, "We're done here," dismissing Leah.

Leah states her answer, but the doctor shows not one iota of interest. "For my family. I did it for my family."

Leah feels a jolt of hope as the doctor looks up, but that soon ebbs away when she speaks.

"Yes. So you will understand why we are doing something others may view as wrong to protect our family. I'm glad we are on the same page."

Leah sinks into her chair.

That was her last chance and she blew it.

# 44

# TESS

Tess's heart sinks when she hears Dr O'Hara suggest they call her parents again. What if something has gone wrong? She knows her mum will take Claire's tale that she's a friend of Tess's at face value. But her dad is a different story. He's pathologically suspicious and probably thinks she's there to steal their silver. What would this Claire person do if confronted? And Sally's 'wake up' comment is just rude and ridiculous. How could she possibly be asleep? She's just thinking. No need for her to be a smart arse.

Sally comes over and crouches down in front of Tess. This is the closest they've been to each other and Tess notices an odour of sour sweat emanating from Sally. Gross. Plus, even though she's probably not much older than Tess, she can see wisps of grey at the front of her hair, which she hadn't noticed before. Tess considers pointing both these facts out. Two can play at the spiteful bitch game. But that thought disappears as Sally takes out her phone.

Tess hopes with all her heart that her mum and dad are okay. Sally speaks quietly and Tess cranes her head.

"Listen very carefully. I'm not going to call your parents."

Tess's brow furrows. "Jenna is distracting Leah so I can talk to you, okay?" Tess nods, not knowing if this is a good or a bad thing. "Now take the phone and put it to your ear." Tess does as she is told, briefly considering calling 999 and screaming down it. "Look at Jenna. Isn't she a genius? I could never have pulled this off without her." Tess screws up her face. Is she supposed to be pleased and impressed by that? They are not on the same side. "She's keeping Leah's attention on her by being irritating. Listen to what she's saying about needing a notebook. It's brilliant. Look at Leah's face. Priceless."

Tess looks across and sees that Leah is indeed entirely absorbed by the doctor. Why is Sally suddenly acting all pally with her? Crouched down on her haunches, Tess could easily kick her over. If it wasn't for her parents' predicament, she would thrust her heels right into the sweaty grey-haired cow's chest.

"Anyway, we haven't got long and Dr O'Hara wanted me to tell you some things. Things she's sure will appeal to you and change your mind. You ready?"

Tess nods, wondering what this magical list of things that will suddenly turn her into a cold-blooded killer might be.

"I've already explained why I'm not willing to kill Leah, and Jenna feels the same. Our families have been through enough and it would be the final nail in the coffin for my mum if she found out I'd done that. But it has to happen and once it's done, I'll be able to get better. I've been completely neglecting Mum and once Leah's gone, I'll be able to focus on her again. She deserves this. I hope you see that."

Tess looks emotionlessly at Sally. She can see many things but not one of them is that Leah dying will make this woman or her mother feel better. She can't even work out how she has put that together. Seeing Leah pay for her crimes the proper sane way, with the police – yes, absolutely. Moving on and being able to focus on her mum again – of course. But setting this room up as some gruesome death chamber and casting Tess in the role of executioner – nope. Not one single bit. No matter what happens, today's events will take Sally from being an irrational obsessive and send her over the edge. She might think she wants this, but she doesn't. Sally's mind is damaged. And Tess is shocked Dr O'Hara can't see that. Unless... What's that French saying? *Folie à deux.* Two mad people making each other madder and convincing each other it's okay. This is definitely like that.

Tess would love to say all of this out loud, but Sally is operating on another plane. So she simply goes with, "Okay." She considers adding that she won't do this for the very same reasons Sally has just stated. Tess's mum has been through enough simply by being her parent. If Tess killed someone, her mum would see it as her own crime and attribute it to her failings as a mother, no matter what the circumstances. It would kill her. There is no good choice to be made here. Tess decides an attempt to appeal to Sally is worth the risk.

"If I did this, and I'm not suggesting I would, it would kill my mum. Come on, Sally, can't you see we're in the same boat? My mum would feel responsible. Please, you have to find another way."

*Do it your fucking self and leave me out of it* Tess wants to add, but she stops short.

"And that's what I'm about to tell you. We have a plan. Now listen and don't interrupt. We're seriously running out of time now."

Intrigued yet ultimately sceptical, Tess agrees. "Okay. Go ahead."

"Dr O'Hara has a patient. A male patient who we have set up to take the fall. I won't tell you everything because the less you know, the better. But trust me when I say he deserves it.

According to our computer systems, he should be in consultation with Dr O'Hara right now. When you kill Leah—"

"I'm not killing Leah."

Sally glares and Tess shuts up, remembering her agreement not to interrupt. But this is bonkers.

"When you kill Leah, we'll call Claire and she will leave your house. Then you'll go to your parents' house as planned. You'll see they are safe and be far away from here. Nobody else will ever know what you have done. Jenna and I will call the police, distraught, and tell them that one of our patients has stabbed another in the waiting room. All of us will be in the clear and justice will be served."

Tess stares deep into Sally's eyes, looking for a hint of anything other than delusion. But there is nothing. And introducing another person into this already convoluted game is mind-boggling. How can they possibly think they're going to get away with it?

"What if this guy has an alibi? Maybe he's currently sitting in McDonald's or with his wife?"

"He's not."

"How do you know?"

"Well, he killed his wife so he's definitely not with her."

Tess tries to let this shocking fact go past her and focus on the point she's trying to make. "Er... okay. But that doesn't mean he's not somewhere else. With people who can prove he wasn't here."

Sally rolls her eyes. "Did you not hear me say that the less you know, the better?"

"I did. But there are so many holes in this. And I don't know why I'm trying to help you, but you're going to get caught. As things stand, you haven't committed a crime, well, not a serious one at least. Kidnapping maybe? If you stop this now, we can all walk out of here. You wanted to make Leah suffer and it's more than obvious you've done that. If you handed her a phone now, she'd call the police and tell them everything. Do that. Get justice the right way."

Tess takes a deep breath. Wow, that was a powerful speech. She's not sure where it came from but it deserves a round of applause. But Sally's eyes are blank. Just dark, empty pools.

"No. This is your last chance, Tess. I wasn't supposed to tell you this, but I will. The man who is taking the fall for this is dead. I killed him last night and nobody will ever find him. I assure you."

Tess recoils in shock. If Sally is lying, her performance warrants an Oscar. Tess believes her wholeheartedly. Someone has already died. Deep inside, Tess has always seen this as a horrible charade that would somehow end with everyone alive. It all feels too ludicrous to be real. But if they've already killed someone...

"We have this all sewn up. It will go perfectly. Now is the time for you to do your bit. You won't take the blame. You'll walk out of here and never have to see Jenna or me again. And if you're thinking Claire won't hurt your parents, you're wrong. You don't know her. She will, and she won't get caught either."

Tess gulps. Her desperate hope that this was all a bluff is slipping through her fingers.

"We have planned this for months. We have thought of every possible hurdle and problem and have multiple solutions to every single one. Every aspect of our plan is bulletproof. Do not underestimate us."

The fierce look in Sally's eyes is terrifying, and Tess has no idea what to believe.

"What about the knife? His fingerprints won't be on it, but mine and yours will be."

"We'll wipe it and say he was wearing gloves. There'll be no fingerprints."

Okay, that sounds semi-reasonable. There will be no evidence that he did it, but there will also be no evidence that someone else did it.

"He was in this room yesterday. His fingerprints and DNA will be everywhere. But none of that is important because Jenna and I will tell the same story. The police already know this man killed his wife. He got off on a technicality. They hate him and won't hesitate to believe he did it."

Tess nods. That does sound like a reasonable story. Albeit a story from one of those true crime documentaries on Netflix, but a reasonable story, nonetheless.

"We have no CCTV cameras in here or outside. The closest one is fifty yards down the street, and we've—" Sally suddenly stops and shakes her head. "Nope. I'm not doing this. Jenna told me not to, and I've already gone way over the line with what I've told you so far."

Tess wants to protest. She needs to hear all of this. Every single tiny detail.

"I'll say this one more time and then that's it. It's over to you. You have to kill Leah. You will stab her in the chest with the knife. You need to make it look like a crazed patient did it. Then you will leave and go to your parents' house. Someone else – a man you don't know, who will never be found – will take the blame. Life will go on for the rest of us. Okay?" Tess feels like she is going to throw up. This can't be it. There has to be another way. "Alternatively, you refuse, then Claire kills your parents. I kill Leah and then I'll have to kill you, too, because of everything you've heard. We'll stage it to look like you attacked each other. Much more risky, much less convincing, and definitely not my preferred option."

Tess stares dumbfounded at Sally. She's moving her mouth just like everyone does, speaking normally and making typical expressions. Yet she just used the word 'kill' about a dozen times without even flinching. It's enough to make Tess feel like she's breaking with reality. Sally stands up, retrieves the knife from the chair Dr O'Hara was strapped to and slides it down the side of Tess's seat, between her leg and the chair arm.

"There you go. Don't even think of trying to stab your way out of here. I'll put a bullet through your pretty face quicker than you can blink."

Sally smiles sweetly and returns to her seat on the sofa.

Tess rests her arm over the knife.

She needs to come up with a plan and quickly.

# 45

# TESS

Sally and Dr O'Hara sit together again. Tess's heart is galloping in her chest. She checks on Leah, who is back to that dumbstruck look she had earlier. She watches her breathing in and out. Will Leah still be doing that in a few moments' time? Will Tess?

The room is eerily silent, there's just the faint sound of collective breathing and the hum of fear and anticipation in the air. This whole thing is a horror show and Tess can't believe the position she is in. She's always been able to keep reality at a distance when needed. To hear people's woes and tragic stories as just that – stories. Tess can listen as her friends and family talk about heart-wrenching things that have happened and not really feel anything. She can just detach herself. But this is different. This is all-consuming and utterly horrific, and Tess feels it deeply in every fibre of her being.

She watches as Sally takes Dr O'Hara's hand. They nod at each other with watery eyes and Tess is sure she can sense apprehension. Have they lost their nerve? Finally realised they have gone way too far? If only.

Sally squeezes the doctor's hand before releasing it and

taking out her phone. She taps at the screen briefly before placing it on the coffee table in front of her. Tess's eyes widen when she sees a timer on the screen counting backwards from five minutes.

Sally speaks. "Tess, you have five minutes. When this timer ends, I will call Claire and tell her to carry out my instructions."

Tess is struggling to breathe and her heart aches with a profound helplessness. "Please."

They ignore her plea, but Dr O'Hara takes the final word. "We won't say anything further. The time for talking is over. Now is the time for action."

Tess looks down at the timer: four minutes and twelve seconds. A minute has almost gone. How did that happen so quickly?

They can't do this. They won't. Surely, they won't.

Tess looks first at Sally and then at Dr O'Hara, a deep pleading in her eyes. She summons every ounce of strength within her. She has to pull them away from this heinous plan. Sally stares through her, completely closed off and unwilling to engage. Dr O'Hara stares at the wall, her lips moving but no sound emerging. Tess turns to Leah, who has now come back to life.

Sally said Claire won't act unless she gets a phone call. If Tess and Leah can somehow overpower Sally and Dr O'Hara and take the phone, could they stop this? They have to try.

Tess wishes she had fought from the very first moment. Spent the entire time kicking and screaming and refusing to engage. She's been far too compliant. And now she has what?

Three minutes and seven seconds.

Sally and Dr O'Hara are in some kind of trance. Holding hands as though in ceremonial prayer. Will their reactions be slowed? If she's going to do something, now is the time.

Two minutes and forty-four seconds.

Tess whispers, "Leah, come on. We have to go." She takes out the knife. Her hands tremble and she almost drops it.

Leah is dazed and clearly misunderstands Tess's intentions. She looks at the knife and starts screaming. Tess tries to calm her, but the woman is lost in her own world. Tess leans forwards and stretches out her arm, the one without the knife, trying to calm her. But to no avail.

Tess recoils as the sound of the gun firing rips through the room. Unconsciously, she protects her head and closes her eyes. Her ears are ringing and she is completely disorientated, but there is no pain at least. She hasn't been shot.

Tess doesn't dare open her eyes. Leah is quiet. Presumably, because she has a bullet lodged in her head. Tess peels one eye open and looks down at the timer.

One minute and forty-one seconds.

She opens her other eye and sees Dr O'Hara and Sally seated precisely as they were, the gun still in Sally's hand. If Tess hadn't heard the gunshot, she wouldn't have believed the woman had moved at all. Tess turns her head, dreading what she is about to see. But somehow, Leah is still alive. Trembling furiously but unhurt. The wall behind Leah has taken the brunt of the bullet. It must've missed Leah's head by centimetres.

Fifty-seven seconds.

Leah needs to snap out of it. Tess stands then squats in front of Sally and Dr O'Hara, recognising she is risking being shot but knowing she has to take the very last chance she has to change their minds.

"You have to stop this!" Neither of them move or speak. Their faces remain stony. They don't even blink.

Tess moans and jumps to her feet.

Twenty-six seconds.

That's all she has. Twenty-six seconds and her life will change forever.

Her parents are going to die. She and Leah are going to die.

Tess strides over to Leah, knife still in her hand. Leah starts wailing again. Turning her body away and holding her arms over her head.

Fourteen seconds.

Tess yells with fear and frustration. "I am not going to stab you. Would you get a grip and help me?"

Six seconds.

Leah unfurls and turns towards Tess.

Three seconds.

Tess takes the knife and plunges it deep into Leah's chest. It glides through her skin and into her flesh so easily that Tess can barely believe it. Neither can she believe what she's doing. Nothing feels real. It's like an out-of-body experience. Then Tess pulls out the knife and repeats the stabbing motion four more times. She moves the knife in and out cleanly, angling her body away to avoid getting any blood on her clothes. If Sally is telling the truth and she's going to leave here and go to her parents' house, she can't be covered in blood.

Tess can vaguely hear the timer going off in between stabs. She doesn't look at Leah's eyes. She just does it.

Tess truly didn't know what she was going to do until those last few seconds. But once it came down to the wire, the choice between her mother and Leah was suddenly very easy to make. There were no other options available.

Leah hasn't moved. The "I'm not going to stab you" line had the desired effect. If Tess was going to do this, she needed to do it cleanly. She wasn't going to stab Leah in the back and she didn't want her thrashing around or cowering in terror. So Tess put her at ease.

They are the worst words Tess has ever said or ever will say. The wickedest lie she has ever told. But she said them for a good reason. She did what she had to do to save her mum. And if

Sally doesn't follow through on her promise, Tess will unleash holy hell on her and Dr O'Hara. They made her a murderer. And if her mum still dies, they will die too. Painfully.

Leah was going to die anyway, of that Tess is sure. If Tess didn't kill her, Sally would have. But now, hopefully, Tess's mum and dad will live. Tess will, too. And in this horrific moment, just seconds after spilling the blood of a woman she only met this morning, Tess vows she will live a better life.

She will make sure she comes out of this a better person. She will spend more time with her mum and dad and treat them with the love and respect they deserve. She will set Joe free and make her own way in the world. Joe is a good man, a kind and trusting man, and he deserves much better than her.

She will learn to value those around her and care about their feelings. She will listen and empathise.

She will become the person she should have been all these years.

And all it took to make her realise that was killing another human being.

# 46

## LEAH

Sally places the timer on the table. Will these be the last five minutes of her life? Will Tess actually go through with it? She doesn't know. Leah considers whether she would kill Tess if the lives of one of her boys or Jeff were on the line. *In a heartbeat*, she thinks. The realisation stuns her, but if today has taught her anything, it's that people, especially women, will go to extraordinary lengths to protect those they love.

That's what all of this is about. What Sally is doing is nothing but misguided, ugly, fierce love.

Leah's stomach lurches as she turns to see Tess pointing the knife at her. Tess says something, but Leah has no idea what and immediately finds herself screaming. She doesn't seem able to control her body or her voice. And what does it matter? She can go quietly or go down screaming. The result will be the same. Leah's cries die in her mouth as a horrendous bang fills the room and she feels a bullet whiz past her ear. She almost loses control of her bladder and swallows down the bile rising in her throat. She waits, frozen with fear, for the next one to hit her.

But Sally and Dr O'Hara remain seated, holding hands. The only sign that the gun has even been fired is a small puff of smoke from the end dissipating into the air. Tess is pleading futilely with the two women now. But there is an invisible forcefield around them and their emotions. No words can touch them now. They are impenetrable. Finally, Tess gives up and staggers over to her, the knife still in her hand.

Leah lets out another involuntary wail. She wants to run. Yet she also wants to curl into a ball and block out the world. Her body chooses the latter. Whatever is about to happen to her, she doesn't want to see it.

But then Tess speaks. "I am not going to stab you. Would you get a grip and help me?"

Leah turns to her in confusion. Help her? What can she possibly help her with? There's nothing to be done here. Can't Tess see they've lost? When that timer runs out, they're both going to end up dead and Tess's parents too. Leah wishes she would just—

Then, suddenly, it happens. Tess plunges the knife deep into her chest. Leah looks down and sees the knife sticking out of her, blood flowing freely from the wound. Leah watches with amazement. Somehow, she doesn't feel any pain. There is tightness and a warmth in her chest, but not what she would describe as pain. She thought it would be worse than this. Leah stares, dumbfounded, as Tess pulls the knife out and stabs her again and again. It's the most peculiar thing to watch. Leah tries to catch Tess's eye, but her attacker won't look at her and she understands why. She wants to tell Tess she would have done the same thing under these impossible circumstances, but her voice doesn't work.

Leah blinks. Her eyes feel odd, like she's looking through a lace veil. But she can't seem to clear it. Leah opens her mouth to tell Tess this isn't her fault, but all that falls from her lips is blood. Tess may have wielded the knife and ultimately delivered the fatal blows, but Sally and Dr O'Hara left her with no choice.

They literally held a gun to her head. What else could she have done? It's a sacrifice of one life to save three. Sort of honourable, really.

At least this way, there is a chance for the others. The blood is clogging her throat now and her chest is heavy and immovable. Everything is starting to fade and she feels herself beginning to disappear. Drifting away from this world and moving on to whatever awaits her in the next.

Leah will never know if Tess will live, but she hopes she does and her poor parents too. The world is starting to close around her and she can't take in any more air. There is no panic or sadness, simply a strange, ethereal sensation.

Leah thinks of her boys and Jeff and says her last goodbyes.

Then the world goes black.

# 47

# TESS

Tess lets the knife fall from her hand. She should probably keep hold of it. Protect herself or wipe her prints off it. But the thought of touching it again disgusts her. She turns her back on Leah's now dead body. There will be a time to come to terms with what she has done but now is not it. Now is the time to go. To get as far away as possible from these two heinous women and be with her parents.

Tess glowers at Sally and Dr O'Hara, her chest heaving. They release their hands and emerge from their trance almost simultaneously. Tess would love to strangle the pair of them. Look what they made her do. She waits for them to speak but instead, they turn and hug each other. Tess has had enough. She pushes past the sofa and heads for the door. Fuck them. They can deal with this shit; she's out of here.

"Where do you think you are going?"

Tess grits her teeth. Dr O'Hara's robotic voice is making her hackles rise. "To see my parents. And I dare you to try and stop me. I've done what you asked. She's dead. Go on, take a good look." She should storm out but she waits for their response. A slithering unease inside her tells her this isn't over yet.

Sally answers this time. "Yes. And thank you, Tess. But I think you're forgetting yourself."

Tess whips her head around and glares at both women, who are now looking over their shoulders at her. A burning rage pulsates inside Tess's head. What the hell does Sally mean?

"No, I don't think I am. It's done. I'm done. I'm going to see my parents now." Tess reaches for the door but stops when Sally continues.

"We have a call to make first. We need to let Claire know and ask her to leave your parents' home. She can't be there when you arrive."

Tess's blood boils with fury and she screams her words. Spit flying from her twisted mouth. "No. You do that. Call her while I'm on my way. Let me go. That was the deal."

Sally's tone is firm. "You've come this far, Tess. Wouldn't it be a shame if your parents still died because you wouldn't listen?" Tess's eyes bore into Sally. She has never felt such pure hatred for a person in her whole life. "Sit down. We'll make the call."

Tess balls her fists and stomps across the room. She is stopped momentarily in her tracks by the horrific sight of Leah's body. Her lifeless glassy eyes are open and staring up at the ceiling. And the blood. There is so much blood.

"Sit down, Tess. And don't worry about her. She can't hurt anyone now. You've done the world a service."

Tess can feel her heart beating in her throat. How can they say that? Leah wasn't a danger to anyone. She did a stupid thing and has paid the ultimate price. A price exorbitantly higher than she deserved. But Tess sits, legs crossed, digging her nails into her palms, and angles her body away from Leah. She needs to focus and do as they ask. Complying with anything these monsters request is excruciating, especially now. But as with everything she's done so far, it is a means to an end.

Sally takes out her phone and dials. "Hi, Claire. It's done." The volume is too low for Tess to hear Claire's response, no matter how much she concentrates. Sally holds out the phone. Tess recoils and shakes her head frantically as though being proffered a poisonous snake. She does not want to speak to her parents' captor again. There's no way she could hold her tongue.

Sally's jaw tenses. "Take the phone and tell Claire you were held up. Tell her you'll see her another time."

Tess reaches out a trembling hand and takes the phone. "Hi… Claire. Something's come up and I'm… going to be a while. I'll see you another t-time," Tess stammers, her voice cracking throughout. She will never meet this woman and would love to take this moment to tell this person who was willing to murder her parents exactly what she thinks of her. But she has to stick to the plan.

Claire's reply is disgustingly cheery. "Oh, okay, no problem, Tess. I'll see you another…"

Tess hears a commotion on the other end of the phone. She's gripping it so hard that her hand is beginning to cramp painfully. Just as she is about to shout and demand to know what is happening, her mum's voice arrives. Tess closes her eyes and feels her body slump. It is the most wonderful sound.

"What's wrong, my love? Your lovely friend Claire says you're not coming."

Tess sniffs and tries to stop the tirade of tears that are falling unbidden from her eyes. *Claire is not my lovely friend.*

"I… am coming, Mum. I'm just going to be a while. I promise I'll be there."

Her mum gives a relieved sigh. Tess will wrap this wonderful woman in the biggest hug when she sees her.

"Well, Claire can wait then." Tess hears her mum call out, "You can wait, can't you, dear?"

"No!" Tess screams down the phone, warranting a stern look of warning from Sally.

Claire speaks in the background. "I'm sorry, Mrs Liu, but I won't be able to stay. I'll catch up with Tess some other time."

Tess falls still. Terrified of moving and somehow changing the course of events. Claire's leaving. Her parents are going to be okay.

"I'll let you go, shall I? See your friend out properly."

Tess manages to control her voice this time. "No, it's okay. Say goodbye and I'll stay on the line."

"Okay, Thérèse. I'll be just one minute." Tess listens closely as her parents say an excruciatingly long goodbye to Claire. Eventually, she hears the door close. Tess has never felt relief like it. Her parents are safe. At last, something good. A silver lining in what has been the worst morning imaginable.

"I'm back, love. It's a shame—"

Tess butts in, not caring how she sounds or how pissed off Sally might get. "Lock the door, Mum. Lock all the doors now and don't answer them again until I get there."

"Whatever do you mean? Are you okay? You don't sound like yourself."

Tess pinches her nose between her thumb and forefinger. "Please, Mum. Just do it."

"Well, okay, but—"

"Now. Do it now." Tess glances at Sally and Dr O'Hara, but they don't seem upset or angry with her giving out these instructions. This strikes her as weird but she doesn't care. She'd be doing it even if they were furious. That woman is not getting back into their house.

Then Tess hears her dad's voice. She knew this would happen. Her mum always defers to her dad when she's uncertain or concerned. "Why are you telling your mother to lock the doors? Was that woman not your friend?"

Tess knows she has to try to smooth this over. Even with Claire gone, she won't believe her parents are safe until she sees them with her own eyes. So she makes something up. "We used to be friends. But she's not very nice. A bad influence, you know. I'm not very keen to get back in touch with her."

That sounds pretty credible and is the type of thing that would appeal to her dad. Tess waits nervously for the verdict.

"Ah, I see. Well, yes, you know what your mum's like, she'll make friends with anyone. But I have to say, I wasn't awfully keen on her just turning up like that. A bit rude if you ask me."

Tess wants to laugh. That's so typical of her dad. What she wouldn't give for him to have just turned Claire away. But even though he appears to be the man of the house, he'll do anything to keep her mum happy.

"And don't worry, we won't let her back in. Now, are you coming or not? Your mum's going to be upset if you don't."

This time, Tess does laugh and she can read the unsaid meaning behind his words. He wants to see her too. And after she's hugged her mum, she'll do the same with her old-fashioned and stoic dad. She's been far too harsh on him.

"Yes. I can't wait to see you."

"Okay then, I'll put your mother back on and I'll see you soon."

Tess smiles and wipes her tear-streaked face. "See you soon, Dad."

Tess hears her parents muttering and waits for her mum. This all feels refreshingly normal, and she wishes she could block out and erase everything in this room and be there with them.

"Well, that was a lot, Thérèse. You had me thinking there was something to be afraid of."

Tess breathes deeply. This could be dangerous. She must remember the rule: do not raise the alarm.

"Sorry, Mum." She leaves it there, knowing that anything she says will likely make things worse. Mum will calm herself down and Dad will help.

"Your dad's just told me Claire wasn't a good friend. She seemed nice to me, but what do I know? She did eat a lot of biscuits though. Impolite."

Tess smiles, wondering how many biscuits her mum would deem impolite. "Look, I better go, Mum. But I'll see you soon, okay?"

There's a pause and Tess worries they've been cut off. But then her mum speaks.

"Okay. You don't sound right though. I can hear it."

The tears return and Tess can't stop them. No, she is not all right. "I'm... er... Yes, I'm okay."

"Oh, mon amour." The outpouring of care from her mum, condensed into just three words, hits Tess like a steam train, even down the phone. Tess turns her back around further, blocking out not only Leah but also preventing Sally and Dr O'Hara from intruding on this moment.

"What is it, Thérèse? You can tell me anything. You know that."

Tess can hardly speak through the streaming tears. She knows she should wait until they are alone to tell her mum any of this, but her emotions are at the surface, straining to get out, and she finds herself letting go.

"I... I know I've not been a very good person, Mum. I know I've been awful and selfish, but I'm getting help. I'm going to do better, I promise. I'm so sorry I've been such a bitch to you and Dad. You don't know how sorry I am." Tess's shoulders shake and she lets every pent-up emotion from today pour out. She is sure she can hear her mum crying, too, but when she speaks, her tone is surprisingly practical.

"You've nothing to apologise to me for. And don't say the B

word about yourself. I won't have it. Now come home. I'll make you some tea and we'll talk. I want to see your face."

Oh, how Tess wants to see her Mum's face too. "I love you, Mum."

"I love you too. Now come straight here. I'm getting worried and I want to see you. Whatever's happened, we can talk it through."

"Okay. I'll see you soon. Bye."

"Bye, Thérèse."

Tess ends the call. She is more exhausted than she can ever remember feeling and can barely find the energy to move. She has no idea how she's going to drive.

Tess gathers herself slowly and turns to give the phone to Sally.

Sally stares at her through cold, callous eyes, lifts up the gun and aims it at Tess's forehead.

# 48

# TESS

Tess is not remotely intimidated. She is spent. She has nothing left to give. She is leaving right now and won't be following any more instructions from Sally or Dr O'Hara. They have no hold over her anymore.

Weirdly, Dr O'Hara takes out a Dictaphone and holds it up to her face. Tess watches in confusion as the doctor clicks the record button and starts to speak.

"Next patient: Thérèse Liu. Date of birth, tenth of October nineteen ninety-seven."

"What are you doing?" Tess says.

Dr O'Hara rolls her eyes and stops the recording. "Can you be quiet, please? This is important."

Tess doesn't want to be quiet. She wants her mum. She's done everything they have asked of her. Dr O'Hara can make her shitty recording when she's gone.

"I don't need to be here anymore. Let me go."

Dr O'Hara shakes her head. "No." Tess waits for more, but the doctor doesn't elaborate.

Tess turns to Sally. "She can do that when I'm gone. That's it. I'm going."

Tess makes her second bid for freedom and Sally sticks her leg out, tripping her up. Tess clatters to the floor, her face landing horrifyingly close to Leah's outstretched leg. The metallic smell of blood makes her retch.

Tess scrambles to her feet, her ears ringing. "What the fuck is going on? I can't believe you actually tripped me up. What are you, five?" Tess straightens her clothes and gags when she sees a smear of Leah's blood on her sleeve. She wipes it on the arm of the chair but it only makes it look worse.

Sally looks at Tess as though she were a disobedient child. "Just sit down and be quiet. If Dr O'Hara says this is important, then it's important. And she won't be changing her mind."

Tess is incandescent with rage. "No. You made me stay and speak to my parents and I did that. But I'm not staying one second longer. You heard my mum, she's worried. I need to get to her."

Dr O'Hara looks up. Her tone is perfunctory. "I need to record your consultation and you need to hear it."

"But why?" Tess feels the urge to lash out. To destroy everything. Until Dr O'Hara fixes her with a look so cold and menacing that it stops her dead. Is she really going to die on this hill after everything else she's done? Is her temper going to make her fall at the final hurdle? This has to be the last thing, surely. And if she stays quiet, it should only take a few minutes. If she keeps arguing, she'll only be dragging things out. But what if they add another thing and then another? They're all in here with Leah's dead body. Tess can't understand why any of them would want to prolong their stay.

When Dr O'Hara clicks record for the second time, Tess stays quiet. Praying with all her might that this will be their last request. "I reviewed Thérèse, preferred name Tess, in my clinic today. Tess self-presented with claims of exhaustion and feelings of poor self-worth. It quickly became evident that these claims were false and Tess confirmed this."

Dr O'Hara clicks pause.

"Come on, get on with it."

After a few moments of contemplation, Dr O'Hara restarts the recording. "Tess displays many of the traits of both narcissistic and psychopathic personality disorders: lack of empathy, egocentrism, impulsive behaviours and a lack of remorse. She craves admiration and displays an unreasonably high level of self-importance."

Tess grits her teeth. She's heard all this before from Sally and whilst some of it is true, she doesn't need to listen to it again. Dr O'Hara is simply trying to humiliate her. But she won't bite back. Instead, she sits, dampening down her building rage and trying to appear as though this is all water off a duck's back. She'd love to grab that recorder and recite character assassinations of Sally and Dr O'Hara. Fucking hypocrites. Tess might have a touch of whatever these disorders are, but these two are off the scale.

"During the consultation, Tess was outwardly charming but aggressive on occasion when challenged about her behaviours. On one occasion, towards the end of our consultation, I did feel somewhat threatened by a burst of rage, seemingly from nowhere, but I was able to de-escalate."

Tess rolls her eyes. *What absolute bollocks.*

"Tess was relatively open about her relationships. She has what appears to be a genuine relationship with her mother, but all other relationships, including her romantic partnership with her fiancé, are for her convenience. She openly admits her callous and manipulative behaviours in her relationships and, again, showed no remorse."

Tess continues to show disinterest. Do they honestly think they can upset her with this? What a joke.

"Tess and I discussed psychotherapy and she is willing. I am hopeful I can assist her in developing techniques to reduce her harmful actions and create more positive outcomes. We do, however, need to be realistic given the severity of her disorder." Dr O'Hara stops briefly before continuing. Tess is sure she's doing this to get a rise out of her, hoping she'll interrupt. But that isn't happening. *Crack on with your bullshit, Doc.* "I do believe that Tess has a propensity for violence. However, she denies any previous violent behaviours and vehemently denies any desire to hurt others or herself. She is challenging to assess given her manipulative tendencies but at this moment, I don't believe there is any risk."

Tess is finding it increasingly difficult to stay quiet and hates that this is on tape. She'll see if she can grab that recorder on her way out.

"Tess and I have agreed on weekly sessions." Tess scoffs. Not a chance in hell. "It is worth noting that Tess's fiancé, Joe, is also a patient of mine and has been for some time."

Tess's eyes go wide. *What?* There is an evil smirk on Dr O'Hara's face.

"Obviously, I didn't share this information with Tess due to patient confidentiality, but I feel I can manage this appropriately and professionally without conflict."

Dr O'Hara stops the recording and stares at Tess menacingly. Provoking her. Tess knows she shouldn't ask. It doesn't matter anyway. She's already decided she's going to leave Joe. She knows he deserves a partner better than her. Someone who actually loves and appreciates him. She won't rise to their bait.

"Can I go now?"

Dr O'Hara gently places the Dictaphone on her knee and clasps her hands together. "You've destroyed him, you know."

Tess ignores the jibe. She won't be taken back in. "Can I go?"

Again, Dr O'Hara acts as though Tess hasn't spoken. "Before he met you, Joe was a strong, confident man. Do you have any comprehension of what you've done to him? Of course you don't, and even if you did, I don't think you have it in you to care."

Tess's lip begins to tremble. "Can I please just—"

"No!" Dr O'Hara's sudden shout echoes around the room and stuns Tess into silence. It's the first time she has raised her voice. "No, you need to listen to this. I told you it was important. Not everything in this world revolves around you, Tess. Other things, other people actually matter, you know."

Tess pleads and begs. Realising they're not going to let her go without her acknowledging and apologising. "I know. And I promise you, as soon as I get home, I'll be leaving Joe. He deserves better. I know now. Trust me, I know. Just let me go."

Dr O'Hara scowls, her nostrils flaring. "You do realise he actually cares for you. I have no idea why. The things he's told me are sickening and do you know the worst part?" Tess shakes her head in desperation. "That you, you, with your manipulative and selfish ways, have convinced him that everything is his fault. He's depressed, he's anxious and he's lost every ounce of self-respect, yet still he feels like he is the problem in your relationship. You only care that you've landed on your feet, wringing out everything you can get from him. And he's been depleting all these years. Sacrificing himself to feed you and your ego."

Tess's heart aches. Genuinely, she thought Joe was fine. He never showed signs of any of this and she had no idea he was seeing a doctor. "I've told you. It's over. I'll leave him alone and stay away."

It's at this moment the fear really sets in. They're not going to let her go, are they? They never were. She's going to end up in a puddle of her own blood, just like Leah.

"Joe can still recover, you know, Tess. He is not beyond help. But he needs to see that you are the problem. That he was cruelly deceived all these years by a controlling vicious harpy."

"And that's fine. I'll tell him. I'll tell him everything."

"He'll find another woman. A woman who will love him. Someone who sees him for the magnificent person he really is."

Tess is taken aback by the strength of Dr O'Hara's words, and it is only when she sees the look of longing in the doctor's eyes that she understands. Dr O'Hara turns to Sally and nods. An instruction of some kind.

Sally, still pointing the gun at Tess's head, reaches behind her back with her free hand. *Oh God. What are they going to do?* If Sally pulls out a knife, Tess will have to try to escape. Two against one is pretty atrocious odds, but there's no other choice. How she wishes she'd kept hold of the knife. Tess won't just sit and let them kill her. Instead, Sally pulls out a phone. A different one than she used to call her parents. Tess plants her feet on the floor and presses her hands into the chair, ready to spring up. She won't go down without a fight.

Dr O'Hara takes a deep breath and, in barely a second, morphs from being utterly composed and calm into an out of control screaming banshee. The speed of her transformation seems almost impossible, and Tess watches in morbid fascination as the doctor continues to scream. She wails and pulls at her hair. She slaps her own face and roars out terrifying blood-curdling cries.

Tess can't move. What the fuck is happening? Mesmerised by the animalistic transformation of Dr O'Hara, Tess hadn't noticed Sally vacate her seat. And it is only when she feels the muzzle of the gun pressed against the back of her neck that she realises Sally is behind her. Tess freezes.

Dr O'Hara, still howling and weeping, taps frantically at the phone.

Tess is left with no choice but to watch and wait.

# 49

## TESS

Stunned into silence by the sight before her and frozen to the spot by the threat of a bullet to the back of her head, Tess knows she is out of options. Why did she ever believe anything these two women said to her? Of course she was never going to get out of this room alive. Why would they take that risk?

Sally already told her they have a suspect lined up. Someone to take the fall for Leah's death. Tess should have known they would get rid of her too. Add her body to the pile. She feels an innate desire to fight for her life, but she can't make her body move even a millimetre. A gun pressed hard against your neck will do that. She watches and listens as Dr O'Hara's telephone call is answered and prays that her parents are not on the other end of the line, that they are not going to make them listen to her demise. Her death will devastate them and she can't handle her parents' pain being the last thing she ever hears.

Dr O'Hara screeches down the phone, "I need an ambulance. And police. Hurry quick, please. Oh God, please." The doctor's performance is astonishing. The way she suddenly turned on this intense hysterical act is extraordinary, not to mention deeply disturbing.

Tess wasn't supposed to hear this call to the emergency services. She was supposed to be far away from here. Driving to her mum and dad's house. She was promised her freedom. But now her body will be found alongside Leah's, and the fact they are making her listen to this is perverse.

"One of my patients killed the other. She's dead. Oh my God, please, someone help us."

There is a pause and Tess can hear the emergency operator talking and asking questions but can't distinguish the words. And then Tess realises. Dr O'Hara said one. *One of my patients killed the other*. Perhaps all is not lost.

"Yes. Me and my receptionist. We've... we've locked her in. But come quickly."

Uneasiness begins to form inside Tess. Why would Dr O'Hara say they've locked Leah in the room? What does that matter? Unless... and at Dr O'Hara's next words, Tess's world comes crashing down around her.

"She's got a knife. She's shrieking and threatening us. She's completely delusional. Screaming that we did it. I don't think she remembers. Please come quickly before she hurts herself. I've never seen anything like it." Dr O'Hara continues to sob and whimper as the operator speaks to her.

Tess gawps and Dr O'Hara winks at her before mouthing, "He's mine now." Tess can't hold back any longer. She twists her body suddenly and reaches behind her, trying to grab Sally or the gun. Anything. She will not let them frame her for this. But her efforts are in vain and the next thing she feels is a heavy blow to the back of her head. It stuns her and hurts like hell, but somehow she remains conscious. Sally crouches down in front of her and pushes the gun under her chin.

Tess is still seeing stars and her words are slurred. "No. She... she's framing me."

Sally pushes the gun harder into Tess's throat and hisses into her ear, "Framing you? You did this. You killed her."

Tess looks past Sally to Dr O'Hara, pushing down the nausea building in her stomach from her distorted double vision. "You made me."

Sally's eyes narrow and the evil grin that appears on her face chills Tess to her very core. "You can tell the police that, can't you."

Dr O'Hara is standing now, beckoning to Sally while still spouting her poisonous lies down the phone. "I just had a consultation with her. She's got a personality disorder, a psychopathic disorder. But I never thought this could... Oh my God, what have I done? I never thought she would actually hurt someone."

Dr O'Hara holds up a splayed palm and mouths silently to Sally, "They'll be here in five minutes."

Sally nods as she strokes the muzzle of the gun down the side of Tess's cheek and tilts her head in a gesture of fake sympathy. "Jenna and I are going to leave now. If you move, I'll shoot you. I don't mind doing that, by the way. Plus, the police already know you're dangerous and you're threatening us. Jenna will back me up. I'll say you came at me with the knife. And you, well, you won't be here to tell anyone anything different."

Sally shrugs and then pats Tess on the head like a puppy before standing up. The strike from the gun has left Tess addled and her head is hammering. The room is swirling. Everything is moving too fast and she is stuck and unable to move. She needs to do something, but what? Sally will kill her.

Tess watches helplessly, her arms outstretched and tears pouring from her eyes, as Dr O'Hara and Sally begin to back away towards the door. "No, please."

Sally holds her index finger to her lips and waves the gun.

Dr O'Hara is still on the phone, interspersing words with cries and tears. Sally reaches behind her and turns the handle slowly before opening the door a crack. All whilst staring directly into Tess's eyes. The sight of the outside world ignites something in Tess and she leaps off the chair and scrabbles around on the floor for the knife. It is precisely where she dropped it and she heaves as she has to retrieve the handle from a puddle of Leah's blood.

But time is running out. Sally and Dr O'Hara are on the other side of the door now and it is closing. Sealing her fate. Trapping her. The knife is slick with blood, but Tess grabs it tightly and lunges for the door. But she is too late. She smashes into the hard wood, pressing her whole body against it. Pushing with all her might. She wrestles with the door-handle and it slides around in her blood-soaked palm before she eventually manages to get purchase. She turns it but nothing happens. They've locked her in. Locked her in with a dead body, covered in blood and she's holding the murder weapon.

Tess opens her mouth and releases an animalistic scream. She pounds the door with her fists and stabs at it with the knife. Sally and Dr O'Hara watch her through the small window. Tess's vision is filled with explosions of stars and she imagines them laughing and mocking her. Tess pulls back the knife and stabs at the glass, but it jars and her hand slides down the handle and on to the blade, slicing through her palm. She grimaces but barely notices the pain. Instead, she continues banging, alternating between smashing at the door and the glass pane. The window is now smeared with blood. A cocktail of hers and Leah's, and she can't see through it properly. Dr O'Hara's and Sally's faces are now a distorted blur.

Dr O'Hara shouts, "I guess all that attention you craved so badly is about to come your way."

Tess hears laughing and she pushes her face up to the glass and screams until her voice gives out. There's blood on her face and in her hair. She can taste it. But none of it matters. This is war.

Tess retreats and drops the knife onto the floor. She needs to find another way out. She tries to pick up the coffee table but it is heavy, and the bulky soft chairs will be useless. There is nothing in the room she can use to smash down the door. She flips over one of the armchairs in frustration. Then she looks up, and tries to wipe blood out of her eyes but instead manages to add more. The ceiling. Could she break through? She grabs the table and tries to lift it onto the sofa. If she can balance it and climb on, she might be able to reach the ceiling and bash her way through it. She struggles and eventually heaves the table onto the sofa, but it topples off almost immediately, crashing down onto her arm. She hears a crack and hot white pain shoots from her hand to her elbow. She's pretty sure she's broken her wrist. But what does that matter now? Tess ignores her throbbing arm and grabs for the knife again. She throws off all the sofa and chair cushions, looking for something, anything. One of them lands on top of Leah. "Sorry." She laughs maniacally at apologising to a dead body, feeling herself descending into madness. This is madness. This is all completely fucking insane.

And then she starts yelling. There is no way out but if she shouts loud enough, maybe someone will come and rescue her. She closes her eyes and screams at the top of her lungs. Her throat burns. And then, she hears the door click open.

# 50

## TESS

People. So many people. All dressed in dark clothing. And they have guns. They're here to take her. They can't. She isn't the guilty one.

"Don't believe them. They did this. I'm innocent. You can't —" Tess scurries backwards, avoiding Leah and her glassy judgemental eyes and plants her back against the far wall. Tess brandishes the knife in front of her and one of the dark figures shouts, telling her to drop the knife. But she can't. It's the only thing she has left. She knows what this looks like. No, what they made this look like. She is covered in blood. It's smeared all over her face. But she can't let them take her. No one will believe her and she has to make them see.

"I didn't kill her! Well, I did... But you don't understand. You need to listen to me."

Tess looks wildly around the room. She just admitted she killed Leah. She wasn't meant to do that. More people are in the room now and they are closing in. She hears the voice again, louder and more insistent.

"Drop the knife."

A part of her wishes they would just shoot. End it all. What kind of life is she going to have now anyway, locked up forever? Tess looks at Leah. She is flanked by paramedics and their equipment but they don't appear to be doing anything. Anyone can see she is beyond help. Poor dead Leah.

Black spots dance in front of Tess's eyes and her mouth has a strange watery feeling. She holds out her hands in surrender and lets the knife clatter to the floor. A rush of bodies swarm towards her, and she closes her eyes and crumples.

She's on the floor. Feet are rushing around her, making footprints in the blood. Even lying down, Tess feels light-headed and her vision is closing in.

Her last thought before she succumbs to the sweet relief of nothingness is of her mother.

"I'm sorry, Mum. I'm so, so sorry."

## 51

## SALLY

Sally and Dr O'Hara are led outside to a police car and helped into the back seat. Swarms of people have crowded to watch the spectacle. Vultures. Have they nothing better to do? An officer stands guard outside the vehicle, but they are alone inside. Sally grips Jenna's hand, and she squeezes back. They have talked through this part and Sally knows she mustn't break from the plan for even a second. You never know who is watching.

Sally is desperate to wrap her arms around Jenna and wants Jenna to hold her so badly. The adrenaline is beginning to wear off and she's starting to feel a bit odd and shaky. But now she and her mum can rebuild their lives. There will be lots of questions to follow but the hard part is over.

Tess pretty much dug her own grave in there: the screaming and tossing of the furniture, her blood-smeared face. The police saw it all. She knows Jenna will be really happy with how that part went. Sally will never be able to show just how much she loves and appreciates Jenna. She risked her life and her livelihood for her and her mum. And it's not just her actions today – Jenna devised everything.

Sally could never have done any of this without her. Jenna helped Sally see this was the only way to put things right with the universe and allow her mum to heal. Sally feels silly for her reticence now. Even yesterday, she tried to convince Jenna to call the whole thing off. But Jenna cares so much for her family and their happiness.

If this all goes wrong, Sally has told Jenna she will take the blame. Jenna tried to disagree but Sally was insistent. Jenna's already done so much for them.

A sudden commotion pulls Sally out of her thoughts. She looks up to see a flurry of bodies and Tess being dragged out and into the back of a police van. Tess can't see them through the tinted windows of the police car and, in any case, she appears completely out of it. She is stumbling erratically and looks as though she might pass out. But she's alive, at least.

This was the part Sally was initially least sure about. Framing an innocent woman seemed unnecessary. But it all made perfect sense once Sally understood how evil Tess really was. Plus, Tess really did kill Leah. There's no denying that, is there?

Despite all of her threats and bravado, Sally wouldn't have killed anyone. She doesn't have it in her. She really surprised herself with everything she did today, particularly when she bashed Tess on the head with the gun. Still, she knew she couldn't disappoint Jenna.

Sally tries not to think about it. Jenna told her not to and showed her how to block everything out and just do what they had planned. It was for the best. And she'd be letting her mum down if she didn't do as she was told.

When it became clear Leah was willing to go to the police and confess everything, Sally really wanted Jenna to change her mind. It seemed like the perfect opportunity to let Leah and

Tess go. She even whispered it in her ear at one point. But all she got was a stern "no." And Sally supposes Jenna was right. This is how it was supposed to be.

Sally looks at Jenna. Her head is bowed, but there is a glint in her eyes and a tiny smirk playing on her lips. Sally copies her. When she's feeling unsure that's what she does, she copies Jenna. Jenna knows best.

She hated it when Jenna was tied up, but they'd rehearsed it relentlessly. The bits where she made fun of her, like saying what she did was money for old rope, were really hard to get through. But Jenna assured her she needed that time to observe the two women and Sally needed to gain control of the situation. Jenna's so clever and kind.

Jenna helped her with everything, like how to recover if she found herself making the wrong facial expression and what to say if she lost focus or drifted off. She gave so much of her time. They rehearsed every night. Sally still can't believe the lengths Jenna went to. She sat with Sally as she learnt her lines and she was so patient, well mostly, when she kept getting it wrong. Sally can still recite them now. She spent hours perfecting her facial expressions in the mirror. At first, Sally was convinced she couldn't pull off masquerading as Jenna. Jenna is clever and brilliant. And Sally is just... well, Sally.

But Sally started to improve and when Jenna praised and applauded her, it was the most wonderful feeling. She perfected the sympathetic head tilts and warm smiles, making sure they reached her eyes. When every part of the plan started to go right, Sally both celebrated and panicked.

She was sure she was going to screw up Tess's consultation. They must have ran through it a thousand times. Jenna playing Tess all brash and selfish, and making Sally act irritated and challenging. It was hard. She is no actress but as Jenna said, practice makes perfect. Sally found herself repeating phrases in her sleep. Panicking she'd overdo the bit when she was supposed to irritate Tess and she'd end up walking out. Sitting here now, Sally finds herself wishing that Tess had walked out. She was so close. But she pushes that thought away. It's just her mind playing tricks on her. Jenna warned her this would happen when the adrenaline started to wear off. She just needs to ignore it.

They spent hours practising their cold stares at each other. Sally learnt how to appear callous and cruel. Perfected the art of goading and threatening. None of it came naturally to her, but she got there in the end with Jenna's love and support. Soon, she was glaring, sneering, and holding a gun with ease. Sally barely recognised herself. She was amazed at what began to feel normal after enough repetition. Even things she didn't mean or want to do. Jenna congratulated her when she finally perfected her hollow eyes. That's one thing she didn't have to practise. It was how she began to feel. She didn't tell Jenna that though. She wouldn't have liked it.

Sally never understood why the consultation with Tess was even necessary. Why did they have to make all those promises about improving her when they were planning to take her down? That seemed unfair. But Jenna insisted they needed to show Tess they were strong and weren't to be messed with. But why did that matter when they had a gun?

Sally only learnt about the part with Tess's parents a few weeks ago and she's barely slept since. Threatening to kill an elderly couple? She didn't think she could live with herself. But Jenna assured her it was all a bluff. That nothing would happen to them. And that must be true. Sally felt guilty about questioning her. After all, Jenna sacrificed everything for her and she was right, Sally was being selfish for suggesting they back out. Everything Jenna does is for the greater good.

Jenna warned Sally that Leah would try to manipulate her.

But Sally hated herself when Leah was serene and agreeable. It was the only time she went off script and felt in danger of abandoning the whole thing. But she'd promised Jenna she wouldn't turn back and somehow, that promise mattered more than anything else.

A police officer enters the car and tells them they can't go back inside and that they'll be taking them to the station soon. Jenna nods before putting her head in her hands and weeping. Sally follows her lead and covers her face with her hands, but the tears don't come.

Instead, Sally rests her hands on her knees and watches as the van containing Tess drives away, followed by two other police cars.

She knows she'll be separated from Jenna once they get to the police station, but Sally remembers her instructions on what to say and how to act. She hopes she can pull it off without Jenna by her side. Another pang of guilt and sadness hits Sally, and she yearns to reach out for Jenna so badly. She needs to hear her soothing voice and her words of reassurance. But she knows she can't. In fact, Jenna has said she can't come back to work with her after today. And that they probably shouldn't spend much time together for a while. Sally understands why but she'll miss her so much. She doesn't know what she'll do without her.

Jenna said that after everything is over, Sally should focus purely on her mum and suggested it might be a nice idea for them to go away somewhere together. Sally would like that but she reckons her mum would take some convincing.

And then a thought hits her. Tess and Leah won't be going anywhere nice. Leah, most certainly, and Tess is unlikely to ever see anything outside of the walls of a prison for a long time.

Sally tries to push these thoughts away and focus on what's

right and just. She has to focus on her mum and their new life together, just as Jenna instructed her to.

But thoughts of Leah and Tess still crawl over her.

And this time, when she puts her hands over her face, the tears fall freely.

# 52

## SALLY

### SIX MONTHS LATER

Sally looks over at her mum as they wait impatiently in the queue for the hospital car park. Mum's post-operative follow-up appointment is in less than five minutes and they're stuck in this one-in, one-out queue with no way to go forwards or backwards. Why is parking at hospitals always so dreadful?

"I think we're going to be late, Mum. There are three cars in front of us and nobody has come out in ages. Do you want to call them?"

Mum takes out her phone and checks the time. "Let's give it a few more minutes, shall we? Then I'll ring. It's so annoying, we left in plenty of time."

Watching Mum do something simple like checking her phone is wonderful. A few months ago, she couldn't have done that. They're here today for a follow-up appointment with the eye doctors after Mum's cataract surgery and laser treatment. Sally doesn't need a doctor to tell her there's been a huge improvement. But what Mum definitely needs to hear is that these developments are permanent. That there are no complications and that, for once, the treatment for her eyesight has gone well.

Sally can see her mum is cautiously optimistic, but they've been burnt so many times and suffered through so much disappointment and despair. Hopefully, today will put all of that to bed.

Just as Jenna promised, once Sally was able to spend more time with her mum and support her better, she came around to the idea of further treatment. It happened much quicker than Sally expected and the results have been overwhelmingly positive. Mum has been taking baby steps, but her house is a much brighter and warmer space. It's not quite back to how it was before she was assaulted, but they are getting there.

Two cars exit the car park in quick succession, and they move forwards and stop in front of the barrier.

"We'll be in soon. I think I'll leave calling them. They must be used to people being late with the atrocious parking."

Sally nods, and in a couple of minutes they're let through the barrier. Walking swiftly to their appointment, Sally notices the apprehension on her mum's face and her fists balled up tightly by her side. Sally doesn't attempt small talk or try to distract her. It will only irritate her and add to her anxiety. All she needs to do is be here for her.

---

Less than thirty minutes later, Sally and her mum are in the hospital corridor hugging each other tightly, tears falling down their cheeks. They've just had the best possible news. The cataract surgery was a success. The laser treatment was a success. There are no complications and her vision will likely get even better in the coming weeks. Sally squeezes her mum tightly. She deserves this so much. She's been so brave and finally, she is reaping the rewards of all the hard work she has put into her recovery.

Mum leans back and studies Sally's face. "I'm so happy, Sal. This feels like a new lease of life. A new beginning."

Sally beams. "You deserve every bit of happiness. I love you, Mum."

They embrace again, not caring that they are partially blocking the corridor or that people are staring. Mum takes her hand and pulls her along the corridor to the ladies bathroom.

"Let's get ourselves cleaned up, shall we? We look a right state after all that blubbing. Shall we go for coffee? And then let's pick up a bottle of bubbly on the way home. We could invite Natalie and Jenna around later. Drink a toast to our happy news."

Sally smiles and nods, trying to match her mum's enthusiasm and pushing away the pang of sadness that hits her at the mention of Jenna's name. "Sounds lovely."

Inside the toilet cubicle, Sally takes some deep breaths. She can't let her mum see she's upset or that the horrible feelings of panic that have been plaguing her over the last few months have surfaced.

Jenna has made it very clear she no longer wants any contact with Sally. She closed her private practice shortly after that horrific day and has gone back to a job in the NHS. Sally doesn't know the details because Jenna won't speak to her, but she overheard Natalie telling her mum. She knows Jenna is doing it for their safety, to protect them both from any consequences, but the way she's going about it feels unkind.

The police only spoke to Sally twice. At Jenna's insistence, Sally stated her role was small. She was manning the reception desk, where she checked Leah in at 9am and then Tess at 10am. Leah returned for a follow-up appointment at midday and Tess returned for some reading materials around the same time. When Sally heard a commotion in the waiting room, she alerted Jenna, who called the police. They stood outside the locked room waiting for the police to come. That was it. Sally had to make sure she got the times right. She had to remember midday, not 11am as it actually was. It was to account for Leah's time of death, Jenna said. The thought makes Sally feel sick.

After Sally told the police her story, they had no further questions for her. She should be ecstatic and filled with relief but in reality, she just feels empty. Sally has no idea what happened with Jenna and the police. She tried to surreptitiously question Jenna on the occasions she came to visit Mum with Natalie and was told in no uncertain terms to leave her alone and move on. She rarely comes now. Jenna has even accused Sally of trying to screw everything up. The last words Jenna ever said to her still ring in her mind.

*You got me into this. Now leave me alone. You got what you wanted.*

Sally tried texting and calling. But her texts went unanswered and her calls were not returned. She wonders if Jenna is struggling to come to terms with what they did. Because Sally most certainly is. And that's putting it mildly. But somehow, she imagines Jenna is doing just fine. Plus, 'You got me into this' does not accurately portray what happened. Jenna devised the plan and carefully mapped out precisely what Sally should do and say. At the very least, they are equally culpable. Sally can't deny that on the day she threw herself into it, but what else was she supposed to do at that point? They'd come way too far and as Jenna kept telling her, they couldn't turn back. Jenna would have killed her if she'd backed out at the last minute. Well, not literally. Although the more Sally thinks about that, she's not so sure.

Sally had only known Jenna in passing before she took the job at her office. Jenna always came across as introverted and shy, so they rarely spoke. Sally has spent hours thinking about how and why she entered into something so unbelievable and unlike her with relative ease. And with someone she knew pretty much nothing about. Jenna rapidly became Sally's whole world and she trusted her completely. When Sally looks back, she can't comprehend why she wholeheartedly believed that the key to her mum's happiness depended on doling out justice to Leah. She was angry and vulnerable and so desperate to grasp the glimmer of hope that Jenna showed her. But that's no excuse. Now, Sally knows none of it was true. A woman has died for no reason and she has blood on her hands. Her mum doesn't even know what happened to Leah, so how could her death have changed anything?

Mum knows what went on at the office. She knows someone died at the hands of another patient. But she doesn't know who or why. Sally has made sure of that. Yes, Sally has been more attentive and more available now she's no longer at work or staying late to run through plans with Jenna. But if anything, Sally is less present than ever. She tries, but she knows she's distant and morose, her mind constantly addled with hideous thoughts and regrets. Her nights are plagued with fitful, terrifying dreams interspersed with bouts of insomnia and self-loathing. Sally doesn't think she will ever sleep well again. And she supposes that's a very small price to pay for what she did. Look at what Leah and Tess lost. Disrupted sleep, by comparison, is a minor inconvenience. Leah lost her life. Tess lost her freedom.

"Have you fallen down the toilet?" Mum's voice startles Sally. She'd been lost to the world, far away in her haunted mind. It's where she spends most of her days now.

"Sorry. Out in a minute." Sally gives herself a shake and exits to be immediately confronted by Mum's concerned face. It's an expression she's seen a few too many times in recent months. The last thing Sally wants is for her mum to feel worried. Especially not today and preferably not ever again.

So Sally does what she always does, she plasters on a smile and tries to pack it all away in her mind and focus on the present. It's getting harder to do and she worries about what will happen when she can no longer mask everything. She's beyond desperate to talk about it with someone. Ruminating and trying to sort it out in her own mind isn't working. And the one person she needs to speak to wants nothing to do with her. She's not sure how much longer she can keep this up.

Sally washes her hands and splashes her face with water. Dabbing a little concealer under her eyes, she groans internally at her haggard appearance. Fine lines have sprung up everywhere and after losing ten pounds in weight very quickly, she looks sunken. She dabs some Vaseline on her lips and shakes out her hair. Still not great, but better at least.

"Right, let's go, Mum."

"Sally, dear. Are you okay?"

*No. No, I'm anything other than okay. I'm an accessory to murder. I've been so completely stupid and I'm so, so sorry.*

"I'm fine. I was just worried about today and trying not to show it. I think I've been running on my nerves and just had a bit of a crash. But I'm fine. In fact, I'm better than fine. Let's go celebrate. Push all those worries away and celebrate your new start." That was so convincing Sally almost believed it herself, and her heart swells when she sees her mum's face light up.

"I know what you mean. It's a huge relief, but I'm kind of exhausted too. How about we grab a quick coffee, pop to the shop for the bubbly, and then have a few hours of quiet time at home before Natalie and Jenna come over?"

"Sounds perfect." They leave the bathroom together and start the short walk to the car.

"I'll call Nat and Grant while you drive. Tell them the good news and ask Nat if she's free later."

Mum puts the phone on speaker and Sally actually laughs

when she hears her brother's booming response down the phone. "Get in!"

Mum laughs, too, and Grant promises he'll be round for a glass of something fizzy later.

"Best get two bottles," says Mum before dialling Natalie's number.

"Oh, absolutely. Maybe even three and they're on me."

Mum bats away my suggestion and shakes her head before Natalie answers the call. "Hi, it's me. I've just been to the hospital and guess what?"

Natalie sounds excited but with a hint of nerves mixed in. "Don't make me guess, Mel. Tell me now!"

"Okay, okay. Everything is looking good. All healing beautifully and I'll probably get a little more vision back too."

Natalie squeals with excitement down the phone. "Aww, I'm absolutely bloody delighted. I knew it. How are you feeling?"

"Proper chuffed. I'm in the car with Sally. She's driving but you're on speaker."

"Hi, Sally."

Sally leans towards the phone unnecessarily. "Hi, Natalie."

"Sally is taking me out for a celebratory coffee and cake, and then we'll head home for a bit. We were just saying we've been running on fumes waiting for this news and we're a bit knackered."

"I can bloody imagine. Well, I'm thrilled you got the news you deserved. Honestly, Mel, I've had everything crossed for you. Can I pop in later if you and Sal aren't too tired?"

"Oh yes, that's what I was going to say. Champagne at mine. Say sevenish? You could ask Jenna too, maybe?"

"Count me in and I'll ask Jenna, but I doubt she'll make it. She's all loved up with her new man and I've barely seen hide nor hair of her in ages."

"Ooh, exciting. I didn't know that." Mum waggles her eyebrows and gives Sally a suggestive smile.

Sally has to hide her look of shock. New man? But then why not? They are supposed to be getting on with their lives.

"Yeah, I haven't met him and given him my seal of approval yet, but she's properly smitten. Joe something, I think. Some rich banker type."

Joe? Surely that has to be a coincidence. It's a very common name and there are probably lots of Joes who are bankers. But Sally has always believed coincidences don't exist.

"Well, do invite her and her new beau if he's interested."

Sally feels her heart fall. Could Jenna and Joe be a couple? They can't be. They were doctor and patient for a start. Isn't that illegal? The hairs on the back of her neck begin to prickle. Could Jenna have had an ulterior motive that day? Sally truly believed Jenna's involvement was purely altruistic.

But if she and Joe are together...

"Where should we go for coffee, love? The usual?"

Sally pulls herself away from her dark thoughts. Even if Jenna and Joe were together, which she's sure they're not, there's no way they'd come tonight.

"Sure, that sounds good." Sally turns and smiles at her mum and notices her staring off into the distance. Her face is pensive and also a little sad. "Are you okay?" When her mum turns, Sally can see tears forming in her eyes. "What's up? Is it all hitting you? It's okay to shed a tear over good news, too, you know."

"No, it's not that." Mum goes quiet and begins fiddling nervously with the strap of her handbag.

"You don't have to tell me if you don't want to. I know you hate me mithering. But I'm listening if you do."

Mum sighs and her shoulders sag. Something is clearly weighing on her. "Remember when I told you about Leah?"

Panic hits Sally like an electric shock. She keeps her eyes on the road and tries to look as nonchalant as possible. "Your school friend?"

"Yes. I've been thinking about her."

"Why?" Sally has so much more to say, but she knows her voice will give away the anxiety currently ricocheting around her body.

"Now, don't get me wrong, I know what happened to me had nothing to do with Leah." Sally stares straight ahead. It feels like her heart is trying to escape through her chest, and she's beginning to feel dizzy. She should really pull over. "But I've had lots of time to think about what we did to her when we were young and I feel ashamed. She was a good friend and I was so horrible to her. I know it's been thirty years, but I think I'm going to see if I can find her and say sorry. Put things right."

Sally's mouth is as dry as a bone and she struggles to breathe. But she knows her mum is expecting an answer. "I... I'm not sure that's a good idea." Sally sucks in air and looks at her mum. Thankfully, she's still looking down, picking at her cuticles and not noticing that her daughter is on the verge of having a panic attack.

"Why not? I feel awful about it. I think she'd appreciate it. I was thinking if things were the other way around, I probably would."

There are a million reasons why not.

*Leah is dead, Mum. I had her murdered for you.*

Sally takes a deep breath and struggles through her words. "Maybe she's forgotten all about it. What if you made her feel worse?"

Mum looks up. "I hadn't thought of that. I definitely wouldn't want that. Maybe she hasn't given me a second thought in years."

Spurred on by hope, Sally speaks more freely. "Probably.

You've only been thinking about it because of what happened. I bet Leah's completely forgotten about it. Wouldn't be good to open old wounds, would it?" A wave of nausea hits Sally. Why did she have to use the word 'wounds'? She prays Mum hasn't noticed her sudden change in demeanour and she adeptly wipes away the beads of sweat that are now peppering her forehead. But thankfully, her mum is back looking contemplatively out of her side window.

"Maybe you're right. I'd like to say sorry but maybe I only want to do it for selfish reasons and that's not right, is it?"

"No. You should just try and forget it, I reckon."

"Hmm. I think I'd feel better if someone had found out. If we'd been punished. I told you before she never did anything about it. Just moved on with good grace. I guess I'll just have to accept that she was the bigger person. I was a right madam back then. I'd have definitely gotten my own back." Mum chuckles to herself and Sally feels another part of her die inside. "Anyway, enough of that. Let's get celebrating, shall we?"

Sally feels like her heart is breaking. At any moment, she fears she may just cease to function. She wants to pull the car over and start screaming and then run far, far away and block out the whole world.

Instead, she pastes on that fake smile she's become so accustomed to, nods happily and says the words she is supposed to. "Definitely, let's celebrate."

# 53

## DR JENNA O'HARA

### SIX MONTHS LATER

Jenna walks into her favourite restaurant and sees Joe already sitting at their usual table nestled away in the corner. Today is their one-year anniversary. She's not sure if Joe knows it's their anniversary or not. He might feel that the months of them being doctor and patient and then Jenna's time playing the other woman to Tess perhaps shouldn't count. But to her, they do. She knew from the moment she set eyes on him that he was the one and eventually, he'd be hers.

Joe stands as she approaches the table and kisses her on the cheek before they both sit.

"Sorry I'm late."

"You're not. I was early." Joe flashes that perfect smile of his and she melts. She would do anything for this man.

Natalie invited them both to a champagne celebration at Melissa's house tonight, but Jenna declined immediately. Seeing Sally is not an option. She's become desperate and needy and needs to move on. Let's call it being cruel to be kind.

The lengthy questioning Jenna received from the police, alongside an extensive investigation into her actions and professional practice that day have been invasive and overwhelming, to say the least. But Jenna has made it through relatively unscathed. She has remained strong and everything is starting to settle. Sally is nothing but a weak link and Jenna won't risk her destroying everything. Now Joe is hers, her life is absolutely perfect, and she plans to keep it that way.

Jenna is glad Melissa eventually went for treatment and surgery and that the results are promising. She thought that would be the case and is relieved the delay hasn't had an adverse effect on the outcome. Melissa is a good woman and deserves to be well. Her positive results today certainly lessen any guilt Jenna feels for having fuelled Melissa's anxieties and encouraging her not to undergo surgery straight away. Advising her that further treatment was likely to make things worse definitely made Jenna uncomfortable, but she needed more time. Pulling off something of the magnitude she was planning couldn't be rushed, and if Melissa had had the surgery immediately and subsequently improved, convincing Sally of the need for revenge wouldn't have been as easy. But Jenna's secret talks with Melissa, alongside Sally's absence due to their preparations, did the trick. One had a knock-on effect on the other. Melissa fell further into despair and Sally became more fraught and pliable. While both of those things were somewhat painful to watch, they served their purpose. Jenna never wanted any unnecessary suffering for either woman, but they needed to play their part.

Jenna did consider finding another victim for Tess. After all, Tess's downfall was the ultimate aim. But when the situation with Leah presented itself, it seemed too good an opportunity to miss. Of course, Jenna couldn't tell Sally about Joe. She introduced his presence gently and subtly at first before progressing to laying it on thick about the effect Tess was having on him. Telling Sally that Joe was downtrodden and depressed was not true.

Joe's sessions were for bereavement therapy. His brother had died in a freak boat accident while on holiday and his bitch of a fiancée couldn't have cared less. Jenna fell in love with him pretty much at first sight. Initially, they focused on his feelings regarding his brother's sudden death. The shock and numbness, the anger and the guilt. He was so open and caring, and Jenna fell deeper in love with him every time they met. They spent a lot of time just chatting about their lives. Well, his life, mostly. And Jenna didn't mind. She wanted to drink in every aspect of this remarkable man that had been brought to her door.

He wasn't backwards about coming forwards regarding Tess either. He immediately revealed he was desperate to leave her, explaining that she was manipulative and cruel, and he seemed genuinely worried about what she would do if he tried to break off their engagement. He was adamant Tess would never leave him, insistent that she wanted to marry him and that he couldn't keep delaying setting a date. Jenna was appalled that he was planning to tie himself to a woman he didn't love because it was better than dealing with the fallout of leaving. It was clear Tess was in love with the life Joe provided rather than the man himself.

Jenna could see how conflicted Joe was and at the same time, something began to grow between them. She was smitten with Joe and he was beginning to fall for her too. But his concerns about Tess were all-consuming and any efforts to convince him to leave proved fruitless. So Jenna decided to step in.

Tess had to go.

Initially, Jenna tried a different tack. Telling Joe she could treat Tess and turn her into a better version of herself, perhaps even influencing her to stand on her own two feet and find genuine love and happiness with someone else. But Joe was adamant that would never happen.

"She's not changeable, Jenna. Not unless it's in her best interests."

So Jenna took another angle. If Tess really was that shallow, maybe paying her off would work? But Joe just laughed.

"She'd spend it and want more. She'd bleed me dry and keep coming back. Tess wouldn't be happy with any amount of money. Her needs would just expand to fill the amount of money available. It would be a vicious cycle."

With both her suggestions vetoed, Jenna began to think a little more creatively, and fuelled by her ferocious need to keep Joe in her life, her ideas became more and more unsavoury. At first, these thoughts horrified her. How could she even think such things? But once, when she jokingly mentioned spiking Tess's food with anti-freeze, rather than a laugh or a shocked response, she got, "Would that work?" from Joe, and she realised just how desperate he was to get rid of her. He'd vehemently denied he was serious and she pretended she believed him, but she saw what was in his eyes at that moment. Granted, Joe is not the type to turn a fleeting evil thought into reality. He'd never hurt Tess. But he wouldn't be sad if she was gone. And that gave Jenna a lot more to work with.

Tess had Joe cornered. She was a leech. Sucking not only his finances but his time and attention. The latter being the things Jenna was craving with an increasing intensity. She'd never felt this way about a man before and as she approached fifty, she was beginning to think she never would. Jenna had never felt any pressure to marry or settle down at the times society dictated to be the norm. If Joe had not entered her world, she'd have been perfectly content to continue her happy and carefree life. She'd never needed a man to validate her and loved her own company. Plus, she had her fair share of fun and short-lived relationships. No stress. No heartbreak. All the benefits. But nobody had ever spoken to her soul in the way Joe did. How unfair that he was stuck in a poisonous relationship with a blood-sucking harridan.

When their sessions came to a natural end, they continued to see each other. Initially, Jenna was okay with their snatched moments and secret trysts. At least she got to see him.

Serendipitously, Sally began to obsess about Leah and after hearing that Natalie had been trolled, a plan started to form in Jenna's mind. Although there was no concrete evidence, Jenna felt sure that Leah was responsible for what happened to Melissa. A random act of violence? No chance. And as they started to investigate, she became more and more certain. So Jenna settled into her role as Joe's other woman and began planning how to take Tess's place. She hated that she had to share the love of her life with that horrible woman, but it was only temporary and the end result would be worth it. Tess would get her comeuppance in the most spectacular fashion.

Joe and Jenna have never spoken openly about what happened to Tess that day. She's sure he knows she somehow had a hand in it, but she's never admitted it and she doubts Joe would ask her directly. Jenna had told him beforehand that Tess had made an appointment with her. He said he knew and had tried to talk Tess out of it, telling Jenna that she was only going for an ego boost. Jenna laughed. Tess had no idea what she was getting herself into.

Joe has ordered their favourite wine and the waiter brings it along with some complimentary canapés and bread.

"Are we ready to order?"

"Could we have a few more minutes?"

"Of course. Take your time."

The waiter leaves and Jenna raises her glass. "You know, it's exactly a year since we met. Our one-year anniversary." She grins but it quickly falls away when she sees Joe's reaction. He's not looking at her and is shifting in his seat uncomfortably.

Jenna tries to rescue the situation. "I'm only joking. No need to look so awkward." She takes a big gulp of her wine.

Joe remains looking at the table, fidgeting with his wine glass. "Look, Jenna, I learnt a lot from my relationship with Tess."

Jenna has an awful feeling she knows where this is going, and she grips her glass so fiercely that she thinks it might break.

"I would imagine you did. But I'm nothing like Tess. We're—"

He cuts her off abruptly. Jenna stiffens but says nothing.

"Jenna, we're not..."

He rubs the nape of his neck. Jenna leans back and takes a long sip of her wine, eying him carefully. "Go on."

"I like you. Honestly, we have a lot of fun. But we're not... we're not going to be..."

Jenna's lips curl at his cowardice. He can't even finish a sentence. How pathetic. "Are you breaking up with me?"

He looks at her briefly before picking up his bread roll and playing with it. What a child.

"No. I mean... there's nothing to break. We're not a couple. Not really. I like spending time with you. But I think you might have the wrong idea. I'm not going to get deep into something I don't want to do again. You must understand that."

He's more confident now. Holding himself straighter, the bread discarded, and his hands gesticulating as he speaks. Jenna doesn't respond, simply fixing him with a steely glare as he begins to stand up.

"Look, maybe this was a bad idea. I should go. I'm sorry, Jenna. I thought you knew this wasn't serious."

Jenna puts her glass down and leans forwards. Her voice is a menacing whisper. "Do you realise what I did for you?"

Joe freezes and sits down slowly. Leaning forwards so their faces are only inches apart. Joe speaks frantically now. His eyes are wide and full of dread. "No. Not exactly. And to be honest, that's one of the reasons I think we should call this off. I know you did something. I can't for the life of me figure out what. But whatever you did, I didn't ask you to."

Jenna maintains her cold demeanour. "That's not the point."

"Of course it's the point. I don't know what happened but the dust has settled now. I'm free of Tess and, honestly, I'm a little afraid about finding out. I don't want to be blamed for what happened. I had no part in it."

Jenna leans in closer so their noses are almost touching. She was afraid of this and, as such, was also completely prepared for it.

"The point I am making, dear Joe, is if I was prepared to go to those lengths to dispose of Tess, can you imagine how far I'm prepared to go to keep you in my life?" Jenna examines Joe's face as all the colour drains from it, the whites of his eyes glistening. "And believe me. I am nothing like Tess. What she did to you was child's play. I could pull off everything she ever did before breakfast without breaking a sweat."

Joe's mouth is opening and closing but no words emerge.

"Now you're going to listen to what I have to say and then we are going to finish our dinner, celebrate our anniversary and live happily fucking ever after. Do you understand me?"

Joe sways slightly and begins shaking his head but remains unable to argue.

"I'll let you in on a few secrets, shall I? Do you remember when I accidentally nicked you with that kitchen knife? Remember, I was cooking dinner for you at your house. I've kept that blood. You never know when things might come in useful." Jenna smirks. "You look a little unsteady there, Joe. Please don't pass out until I've finished. You'll want to hear all of this, I assure you."

Joe looks utterly dumbfounded and his lips begin to quiver. Jenna reaches out and gently strokes his cheek.

"Oh, and it's not just blood. I've saved and frozen several semen samples. I'm a little old for insemination but who knows? It could work, and if not, there are other ways I could use it. Ways that could make you look like a monster."

Joe suddenly comes to life. Sitting back and puffing out his chest.

"I know everyone you know, Joe. I know their families. I know everything. And I have recorded tapes of all your consultations. You know, the ones where you had violent outbursts. Oh, you don't remember? Ah, well, never mind, it's all on record. Remember when you admitted to thoughts of violence, of assaulting women, or murder? No, well, that's strange because I have all the evidence. Now, pick what you want to eat to celebrate our anniversary. I think I'll have the duck salad followed by the lamb. Why don't you try the sea bass?"

Joe clumsily attempts to stand. Knocking the table and sloshing red wine onto the white linen. "You're nuts. I'm out of—"

Jenna grabs her bread knife. "No, Joe. You're not going anywhere. If you stand up, I will ram this knife through your palm and say you threatened to stab me. Or maybe I'll stab myself with it and blame you. I'm a doctor, remember? I know how to make it look good and bloody without really hurting myself. If you think Tess had the ability to ruin you, I will tear you into a thousand tiny pieces. I earned this."

Joe sits, his chest heaving, looking wildly around the room as though searching for a saviour.

"And another thing, have you checked your basement lately? Good luck explaining all those knives, ropes and poisons you bought. And you did buy them by the way. You've got a post office box. That's the kind of thing crazed killers do, right? Look at me, Joe. I am ten, no, more than that, one hundred steps ahead of you."

Jenna sits back and hands Joe his glass before surreptitiously sliding something under his napkin. Joe is too bewildered to notice or care. "You should apologise to the waiter when he comes back for the mess. Now, let's raise a toast." Joe looks like he's about to cry. "Aww, it's so nice you're being emotional about our anniversary. I'm guessing you were probably thinking of proposing?"

Jenna picks up her knife again and runs it seductively through her fingers. "Take a look under your napkin."

Hands quivering, Joe reaches under his napkin, pulls out a velvet box and opens it, his mouth hanging open. Inside is a beautiful diamond solitaire ring. It cost a fortune and Jenna already knows it fits perfectly.

Jenna smiles and winks at Joe before standing up and flinging her arms in the air. "Yes. Yes. Of course, I'll marry you!" She wraps her arms around him and whispers in his ear, "Act. Happy."

The whole restaurant applauds and Jenna sits down, slides the ring on to her finger, and graciously accepts the congratulations from around the room.

Tears fall down Joe's face as the waiter brings over two glasses of champagne.

"Don't worry about him, he's just overwhelmed."

She gives Joe a smile full of love and warmth as she drives her heel into the top of his foot under the table. He barely reacts to the pain. Instead, slack-jawed and disorientated, Joe picks up the champagne. Jenna clinks her glass to his and takes a long satisfying sip.

Everything is perfect.

# 54

## TESS

### SIX MONTHS LATER

Tess sits on the bed in her stark room, staring blankly at the wall. It's what she does every day. She refuses visitors, ignores any other patients or staff, and only eats enough to stay alive.

Outwardly, she is a broken empty shell.

She fought at first. Oh, how she fought. But nobody listened. And so she simply stopped.

She takes her medicine. Or so they think. She is quiet and obedient and never causes any trouble.

When the doctors come in, they talk about her like she's not there. And that suits her just fine. They think she's in some kind of partially conscious state. *Post-traumatic catatonia*, they call it. She doesn't care. They can think what they like.

Nobody can get inside her mind and see what's actually happening there.

But Tess is biding her time.

She clenches her fists tightly and relishes the pain that spears her palms.

She will not sit here for the rest of her life. Tess has plans. She just needs to wait for the perfect opportunity. It will come and she will be ready when it does.

Dr O'Hara and Sally won't know what hit them.

THE END

ALSO BY CHARLOTTE STEVENSON

The Serial Killer's Son

The Guests

The Family Next Door

# ACKNOWLEDGEMENTS

I can't believe it's been over a year since I released a new book! Thank you from the bottom of my heart to the team at Bloodhound Books for continuing to believe in my stories and supporting me every step of the way.

A huge thank you to Ian Skewis for editing *The Patients*. It was our first time working together, and it was an absolute pleasure. A massive thank you to Patricia Dixon. I admire you and your work so much, and I still have to pinch myself that I now get to call you a friend. Thank you for all of your encouragement and kind words. To Tara Lyons, I am beyond grateful for your guidance, support, and friendship. You are a ray of sunshine, and I appreciate you more than I know how to say. And to fellow Bloodhound author Jocelyn Dexter. I think of you as my 'writing wife'. I'm not sure I could write a book without several hundred messages back and forth between us now. Long may it continue.

Thank you, as always, to my wonderful family. My husband and our three amazing children, who always believe in me. And I promise I'm doing my best to get one of my books onto Netflix, kids! To all of my wonderful friends, old and new, who continue to encourage and be there for me. Your support means the world.

I'm a huge reader and have been an active member of the online book community long before I became an author. It is a space filled with wonderful people. Special thanks go to Daniel McBreakneck, Mark Fearn, Nicola Winter, and Caroline Reid.

All truly fantastic human beings who give so much to authors and readers alike.

And a final thank you to anyone who has ever read any of my books. I appreciate you more than words can express. Writing is a safe and happy space for me, and every single one of you has played a part in keeping me on this journey.

*The Patients* is the first book I've written to unfold in real time, and with an all-female cast. Were you Team Leah or Team Tess? For me, there are no wholly bad and no wholly good characters in this story. Okay, so perhaps there are one or two pretty nefarious individuals... But just as in real life, we are all flawed. In my mind, this isn't the end of the journey for (almost) all of the characters in this book. It's only the end of *this* story. Every ending is a new beginning.

# A NOTE FROM THE PUBLISHER

**Thank you for reading this book**. If you enjoyed it please do consider leaving a review on Amazon to help others find it too.

**We hate typos**. All of our books have been rigorously edited and proofread, but sometimes mistakes do slip through. If you have spotted a typo, please do let us know and we can get it amended within hours.

**info@bloodhoundbooks.com**

www.ingramcontent.com/pod-product-compliance
Ingram Content Group UK Ltd.
Pitfield, Milton Keynes, MK11 3LW, UK
UKHW041539230226
10876UKWH00041B/474

9 781917 705417